FILMS
have given me
TRUST
ISSUES

Films Have Given Me Trust Issues © 2024 Ben Tobler

All Rights Reserved. No part of this book may be reproduced in any form or by any electronic or mechanical means including information storage and retrieval systems, without permission in writing from the author. The only exception is by a reviewer, who may quote short excerpts in a review.

This book is a work of fiction. Names, characters, places, and incidents either are products of the author's imagination or are used fictitiously. Any resemblance to actual persons, living or dead, events, or locales is entirely coincidental.

Cover and internal design by New Found Books Australia Pty Ltd

Images in this book are copyright approved for New Found Books Australia Pty Ltd
Illustrations within this book are copyright approved for New Found Books Australia Pty Ltd

First printing: SEPTEMBER 2024

New Found Books Australia Pty Ltd
www.newfoundbooks.au

Paperback ISBN 978 1 9231 7233 3
eBook ISBN 978 1 9231 7245 6
Hardback ISBN 978 1 9231 7257 9

Distributed by New Found Books Australia Pty Ltd and Lightning Source Global

A catalogue record for this work is available from the National Library of Australia

More great New Found Books Australia titles can be found at:
www.newfoundbooks.au/our-titles/

*We acknowledge the traditional owners of the land
and pay respects to the Elders, past, present and future.*

FILMS have given me TRUST ISSUES

BEN TOBLER

*To all my teachers who believed in me when I doubted myself:
Kate Bricknell, Cherie Stoessel, Steve Higginbottom and,
especially, Dr. Iain Spence whom I will never forget. My
'Barraba Dad' Martin Unwin and Mrs Susan Dolby my last
Head Teacher and mentor.*

Acknowledgements:

I'd like to acknowledge Ashley Emmerton, and Gabriel Radley for their feedback and support. Brad Hunt for his ongoing friendship, support and tolerance. My Year 11 Advanced English Class of 2022 (Ellie, Ashley and Kye) for motivating me to actually write again. Mum, Dad and my sister Amy for their support, unconditional love tolerance. My children Connor, Dominic and Charlotte, Daddy loves you all so much and most importantly, my loving and ever patient wife, Rebecca Tobler, who has done more for me than I can ever repay.

PART I:
'Stranger Than Fiction'

CHAPTER 1

I'm forty years old, alone, and I'm stuck in a job that's a physical and emotional drain on my already broken body and mind. Realistically, what could suck the life out of someone more than administrative assistant; it was the very definition of mundane. It was the first Tuesday in February and my phone vibrated on the nightstand, erupting in a cacophony of music far too upbeat for this time of the day. Why I'd chosen an upbeat Britpop number as my alarm still confused me.

Most people dread Monday, not me. For me, was the day that broke me a little more than most. The simple thought of sitting through another pointless meeting after work made me sick, or was that just the effect of the red wine and pain killers from last night?

Rolling out of bed, I reluctantly covered my naked body with a thin robe that I realised, upon tightening the cord, needed to be washed. Just that simple act of dragging myself out of bed, of accepting that I need to function as an adult, was becoming increasingly difficult. The robotic nature of my morning kicked in; it's the same monotonous series of pre-programmed actions. Rifling through my walk-in robe in an attempt to find my favourite skirt, I realised I couldn't even be bothered making my bed. Failing to find the desired outfit, I slammed the door and took the long way to the bathroom, visiting the kitchen to turn on the coffee machine and the television along the way.

I never actually watch the television, but in a weird way I feel like I'm in a de facto relationship with whichever male happened to grace the screen. This morning I was met with the baritone voice and cheeky attitude of some nobody actor from what appeared to be a shitty 1980s comedy. If I'm not streaming, it is usually some random film filling the background of my mornings. Part of me longed for the company of a real man, but If any male contact reflected my usual, regrettable one-night stands, then it's probably best I steer clear.

Stepping out of the hot shower I was struck by the rapid change in temperature. My bathroom, with its high ceilings, to my disdain, took away the impact of the built in heater. The shower was cathartic, while stepping out and drying off meant re-entering reality.

Drying my hair, I shuffled through the sitting room. I heard the subtle overtones of the credits begin to roll as I began to contemplate my commute and what shit I would inevitably face at work.

Fuck! The credits ... please, not the credits! Fuck!

I must have spent too long enjoying my coffee, or got lost in the warmth of my shower. Either way, I was going to be late. Throwing on anything I could find that remotely matched, I brushed my hair and fumbled with some far from practical shoes. Tears started to well.

'I can't do this anymore.'

Falling back on my bed, one shoe still laying haphazardly on the floor, I began to cry in a way that felt foreign. My mind blank, devoid of any logical thought, I drifted into black, tears streaming uncontrollably down my face.

Around 11am, the phone rang. Still on charge next to her bed, I was violently awoken by the vibration and ring tone. A quick glance at the time as I reached over to answer startled me into a state of complete consciousness. Only one thing came to mind: *Tuesday, 10:58am and I'm waking up from some childish emotional outburst ... Fuck!* I knew who was calling, but I didn't know what bullshit I would have to swing in order to avoid another black mark against my name; the kind of black marks that you earn when you just don't give a damn about your job.

Answering the phone, I was greeted immediately with the clear and uncaring voice of my supervisor. 'Hannah, where are you? What the hell is going on?' There was an attempt at empathy with a very unconvincing, 'Are you alright?' tacked onto the end. There was silence, a silence so striking I almost became lost in it. 'Hannah? Are you there?' My boss had clearly had enough of the dead air.

'Ryan, no ... no I am not alright.' Struggling to think of an excuse that still had some semblance of truth, I managed to convey a somewhat sincere apology. 'I'm sorry, Ryan. I really am. I ... I ... must have fallen in the shower and hit my head pretty bad. I came to about ten minutes ago on the tiles, water still running with a headache and a decent sized gash. I'm getting dressed now and heading to the hospital.' Pausing, I considered the implications of my lie. *Fuck, that might have been too much detail. Is he going to buy it? Why did you mention a fucking head wound? Stupid, stupid girl!*

Ryan must have paused as well, considering how to respond. I knew he was pissed but also that he was clever enough to try and convey a façade of actually giving a shit.

'Okay, stay right there and for fuck's sake do not try and drive yourself to the hospital. You don't have to be a doctor to work out you're concussed. I'm calling an ambulance now ... not negotiable. Do not go anywhere!'

He hung up and I knew I might've have gone a little too far. Strangely, I didn't immediately panic. Instead, I was struck by the fact that Ryan actually seemed worried. He actually sounded like he cared about my wellbeing.

'Fuck!'

The panic set in.

No doubt Ryan would tell the operator I had hit my head and

had a wound. The paramedics were going to expect a cut and blood ... and a concussed forty year old woman. I ran into the bathroom and looked in the mirror. My shoulder length auburn hair was still half done and my pale complexion still held the signs of my emotional outburst. My puffy red eyes, glazed, held my attention and brought back a sharp memory of my breakdown and accompanying shame. How was I going to pull this off in a way that didn't result in me dishing out a self-inflicted head wound?

I stared at myself for what felt like hours, hoping that said head wound would suddenly appear. Based on the actual progression of time, I knew the ambulance wouldn't be far off and I couldn't be caught out in this childish lie.

'Why the fuck didn't I just say I was ill and forgot to call in? Stupid girl! Stupid!'

Nothing left to do but bite the proverbial bullet and come clean ... or self-inflict a head wound and feign a concussion; tough choice.

The next thing I knew, I was staring at myself in the mirror again. This time though, I held small paring knife in the right hand.

'At least this knife will actually get some use.' My poor attempt at humour was met with the obvious silence of an empty house. 'Deep breaths, Hannah. You can do this!'

I had to be quick; the room was filling with steam, fogging up the mirror. To complete the façade and stage the perfect lie, I ran the hot water and really set the scene. Raising the knife to her head, hesitantly at first, I studied the landscape of my forehead.

'Deep breaths.'

With one swift motion the knife cut through flesh, parting my skin with an almost exaggerated ease. Blood wept from the wound, reminiscent of my tears from earlier. Unfortunately, the tears turned into a stream and I realised that I'd got a little carried away.

Moving gingerly to the shower I turned off the water, in case I really did pass out and hit my head. I attempted to wipe the blood away with a towel, hoping to stem the tide before the ambulance arrived. I mustn't have been thinking straight because I decided it would a fantastic idea to throw the knife, the evidence of my deception, into the toilet ... a completely logical place to hide a bloody knife. Walking to front door, I unlocked it before collapsing into my favourite recliner.

I sat back, waiting, still wondering why the hell I'd gone through with this little performance. Why was I wasting the time of the paramedics who were no doubt on their way. It was at that point I registered the pain: a sharp, unsurprisingly nasty sensation emanated from the deeper than expected wound on my forehead. Sitting there, staring at the wall, waiting, I pondered my life and the absurdity of the predicament I'd put herself in. The pain...that sharp, unnecessary pain, triggered this moment of self-loathing. It was the pain, and the fact I enjoyed it, the fact it made me actually feel something physical.

You're a hot mess Hannah, was the last thing that came to mind as I sat there, waiting.

CHAPTER 2

The ride in the ambulance was far from pleasant, filled with awkward questions and an ever present sense of embarrassment lingering. I knew, deep down, that the paramedics didn't believe my story but I was too deep now and had to persist. The vehicle slowed and I assumed they were pulling into the emergency bay at the hospital.

Here we go. Deep breaths.

'Control yourself, Hannah,' I whispered to herself.

As the back of the ambulance opened I was greeted by a nurse with a wheel chair. A nurse who, based on her perfect face, petite figure and 'light up the room smile' didn't have a problem in the world. *Could this get any worse?* I hung my heard as the nurse helped me out of the ambulance and into the wheelchair.

Her hospital name badge told me this was Katie, even her name sounded perfect, and as I slumped back into the chair and accepted the ride I couldn't help but admire the girl, quietly wishing I looked like that.

As I was stitched-up, I tried to pay semblance of attention to the questions directed my way, but I was quietly contemplating my situation, nodding along. All I could think of was the steam filling the shower, fogging the mirror and slowly hiding my reflected façade; then the pain, that sharp cut freeing the crimson of my blood. The sensation was almost too much and I wasn't sure whether I wanted to laugh or cry.

Katie must have registered the not-so-subtle change and she put arm around me and squeezed tight. 'Hannah, I need you to lay down for a bit, you've had a rough day.' She adjusted the bed and almost pushed me down onto the cold, firm bed. Deep down, I wished she had pushed harder, I deserved it.

'I'll get you a cup of tea. Is there anyone I can call for you? You don't seem to have a phone with you.' She spoke with a sense of empathy and what appeared to be genuine concern for me. She gingerly shook my head and begun to consider just how vulnerable I must appear to her: naked except for my underwear and a thin hospital gown, a stitched-up gash and, more concerningly, no phone. 'Hannah, I've got you a cup of tea. Milk and sugar?'

I hadn't even registered that Katie had left, let alone returned with a cup of hot tea and a standard pairing of hospital biscuits. I didn't answer, instead reaching for the tea and one sachet of sugar.

'Thanks so much. Do you know when I can go home?'

Katie paused and, as the moment of silence was broken by the gentle tear of a sugar packet and an apparent fart and moan from the gentlemen in the bed next to me, I knew I wasn't going to like her response. 'I really don't feel too bad, honestly. I don't particularly want to spend the next few hours sitting around feeling sorry for myself.' With a smile and a forced laugh I added a quip about how I couldn't cope without my phone for that long; social media was calling.

I could tell from the compassionate expression that nurses are so good at putting on, that I wasn't going to like what came next. 'Well, I can tell you that you certainly you won't be here for a few hours. The doctors have decided they'd like to keep you in overnight. Just to keep an eye on you.' Katie smiled again sympathetically, trying to convey a sense of understanding.

'Fuck!' That's all I could come up with as I contemplated the clusterfuck that I created.

I had a fairly good idea of why I was being kept in, but I still felt the need to confirm my fears. Contemplating my line of questioning, I once again boarded my wheelchair and was pushed with relative speed through the dark, sterile corridors of the hospital. I considered trying some light conversation to cut through the silence but there was nothing that came to mind that could distract me from the fact I was confident these medical professionals thought I was crazy.

In retrospect, it was obvious. The clean, almost surgical, cut reeked of deliberate self-farm. A deep, emotive reaction of *fuck!* went through my head, swiftly followed by realisation that I swear way too much. I really didn't think this through very well, and my self-assessment of being a 'red-hot mess' was pretty much confirmed.

There were two positives to this unexpected hospital stay: the fact I got a private room, and the young, strapping doctor whose care I was under. I couldn't help but wish that he was available to 'care' for me in a different way, one that was far too inappropriate for my current situation. Besides, she saw herself as a pragmatist and despite acknowledging she was far from an complete aesthetic disaster, she convinced herself someone of his 'quality' was way out of her league. This had been a topic of frequent conversation among my friends, all married and living the dream of domestic bliss. Samantha, particularly, kept insisting my single status was due to a lack of confidence and, in the eyes of my oldest friend, Michelle, an unwillingness to 'show a bit more skin'. This was a bit rich coming from the most conservative dresser out of the group.

'Put it out there, show some flesh. If I had boobs like yours, I'd be showing them off.'

I always blushed and fobbed off statements like this, insisting I was quite happy and content with the occasional encounter and one-off adventure.

This wasn't entirely true. Despite occasional confusion and uncertainty, I wanted more than casual sex and an awkward morning, 'Seeya, thanks for the use of your penis.' The problem was, and always had been, that I didn't think I was capable of a proper, big person relationship. All the blind dates and "completely random" meetings with her friends who "just happened" to have a single male friend with them, and I still hadn't been convinced to do the relationship thing.

It wasn't that I didn't want to ... it was like sky diving or bungee jumping: I really, really wanted to do it but I didn't know whether I could sign up and pay the money, let alone jump. Once again, a red-hot mess.

Dragging my eyes away from the doctor's arse as he left the room, I settled into the hospital bed, contemplating the "conversation" the doctor had arranged with one of the hospital's "support" professionals in the morning. *How the fuck am I going to explain my way out of this without them thinking I'm batshit crazy?* What I should have added was ... *without me acknowledging I am batshit crazy ... and maybe need some help.*

PART II
The Secret Life Of ...

CHAPTER 3

'␀ve told you before Mum, I am not going for coffee with Miriam's son. No negotiation.' I moved the phone away from my ear to avoid the excessive volume of my mum's nagging. Moving in to end the conversation, I paused before engaging with the last maternal tirade. 'No, Mum. And you can tell dad that no amount of money, short of the price of a new house in a decent area of town, will convince me otherwise! This conversation is over … I'm forty years old, I can look after my own relationships. Believe it or not, I am capable of caring for myself!' My voice returned to the normal emotionless tone. 'Right, I'll see your Saturday at lunch. Love to dad.'

With that, my mother's weekly attempt to set me up ended in the same way they all ended. Putting my phone in the back pocket of my jeans, I concluded that I needed to find something else to do on a Saturday lunch and, maybe, just maybe, change my number.

Two weeks after the embarrassment of my hospital adventure, life had pretty much returned to normal. The little "conversation" I had to have with, who I was sure was the hospital psychologist, was not as bad as expected, it was actually quite cathartic. That being said, I still couldn't bring myself to admit the true reason behind the now famous head wound.

I'd decided that I'd rather be seen as batshit crazy rather than accept the fact that I'd cut my head open, wasted the time and resources of the ambulance service, all to avoid the repercussions of being late for work.

Trying to justify this in my head, I acknowledged the fact that the reason I was late for work was because of, what only could be classified as an episode or emotional breakdown. Personally, I blamed the booze and the medication, but I'm not sure that made things any better.

One positive did come from this hospital visit: I seemed to have acquired a new friend. I'd been having a coffee a few days later in the city and the nurse, Katie, walked into the café.

We'd ended up sitting together and as it worked out, we had a few things in common: music, books, an intense love of all things Hemsworth. I'd only had to lie once to Katie, and in an effort to maintain this lie, I was trying develop some kind of appreciation for Taylor Swift. That was a tough pill to swallow, with me being the polar opposite to your everyday "Swiftie" but I at least knew some of her songs now. We also had the shared experience of being hopelessly single. Though Katie was little more desperate than me though. Far too desperate for someone of a meagre thirty-five years of age. I briefly considered getting Katie in touch with my mother; surely she'd have someone to set her up with. On the other hand, I didn't think I'd wish that on anyone.

Early on in this fledgling friendship they'd agreed to never mention the "hospital incident" which it had become known as. It was a good arrangement. I didn't feel under the pump for my deception and Katie avoided obvious discomfort and, possibly, some kind of code of conduct breach. We picked up on a shared cynical view of life and we genuinely just "clicked". I was always pretty reluctant to rush into any kind of friendship but this really did just feel right.

Katie and I had breakfast one Saturday morning before her shift at the hospital started. Saying 'yes' to meeting at a café in the city at 7am when I lived forty minutes away with no reason to be there, seemed somewhat desperate in retrospect but the pancakes and company made up for it.

Our friendship certainly did go to a whole new level that day, when

Katie invited me to a late dinner and band at a local pub. I hoped the speed of my acceptance didn't reinforce the earlier desperation but, fuck it! I was going to the pub to see a band with another single friend, "single" and "friend" being the optimum words.

Katie rushed off to her shift after we'd agreed to meet at her place at 7pm. Conveniently, this was only a ten minute ride from my place and located in a rather posh area. Despite being already wired, I ordered another coffee and sat back and savoured the blueberry pancakes I'd just indulged in. *Shit! I wish I had known about tonight before hammering a stack of blueberry pancakes. Fuck!* I finished my coffee, nervous now of the impact of breakfast on my waistline and wardrobe.

I was in the city and had nowhere to be or anything to do until tonight. I contemplated another coffee but, with the shops beginning to open around me, I had a rare moment of clarity. Suddenly, I had a plan for the day.

I'd decided to treat myself to a new outfit for tonight. I was talking complete outfit, shoes, accessories and all. Besides, trekking around the city all day would help remove the guilt from the pancakes. I just had to stay clear of Chinatown at lunch time to avoid adding to my food guilt.

Walking through the first store I encountered, one I regularly frequented when in the city, I was met with a familiar quandary: what to buy? Do I go classy, casual, slutty? *Fuck. I wish someone was around to ask, Katie in particular.* I really didn't want to show up in my standard, "I have no fucking idea what to wear" outfit which was a little black dress and black heels. That dress was cursed, I was sure of it.

The last time I'd worn it was to a dinner with Anna, one of my married friends. Very domesticated and down to earth she is, good family woman and quite conservative. So, it came as quite a surprise to all when I'd arrived at a casual dinner with Anna and her sisters, one of which went school with us, in a relatively short little black dress, high heels, 'going out' make-up and sporting a new hair style. While that didn't sound inherently bad, it was certainly quite a contrast to the jeans and shirts the others were wearing.

I'd felt like a fucking idiot, which may have led to me excusing myself early to write myself off at the bar of a nearby pub. This then may have contributed to me going home with some random guy who, so he'd told her, worked with a prominent sporting club as a physiotherapist. Seeing his naked body in the somewhat coherent state of the morning after, certainly led me to question his story.

Basically, that dress had led to a vicious cycle of bad decisions so I was determined not to wear that night. Resisting the temptation to text Katie and get some kind of clarification of the night's intention, I eyed a chic little number. I thought the colour was apricot; with a, spaghetti strap, conservative, but still short enough to turn few heads; theoretically anyway. Fleecing the only size 12, I made a b-line for the change rooms grabbing another dress on the way in the same style but in a light blue.

Now for the situation I always dreaded: the moment I figured out if my rose coloured vision matched the reality of it all. I stood there, scrutinizing my near naked body to, what most would say, an unhealthy degree.

'I'm not that bad … surely. Decent boobs, petite … ' I trailed off as I realised that I'd been thinking out loud. The snigger from the change room next door confirmed the fact I'd given someone some level of amusement. *Mental note, don't leave until you hear that the amused customer is well gone.* As I slipped into the apricot dress I made a quiet note of the fact I would need a new, sexier bra, on the off chance I actually ever found myself in a situation where I'd give a shit about what a guy thought. *Perfect fit, surprisingly. This never happens.* I actually liked the way it looked on me with the fresh form of the material accentuating my strengths and hiding the flaws.

I didn't even bother trying on the blue number, I just stood there, hands on hips eyeing myself, trying to build my self-esteem. This moment of self-admiration and/or loathing would also delay my departure long enough for my booth neighbour to hopefully depart. Changing back into my street clothes I made my way to the counter with a new-found confidence, a swagger that seemed to have stemmed from actually finding something that a) fitted b) looked ok and c) didn't require me to take on a second job as a waitress. For the first time is a long while, I left a store feeling relatively happy and somewhat confident, a feeling I certainly hadn't been expecting.

The rest of the day was filled with a feeling of giddy anticipation, coffee and a rather eventful train ride home. I'd never expected to see a penis this early in the day, especially one belonging to a rather hairy twenty-something gentlemen who seemed to have been indulging either an elicit substance or have drank his body weight in booze. He was quite impressive, as he appeared to have no problems getting things happening "down there" despite his inebriated state. But his enjoyment and merry making was cut short when two rather unimpressed police officers boarded and kindly escorted him off the train.

For the sake of the unsuspecting commuters, I hoped they would force him to cover his cock before escorting him through a crowded station to the inevitable cold of a waiting police van. In a perverted kind of way, I hoped it would be cold enough to remove any visible signs of arousal and remove any thoughts of penile grandeur he held.

Adding to my sense of self-perversion, for the next few minutes I struggled to avoid the thought of what level of ugly his penis took on while flaccid. What the actual fuck was wrong with me? Was I really so desperate and perverted to fixate on the size and appearance of the cock of a stranger on a train? Apparently, I was; leaving me to conclude that I was either incredibly desperate, incredibly crazy, or just a dead-set pervert ... the jury was still out.

7pm couldn't come soon enough. I was keen, remotely confident and, surprisingly, not feeling like I needed to assume the foetal position and cry. Opening the door, I kicked off my shoes, dumped my shopping bags and hightailed it to the kitchen. My breathing was laboured from, presumably, the anticipation. The cure was obvious and one I resorted to far too frequently; wine! I knew I had a lovely bottle of actual Burgundy ... from France ... fancy and quite expensive. I pushed it aside and found a $10 bottle of pinot. The best thing about cheap wine was the fact I didn't need to a) find a corkscrew and b) try and open the bottle quickly without fucking it up. Pouring a rather tall glass, I knocked back a significant portion while surveying my place.

My "not giving a fuck" attitude was really starting to show with a sink full of dirty coffee cups and a single plate, while the coffee table, ironically, was topped with a few magazines, two wine glasses and an empty bottle. Why two wine glasses? I assumed I'd just been too lazy to return one to the sink and add to the pile of dirty dishes.

I should make some effort to get ready early. I needed to impress and leaving make-up and hair to the five minutes before I needed to be looking for an Uber would only end in me looking like child sneaking a go at mum's 'big people' make-up, and not for the first time. I locked my door, grabbed my shopping bags and, importantly, the wine, and moved into the bedroom.

Putting on some music I parked myself on the edge of my unmade bed to plan her approach for the next few hours. Getting ready to go out was, after all, reliant on a military-like routine, planning and a strategy, that would result in me looking sharp, sexy and single.

I came up with the following: finish my wine, layout my outfit, organise another wine for the shower (shower drinking is awesome!), shower while drinking said wine, get dressed, check the wine situation, make-up, and hair.

Controlling the wine before leaving was somewhat essential. I needed enough to calm myself, take away the nerves and develop some inspired confidence, but not so much that I turned into an overtalkative, drunk, and desperate mess.

Slipping out of my clothes was refreshing, almost like a rebirth of sorts as the stench of public transport and the masses seems to have been absorbed into the fabric. Whenever I was changing, I always seemed to think about getting a tattoo and where I should put it if I ever actually followed through with it.

Would it just be an act of rebellion against my mum? It was something I'd really wanted to do in my teenage years, or a way of making one part of my body look how I want it to. Either way, I promise myself that one day, despite my fear of needles, I will go through with it. Maybe a cute little tattoo of a bottle of wine would be appropriate, considering they say you need to tattoo something important to who you are.

As I stood there waiting for the water to heat, I concluded that this very night started right here, several weeks ago. Here I was now about to shower and dress up and go for a night out with this beautiful, kind and confident nurse who through, what a more positive person would call fate, I ran into again at a coffee shop. I still couldn't believe we'd clicked and that she actually appeared to genuinely enjoy my company. Doe-eyed, I stood there contemplating my current "Katie-centric" emotional state until I was brought headlong back to reality by the ever-increasing steam fogging up the glass. I was proud of myself as I stopped myself making a stupid, clumsy error and stepping into the obvious scalding heat of the water.

I paused, tried to gain a semblance of focus, turned down the heat and moved into the warm embrace of the downpour; after grabbing my glass of course. As I rested my wine on the rather unstable soap rack, I contemplated the grimy state of my tiles. A kind of funky looking mould was taking over a few locations, making the grout its own. Taking another sip from my wine, I promised myself that if tonight actually went well, I would try and sort my shit out and make my place less of a proverbial pig stye. I was very aware of the need to really wash that dirty "I've been in the city" vibe that somehow manages to worm its way into every crevasse of your body, before I finished my friendly shower wine. I was concerned the less than subtle aroma of my coconut body wash would ruin the ... something posh sounding ... of the wine but as it happens, it takes a lot to totally wreck a cheap bottle of red wine.

    I must have taken longer in the shower than I thought. I got overcome by the miasma of steam, hot water and the tingle of the wine. The lingering, sweet aroma of coconut exuded from my pores as I dried off. Wrapping the towel around my body, I find another clean towel and go to work on my hair. Standing in front of the mirror I consider what the actual fuck I am going to do with it. In my haste and anticipation, I never actually thought how I would attempt to style my shoulder length, currently dishevelled, hair. Throwing my pretence of a battle-plan to the wayside, I decide it's best that I "own" my lazy hair. I decided on a messy, undone look. I brushed just enough to keep my waves textured and tousled. Pairing this with my relatively long, choppy fringe, reeked of a lazy, sultry, sexiness while, at the same time, it was casual enough to work for whatever Katie had in mind for the evening.

    Getting dressed is, for many, an artform and I found the process of selecting underwear the hardest part. I continued to have these delusions of finding a classy gentlemen, one that I could take home for a torrid, sweaty night of passion but have him still be there in the morning after the alcohol wore off. Two things struck me about this scenario: 1) these are not the type of guys I bring home, when I do manage to hook-up and 2) I am, and always have been, a romantic failure. I honestly believe, I am destined to be one of those crazy cat ladies, except for the cats of course ... I fucking hate cats!

All the while these delusions went through my wine-soaked head I had managed to shift into autopilot and dress myself in sensible, plain underwear and the dress I picked up today in the city. Now, the litmus test: will it look as good on me now as I thought it did today? Approaching the mirror, I closed my eyes, stood tall and braced myself. Butterflies fluttered in my stomach and impending dread flowed through my mind.

I tried to think positive. 'I **will** look hideous in this dress! It **will** highlight every flaw on my body and it **will** make my hair look like a poorly constructed birds nest.' At least that is some kind of positivity I guess. Forcing myself to open my eyes and raise my head, I was greeted with something I didn't expect. I actually looked half-decent!

I kind of looked like a movie star, all be it one of the plain looking bridesmaids in a Hollywood romcom. I turned side on, I did a swirl and I checked my arse out as best I could from over my shoulder. It might have been the red wine messing with my head but the tears I expected were replaced with a little smile. I guess my positivity worked after all.

Forcing myself away from the mirror I rushed off to do a simple make-up job. I contemplated the glow look but I get enough of a shine on after the inevitability of cocktails. Deciding on a simple gloss on my lips, one part of my body I am quite proud of, I went for a pigmented blush, gradually building up the colour on my cheeks to a level I was happy with ... I just wanted a "pop" without being too over the top. That was it, I was done ... I think. I felt comfortable, cute and the most confident I have been in, well ... years. Grabbing my clutch and phone I dashed to the door, giddy with red wine and anticipation. Now, challenge number one of this evening: get a cab that doesn't stink of sweat and stale coffee.

CHAPTER 4

The trip to Katie's place was surprisingly smooth and painless. I didn't wait long for a cab, it didn't stink, and the guy knew exactly where to go and had absolutely no interest in small talk. It was the very definition of a perfect cab ride.

Pulling into Katie's street was a surreal moment; it was a lovely street with a line of cute, well-kept houses and immaculately kept lawns and gardens. It even had a green space, one that wasn't just an abandoned block. It was obviously maintained by the local council with love and care. The rose garden sported an impressive array of colours in an organised and weed free bed. The grass itself was incredibly uniform in both height and colour giving the area, and the street, an incredibly welcoming feel.

As the car slowed down, I took a quick glance at the metre and, while I somewhat expected it, the cost took me a little by surprise. Pulling into the driveway of a rather large looking brick house, I prayed that this wasn't a big practical joke. What if I'd been deliberately given the wrong address? It had happened in the past with a guy who, I naively, thought was relationship material. That prick got his own though, he ended up getting one of the HR women at work pregnant. Oh, it gets better: he was engaged at the time, she was married, and it turned out to be twins! I'm not normally a bitch, but regardless of how many times he apologised for his immature "prank", I couldn't help but take a perverse pleasure in his self-imposed misery. I think the Germans call it *schadenfreude* and I fucking loved it!

As I paid and received absolutely no farewell from my cabby, just as I liked it, I realised the address she had given me, 4A, was actually a cute little flat located behind the house in a subdivided double block. The path to her place was paved in flagstone and bordered by an adorable and immaculately manicured hedge giving it an almost fairy tale feel to it.

The sun was getting low as I reached her door. Anticipating my arrival, Katie had left a light on above the door in a welcoming touch. It is details like this that I wouldn't have thought of, probably because I would've already had a few wines by now in preparation for the night. I rang the doorbell and waited and stood there thinking just how perfect her place was, just like her near perfect figure, appearance and personality.

I checked my phone, 7.05pm, very unusual for me, but the wine was helping me keep it all together.

This isn't a fucking date, Hannah. Keep it together! It's a girls night out with a new, albeit amazing, friend ... calm down! As I heard footstep approaching the door, gorgeous high heels no doubt, I considered the real possibility that I had built the night up so much that it would end in some level of disaster or me doing something – or some*one* – stupid. I needed another wine to settle me down, calm the nerves. The wine from earlier, coincidently, also chose that very moment to want to exit my system. At least I knew how to open the conversation now;

'Hey Katie, I love your place, you look beautiful and where is the bathroom?' The footsteps stopped, the door started to open ... here we go, showtime.

CHAPTER 5

Standing in front of me was Katie, bathed in the back lighting of her home. She exuded confidence and grace with her hair done up in a messy bun and her little black dress. Little. Black. Dress.

I'm even happier now I didn't go with my fallback option; Katie looks a hell of a lot better in her LBD than I ever did. She grabbed me by hand and led me into a living area which, surprisingly, was messy ... maybe more so than mine. This made me feel somewhat relieved and happy that she was not completely perfect.

'Perfect timing, I just opened a bottle of bubbles. You keen?'

I'm always keen for bubbles but I needed to stem my enthusiasm, and avoid giving her the impression I'm a raging alcoholic. 'Sounds good but, first I need to visit the little girls room.'

I felt slightly embarrassed and with one of our first interactions for the evening involving my bodily functions, I started to regret the shower wines. She directed me down a small hallway to a comfortable sized bathroom.

Her shower was immense, taking up a rather large proportion of the room. It was so very impressive. A rainfall showerhead covered most of the beautifully tiled shower cubicle and was very much a thing of envy ... Anyone who says size doesn't matter obviously hasn't encountered a shower head of such size and beauty. Wanting to randomly take a shower at this point would be inappropriate, crossing that line between eccentric in a cute way and outwardly strange.

Drying my hands, I move back to Katie's living area but I am intercepted and handed a rather large glass of sparkling wine. Some music, which I couldn't identify, radiated from a Bluetooth speaker and we settled around a bench to, hopefully, discuss the evening.

Katie complimented my dress to which I responded with, 'You too.' Cringe ... so very cringe. Ten minutes in and my nerves have already made me look like an idiot. Having this gorgeous friend compliment my appearance made me feel strangely sexy, continuing to build up my confidence. I maintained some level of hope that this new-found confidence was not going to be shattered by the end of the night.

'So, I'm thinking we have a few drinks here and then head to a pub about five minutes away in an Uber; it's usually pretty buzzing. They do a great meal there as well and dinner would probably be a useful addition to the night, but it's optional I guess.'

There is no way dinner is "optional". Without something solid and non-alcoholic inside me I'll be anyone's by nine. This is something I am really trying to avoid: both the "drunken mess" thing and the picking up some random guy thing. I think either could detract from my new social confidence.

Three glasses of bubbly later, we decided to make a move. The conversation we had highlighted two things: unlike Katie, my job was fucked and the cause of massive emotional and physical issues, and that Katie appeared to be even more perfect than I'd originally thought.

It genuinely felt like we had been friends for years with the ease of conversation and the awkward topics (like my levels of craziness) that we could talk about without me shutting down.

She seemed to think that I needed have a conversation with Ryan, my boss, about where I was at and what could be done to try and help from the employer's perspective. The problem with that was, that other than the slightest hint of compassion from him during the infamous "head incident", he has exuded nothing short of a heartless prick kind of vibe. I was already concerned that people around the office were talking about the incident and assumed it was a classic self-harm, cry for attention from a broken girl kind of deal.

'Fuck them!' Katie said with a slight slur. Her training and wealth of knowledge had obviously kicked in, despite the bubbles. 'You know, it really is their responsibility to help with mental health issues in their staff. This Ryan needs to man up and take some actual responsibility for the health of his staff.' She sounded so professional and caring but the giggle that proceeded the statement indicated the booze was starting to take a hold.

I was incredibly relieved. I really didn't want to deal with this right now, everything about the work situation and how I felt was fucked-up enough without it taking over the conversation on a night out.

The booze certainly produced a more "out there" side of Katie that went beyond her regal confidence and presence while sober. 'So … ' – she gave another childish, but cute, giggle – 'this Ryan, is he cute? Ok, let me rephrase … ' – another giggle – 'is he fuckable? Really, if he is, you might need to strap on and go for a ride.' Her giggle turned into a laugh and I blushed so hard I could feel the heat radiating from my face.

I had absolutely no idea what to say; honestly. I had felt so much disdain towards the man that I hadn't ever really thought about him or looked at him in that way. Even on day one, his obvious arrogance prevented the pervert within me from checking him out in a either a sexual or romantic way.

Katie was clearly waiting for a response. She must have been able to detect my discomfort at the question which, I am fairly confident, made her more intrigued to hear my response.

Okay, Hannah, think quick. What did I think of Ryan? Was he cute, sexy or physically attractive in anyway? Fuck, the man was at least ten years my junior! He had been at the core of so many of my work issues with his blunt, almost confrontational, demeanour and ability to make me feel so immensely underappreciated so why would I even consider looking at him in that way, even for shits and giggles.

But now that I thought about it, he did have quite a nice arse. I sure as hell saw enough of it as he walked past my desk frequently, barely acknowledging my existence. I guess, in retrospect, he wasn't *that* bad to look at. He had that strong, chiselled facial structure with immaculately manicured stubble. His dark eyes exuded dominance and strength which was in complete juxtaposition to his smile. His smile, what little I saw of it, was subtle but hinted at a possible tolerant side to his personality. His body filled his suit well, highlighting his natural shape and build. There was no sculptured gym Adonis physique, just a regular male body.

Wait ... how the fuck did I actually know all this? It was amazing how much detail I'd apparently taken in about the guy who had made my work life miserable.

Katie looked at me with an eager expression, obviously wanting a saucy response. I had no idea what to say so I decided to disappoint her and go with underwhelming, 'He's okay, I guess.'

I wasn't quite sure where to go after that or even how to respond to Katie's wry smile.

In typical fashion, I finished off my drink and quickly changed the topic. 'I need more to drink.'

Katie laughed as she coerced herself off the low, leather coach nestled in her living space and made her way to the kitchen to, presumably, get some more wine. 'Hannah, how would you feel about ordering in and just kicking back here? I'm really comfortable and rapidly losing any motivation to go beyond my front door. I've got plenty of wine and we can order in some dinner.'

Staying in certainly had its merits; I was already quite tipsy and staying in guaranteed I wasn't going to make an arse of myself in public. 'New dress, just for tonight but you've certainly sold me on staying in. I don't actually know if I could tolerate another cab ride in all honesty.' I kicked off my shoes as I got up and made my way to the kitchen, I couldn't wait any longer for that drink. I needed to erase any memory of my thoughts about Ryan.

'Save the dress. We can try it out again in a few weeks when I'm not rostered on over the weekend. You look really cute in it and I'd hate to see it go to waste.' She winked at me as the cork popped and a fury of bubbles erupted from the bottle. Pouring two glasses she excused herself.

'I'm just going to change out of this dress if you're okay with that? I'll only be a few minutes.' I didn't have the heart to tell her that I would have preferred she stayed in it. There was something quite depressing about sitting around in a semi-formal dress, with the make-up and hair of a woman ready to tear up the town, while the only other person in the room was wearing relaxed casual.

'I can give you something more comfortable to wear, if you'd like?' As if she'd read my thoughts, Katie's voice echoed up the short hallway from what was obviously her bedroom.

I really wasn't sure what to say. I desperately wanted to change but from a glance, Katie was about a dress size smaller than me. There was quite an awkward silence which was eventually broken buy Katie telling me to have a look through her robe and put on anything I want if I felt like it. She appeared again, this time wearing a cute white tank top and a pair of jeans which accentuated her amazing figure.

Taking a sip of her drink, she grabbed my hand and led me up the hall and into her room which was strewn with clothes, including several work uniforms and the dress from tonight. I'd finally met someone with a more disorganised bedroom than me. I even saw a bra that had somehow lodged itself on the top of the window, perched precariously on the blinds. I tried to avoid thinking about how it got up there but, in my mind, it was either a fit of passion or the sheer relief of stripping off after a long shift.

'Don't be shy, honestly. You can't swan around all night wearing that while I look like this. What if someone comes knocking?' She directed me towards a rather overflowing robe, outfits appeared to be barely contained within the confines of the space. There didn't appear to be any rhyme or reason to the "organisation", it was daunting to say the least.

Stripping down to just my underwear in the bedroom of another girl was something I'd never really done. Even with my oldest friends, this had never happened. I was always uncomfortable with my body and was reluctant to even wear a swimsuit around others. The thought of putting myself in such a vulnerable situation awakened the fears of stares and silent judgement I'd so feared when I was younger.

Manoeuvring out of my dress I detected the subtle hint of coconut lingering on my body, despite the nervous perspiration that had begun to form. Feeling incredibly self-conscious, I begin to search the very back of the wardrobe, hoping to find some older clothes that I would feel less bad about spilling red wine on.

I picked out a simple blue blouse and an old pair of jeans shoved right in the back corner. Based on the creases and musty odour I could tell they were quite old. As I begun to shimmy into the jeans, I had a horrible thought: what if they didn't fit me.

I paused at my knees and took a deep breath. So far, so good, but I was trying to form a contingency plan in my head.

What if nothing fit? What I have to wear nothing at all? That was all I could come up with. That's how much the thought of not fitting the clothes of this gorgeous, trim girl, mind-fucked me.

Deep breaths ... you can do this. Say a prayer, hold it in, and think good thoughts. Regretting every muffin and serving of French toast I held my breath and pulled the jeans up. I couldn't believe it! They actually fit, and they were quite loose, in all honesty. Katie must have been a little bigger previously, which would explain their location in the back of the wardrobe.

Maybe she kept them as a reminder, as motivation, or maybe

she was like me and kept them as a contingency for when those few extra kilos inevitably return. Buttoning the shirt, which fit perfectly, I brushed myself down and turned side on to check myself out in the mirror.

I normally hated my reflection, avoiding it like non-alcoholic wine, but I couldn't resist. I looked okay, the combination actually worked. That's twice in a few days I hadn't wanted to drown myself in cheap booze.

'Hurry up, your drink is going to end up drunk if you don't get a move on. My room really isn't that interesting but if your snooping, do yourself a favour and avoid the bottom drawer.'

I heard Katie laugh from up the hall. Shutting the door to re-join Katie I oddly regret not checking out her bottom drawer. Maybe there was something truly scandalous like stolen medication from her work, but I'm confident the contents of hers closely resembled the contents of mine.

Katie had found us some new glasses of the fishbowl variety and filled them to a level that, in public, would have been ridiculously unacceptable – I know this from experience.

Flipping through her phone, she lifts her head and looks me up and down. 'Back of the closet, I'm guessing. I can't remember the last time I wore those.' She pulled back, apparently realising the slight size difference between us may have caused the delay in getting changed. 'It looks good on you, a little big, but the colour really suits.' Katie paused slightly as she shifted position, eloquently crossing her legs. 'You probably picked up that I used to be a little bigger. I'm not ashamed of how I was, but I also can't say I'm unhappy that I dropped a few. Running around doing long shifts in a public hospital will do that to you.' She laughed, handing me the wine, which I drank with far too much enthusiasm.

I pretty quickly lost track of the amount we'd drunk, which had removed any lingering nerves. Laying back on the couch, contemplating the need to order dinner, we become a lot more philosophical and by philosophical, I mean honest about ourselves. Katie, obviously the more confident of us, broke the light-hearted conversation.

'So, when we first met in the hospital, what was the deal? I've seen enough to know that the cut was not caused by hitting your head.' I could tell my body language changed immediately, I withdrew, both physically and mentally, trying to find some sense of safety from the question. 'You did it to yourself, didn't you? We all knew it, which is why we sent you to speak to the resident psych.' Taking another sip of wine, Katie sat up and edged a little closer towards me, sensing my discomfort. 'You obviously weren't trying to do yourself in, because no one in their right mind would think that was going to do the job. The doctor suggested it was a cry for help, an attempt to get someone's attention.'

I took another sip of wine hoping it would settle the butterflies building in my stomach.

'We don't have to talk about this, honestly,' she said, lowering her voice and placing her hand on my leg. The physical contact was nice, comforting, distracting me a little from the tempest brewing in my head. 'I was worried about you, I guess. I've been hoping that my instincts were right and there some just some wacky story to explain it all.'

Sitting up and finishing my glass of wine in one gulp, I accept that the reality of my situation: she was good at loosening my tongue, very good. 'Okay, but try and keep your laughter to a minimum.' I try and put on a façade of confidence as begin to try and explain "that night". 'Long story short … I'm a red-hot fucking mess!'

CHAPTER 6

I don't know whether Katie was going to laugh or cry. There was an awkward moment of ghostly silence as I stared uncomfortably at her, waiting for a reaction. All I could hope at this point was that this one act of stupidity wasn't the deal breaker in this blooming friendship. I'm sure there will be something in the future that will serve the same purpose.

'Wow … you need help.' She managed to get out with a wry smile. 'I'm actually impressed you went through with that just to justify being late to work. What I am more worried about though is the breakdown that came before all of this.'

Katie seemed genuinely concerned, something I wasn't particularly expecting. I guess I'd expected her to be a little more judgemental and I little less understanding. This spoke bucketloads about my other friends who, I have no doubt, would laugh to the point of rupturing something and then proceed to remind me of the event at every possible opportunity afterwards. Not that I'm saying they're bad people, but I always seem to be the butt of all jokes. I've always seen myself as the proverbial runt of the litter; not married, not as attractive and lacking in their social graces and lifestyles.

Don't get me wrong, I like them, and they like me, I think, but being the only single one and not a member of the suburban dream club, I will always be the odd one out. They are going home to their husband, kids and immaculate houses, while I'm going back to my messy, disorganised apartment; occasionally with some random 'gentleman' from the bar. Living the dream!

The mood went a little sombre after my revelation, Katie wanted to talk about my breakdown in a way that I had no doubt would make me uncomfortable. She topped up our glasses, which I am sure she realised would be required, turned off the music and sat on the couch opposite me in a position that reeked of the "I'm going to psychoanalyse you, but in a nice way" vibe.

'So, what's up? Really? Just talk at me if you want, I'm happy to just listen.'

She sounded so caring and actually interested in what was going on, that I actually felt like giving her a rundown of what was going on in my head. My goal was to avoid tears and to try and keep it as brief as possible. I really wanted to get back to having a good time.

'As I said, I'm messed in the head. I didn't think I was always like this but it is something; I feel like I've learned to live with it. I'm medicated for a few things, bipolar, anxiety, depression … you know, all the good ones … and sometimes they just kick into overdrive and over power the meds.' I looked at Katie for a reaction, any reaction.

'I knew all that, I've seen your medical records, it was a part of my job. What I want to know is what happened on that particular morning that caused it?' I really had to think about that. It seemed such a blur and just so long ago.

'I think I'd just had enough … of work, of routine, of my life, of everything. Doing the same thing every day, going to the same shit job that I fucking hate and coming home to an empty house. It's all very confusing, even for me. I don't want to be in a relationship, but I want someone or something different. I am happy with my random flings because, deep down, I don't think I am capable of a functional relationship.' I paused, realising that I was starting to evacuate my mind of all these little thoughts and eccentricities that have lived rent free in my head for so long.

'I really don't know what I want. I think that's what got to me, it just overwhelmed me. Sitting there, putting on my shoes staring that this sad little world I'd created for myself and not knowing if I wanted more or not. I'm forty and I've got my mum trying to set me up with her friends' sons, most of which are either too young, too old, way out of my league or, generally, just fucking creeps.'

Katie took another sip of wine, which I mirrored. After all, it would be rude to not indulge. She stood up and walked over, sitting on the couch next to me, obviously to provide some level of comfort. 'You know what, I'm thirty-nine and I'm in a similar situation. The only real difference is that I love my job and I'm not on the meds. Although, some of that shit you're on is pretty amazing. You could make a fortune selling if you're after a quick dollar.

'You at least have time for the occasional fling, I haven't had sex in six months or been on a proper date in over a year. Oh, and might I add, the last guy I slept with was, hands down, one of the most fucked-up men I've ever met. Get this, next morning, he asked if he could make breakfast. I showered, got dressed and came out to him eating the French toast that he'd made for himself... none for me, just for him. When he eventually fucked off, he left me fifty dollars on the bench! Who the fuck does that?' There was a pause while we took another mouthful and I had a chance to ponder what she just shared. 'Sorry, this was meant to be about you I should have—'

I interrupted with a little more vigour than I expected. 'Wait, you're trying to tell me you're thirty-nine? No fucking way you are that old, you look way too good to be pushing forty.'

Even to myself, I sounded much more intense than I expected but I was genuinely in a state of shock. This girl was twelve months younger than me while everything about her from her figure, demeanour and, most notably, breasts, were reminiscent of girl in her early thirties, at a push. 'How do you do it? Honestly. Sheep's placenta, animal sacrifice? Please don't tell me its eating healthy and training hard, because I'm really sick of that kind of talk.'

Katie laid back in her chair next to me and laughed. 'You try eating healthy and exercising regularly with the shifts and hours I pull? My diet usually consists of coffee, booze, and some type of food I acquire along the way. As for exercise, I'm on my feet all day at work, but that's about it.'

What do you say to that? I kind of felt cheated by life in that regards. I could live off of leaves and fresh air and still not drop a dress size. I laid back as well, sighed and had another drink. We both looked surreptitiously at each other from the corner of our eyes and burst into laughter simultaneously. 'I must say, I've always wanted to sacrifice a goat.'

CHAPTER 7

'm not sure if it was the emotional interlude or talk of a goat and sacrifice that brought on the insatiable hunger ... who am it kidding, we had clearly reached that magical point when drinking that eating become a necessity. The Thai food we'd already ordered on UberEats meant we didn't have to try and act somewhat sober enough on the phone to convey our order. My pronunciation of Thai food was sketchy at the best of times, so any drunken version may have resulted in some level of offence.

Katie ordered, which took away added pressure, while I rifled through her shelves looking for some more booze which, realistically, neither of us needed. I'm just thankful we are not at the pub because it is in this type of state that usually ends in me making bad choices, usually in the form of a Cameron or David. I was really enjoying the casual comfort of Katies clothes and the way they made me feel somewhat better about myself. There was no logical reason for it but, then again, my brain was wired in a way that logic usually played second fiddle to impulse, stupidity and a sense of self-loathing.

'Okay, dinner should be about thirty minutes apparently, plenty of time for more pre-dinner drinks,' I said, sticking my head up from behind the kitchen shelf. The rapidity of movement was not the best idea. The head spin was incredibly disorienting and, embarrassingly, required me to hold myself up using Katie's kitchen bench. With a smile, Katie suggested pre-dinner drinks might not be the best idea but I wasn't entirely confident in her sincerity in this matter.

'By the way, wine is next shelf over. Just saying.'

Regaining my equilibrium I reached in and grabbed a bottle, any old bottle. At this point, any level of wine appreciation had been eradicated and replaced by the simple desire for it to be good enough to stay down. It turned out I'd grabbed a bottle of pinot noir, and it looked a little better than what I deserved, but before I could question my choice Katie had the screw top off in a swift, purposeful motion and had begun refilling my glass.

Sitting down at the stools facing her breakfast bar there was a moment of silence or, in my case, clarity. I honestly thought, at that point, with a head drowning in wine and emotion, that this girl sitting across from me could save me.

CHAPTER 8

The UberEats guy was disappointingly average in appearance, usually my kind of man. He seemed incredibly excited to be delivering to two drunk girls, one of which was drop-dead gorgeous. I dare say his mind went to the copious amounts of porn he'd watched and the possibility that, in the most generic of porn premise's, we would have no money and would have to pay him in 'favours'. If that was the case, he was going to be incredibly disappointed with the very traditional and impersonal payment method.

She did, however, add in a sexy wink and gentle, deliberate physical contact in the form of her hand brushing his arm. No wonder he left with a smile. I wouldn't go as far as to say she enjoyed it but … fuck it, yeah she enjoyed it. That power she had over this guy with just a simple wink and an innocent touch. Men really are led by their cock when there is a pretty girl involved.

The rich aroma of curry filled the room as Katie walked into the kitchen brandishing a brown paper bag holding our dinner. There was a much-needed break from the wine as we sat and ate the steaming bowls of green curry and rice Katie had ordered. The warmth and richness filled my stomach, a panacea to my hunger after the ever-developing state of intoxication.

I was incredibly self-aware of spilling the thick, vibrant green sauce on my borrowed outfit as I enthusiastically finished my bowl. Embarrassingly, I noticed Katie was only halfway through hers as I sit back and bask in the afterglow of what was a stunning example of Thai cuisine. I had to stop myself from commenting on how it was better than sex, but that would be a slight exaggeration. That is, unless you take into account my last two or three partners, and I use that term loosely, of which one could only describe the act as being not even as good as a petrol station sandwich.

I sat, watching Katie finish her food with a grace and elegance befitting one of celebrity status. That however, was fleeting as a burp managed to escape her, shattering the façade. I wasn't sure how to react but deep down, I enjoyed a further confirmation that Katie was not the perfect specimen of femininity I'd once thought.

She laughed, which was a relief, and excused herself as she reached for her glass of which contained only a small mouthful. 'That was really good, I haven't had Thai that good in a long time ... not that I actually eat a lot of it.' I said. In fact, I can't actually remember the last time I had eaten it but, I did exclude that little piece of information.

Dinner kind of paused the festivities as we both came to grips with a full stomach. The laughing and childish silliness from early had been replaced with a level of civilised conversation, slurs and all.

I had entered a very pensive mindset, unsure of whether to talk to Katie about my earlier epiphany. While I wasn't sure how she'd react, the alcohol overpowered my conservative nature. Interrupting our talk of our respective neighbours, I hit her with this somewhat embarrassing revelation ... right out of left field.

'This is going to sound crazy and kind of intense, but hear me out ... please. I know I'm kind of broken and I've came to terms with that, I deal with it.' *Hold back the tears, Hannah, you have to finish it now.* 'But for the first time in forever, I kind of feel ... less broken. I know, this sounds stupid and ridiculously soppy but, I think it's being around you and I think you can save me.'

I paused, waiting for reaction from her; hoping that would be some kind of cue from her to reassure me, make me feel a little better about the shit I just said. After what felt like an eternity, she shuffled forward, placed her wine glass on the coffee table and smiled, I think.

Her full, red lips, slightly stained with the red wine, drew my attention as I contemplated the potential implications of my statement. Typical, I start something, get to the point of no return and then consider the potential ramifications. I realised, at that point, just how vulnerable I felt. I put myself out there, expressing something incredibly profound and personal to a girl I had only known for a very short period of time. I clicked with Katie and already had internally acknowledged that I saw her as the best friend I always wanted, and needed, and here I was, potentially, risking it with some creepy intense comment that made me sound even crazier than I am.

I knocked back the rest of my wine, the harsh intensity making me visible wince. That is clearly why wine is meant to be sipped and not devoured or, in the case of this one, possibly not drank at all. What the fuck have I just done?

CHAPTER 9

'Is that all? Christ, I thought you were going to ask me out or something. I'm not gay, but after this much wine I would have found it hard to say no.' Katie laughed and I relaxed a little more, eliminating some of the stress of the choice I made. 'You're not broken, you know that right? You're slightly cracked, but far from broken. If you'd worked where I do you'd know what broken really is. We had some guy brought in the other week, it was his third time he'd been in after messing himself up. He was hearing things; voices telling him ... things. That is broken.'

I hung my head a little, embarrassed and filled with this sense of selfishness and disgust at myself.

Katie continued, 'I'm not trying to detract from what you are going though, please don't think that. It's just that broken is REALLY bad and you are not broken, despite what the psych at work put in your record.' Katie reached over, refilling my glass, taking my hand in the process.

Why the fuck did I drink so much? I'd crossed that magical line that separates horny drunk from emotional drunk. Hannah could see I was struggling, I think she could sense my vulnerability and the sense of fear that was brewing inside me.

'Hannah, I'll be incredibly honest with you. I am not going to save you.'

Katie's words hit me with a force that reverberated violently, making me feel physically ill. I could feel that metaphorical crack she spoke of, very quickly turning into the break I feared. As she stared at me, her eyes revealing the subtleties of impending emption.

I tried to reassure myself in the fact that I'd be fine being broken. I'd existed in that state for so long that I almost took solace in the fact things would return to normal ... the daily drudge, the banal mediocrity. Hey, at least I still had booze and my medication, so it wasn't all bad.

I tried to avoid eye contact with Katie but it was harder than I thought as I kept being drawn to those blue eyes and full lashes and that look of what seemed to be pity.

Katie took my other hand and squeezed. She appeared to be transfixed on me, her expression taking on an appearance unlike anything I have seen from her before. In that fleeting moment, she looked different, a pale shade of the vibrant girl who just five minutes ago brimmed with vigour, confidence, and red wine. 'Hannah, I'm not going to save you ... ' *Fuck, we've already been through this, just put me out of my misery. Get it over with girl!* ' ... but maybe, if you're up for it, we could save each other.'

I certainly hadn't expected that. It came from left field and threw me for the proverbial curve ball. I had to resist the urge to tell her, "You can't fix what isn't broken" but I had enough self-control and common sense to just keep my mouth shut. Despite this revelation she still exuded grace and confidence in her presence, in the way she sat but, for the first time there was a hint of vulnerability in her eyes.

'I'm a little broken, Hannah. I don't know what I have in my life other than work and, like you, I don't know whether I want anything else. I honestly think we can help each other; I really do.'

I reached over and put my hand on her knee with the intention that this awkward physical contact might actually help her, provide her with comfort and a level of assurance. I hadn't prepared myself for this eventuality but the thought of a relationship of mutual support with Katie filled me with terror. How could I help someone when I couldn't help myself? However, going through it all with someone else along for the ride provided a level of comfort that I didn't really expect. I could tell she was waiting for something from me, some kind of reaction or response. I was nervous as fuck! I'm sure she could feel my hand shaking as I shifted position, my brain ticking over, desperately trying to formulate a perfect response.

'We can definitely do this together. The question is, how are we going to go about it?'

CHAPTER 10

The point had come in the night when even I could acknowledge the need to stop drinking. My head was heavy and my stomach was starting to churn, creating a rather unpleasant, yet familiar, feeling. That could also have had something to do with the revelations and repentance of the last few hours, but I have no doubt the copious amounts of wine consumed was the primary cause. I looked over at Katie who, for the first time since I'd known her, looked somewhat deflated. Two broken girls, sitting here, drunk out of our gourds trying to keep it all together.

Katie stood up and moved towards the kitchen, depositing her empty glass on the bench. 'Right, another drink?'

I couldn't help myself but laugh … and I mean REALLY laugh. The kind of laugh that only appears on special occasions and inappropriate moments erupted, filling the room. Katie just looked at me. I could tell she was trying to maintain a straight face; it didn't work. To anyone on the outside looking in, they would have been met by the sight of two obviously drunk girls laughing hard and loudly at each other without rhyme or reason.

'I probably shouldn't,' I managed to somehow answer, despite the laughing fit. 'It's getting late and I really should be getting home. Besides, if I keep drinking, I may very well end up back at your place of work with another self-inflicted injury and a date with a stomach pump.'

I brought myself under control as I realised that tonight was ending.

'If you are going to hurt yourself again, call me first so I can tell you if Dave is working. He works admin, he's as dumb as dogshit, but he is one fine specimen of a man. If he's working, it's worth the visit.' Katie's words were slurred, but still very sincere. I got the sense that she really didn't want me to go. 'You're welcome to crash here if you'd like. The couch folds out or you're cool to share my bed if you promise to keep your hands off me.'

I hadn't expected the invitation to stay … no one invited me to stay and that includes family and guys I sleep with. The cogs in my brain engaged as I tried to diplomatically decline. One of the triggers of my anxiety was the need for safety and security that my own house and bed offered. The vulnerability of staying somewhere else was scary and made my heart rate and breathing increase just at the thought of it.

'I can't, sorry. It's a long story … the whole broken thing and all. I'll explain when I'm at least slightly sober.'

It didn't faze Katie at all, which was a welcome reaction. 'Do you want to catch up for lunch tomorrow and a debrief? We probably need to work out exactly how we are going to go about this thing.'

I agreed without any hesitation at all, though the thought of food at this very moment resurrected the churning beast within my belly. 'I'll give you a call in the morning then.'

Katie called me a cab, which seemed to arrive very quickly. 'Leave your dress here. I'll bring it with me tomorrow.'

The last thing I remembered before leaving was a drunken hug at the doorway, which was beneficial to ensure we both remained upright. Falling into the cab door, I realised I probably should have brought my shoes with me.

Needless to say, the cab ride home was a haze. The good news was, I avoided painting the backseat with vomit – always a win after drinking. Now we come to the bad news: my bathroom floor and toilet weren't spared the same fate.

I had felt it brewing as I fumbled with my keys in an effort to open the door as quickly as possible. Luckily, I had no shoes to slip off as I threw my handbag on the floor haphazardly and darted towards the bathroom. By sheer chance and good luck, I had left the light on which made the cascade of crimson red that erupted from me as I fell to my knees much more horrifying. The cold caress of the porcelain provided no respite as I focused on trying to get as much in the bowl as possible. Unfortunately, I failed.

After the torrent faded and my stomach started to settle, I surveyed the damage. Having had some experience in the field of late-night cleaning, I anticipated this clean up would be a solid ten minutes of work but it could definitely not wait until the morning. As I kneeled there, knees aching from the cold tile floor, mopping up the consequences of my night of drinking, I pondered the reality of the paradigm shift in my evolving friendship with Katie.

I smiled. I finally had a friend that understood just how fucked-up I really was and wasn't scared off by it. A warmth, a glow that I hadn't felt in a long time, filled me ... and it wasn't associated with the borderline alcohol poisoning.

After the clean up, which was quite effective if I do say so myself, the turgid smell of vomit had disappeared. It made cleaning my teeth a whole lot more bearable, and as the minty freshness filled my mouth, a sense of emotional exhaustion overwhelmed me. Positive it wasn't just the alcohol, I wiped away a subtle tear as I staggered to the kitchen for a glass of water and my pills. These were the pills for the bipolar, not the painkillers I'd relied on for so long. I had the clarity to know that the danger of mixing them with copious amounts of wine outweighed the brief euphoria.

Gulping the pills, and what felt like a litre of water, I switched off the lights and made my way gingerly to the bedroom. I stripped off my clothes, underwear and all, and briefly enjoyed the fresh, cool air wafting in from the open window. The emotional fatigue was replaced by sheer physical exhaustion, and I slipped into my cold bed contemplating how thankful I was we didn't go to the pub. Not just for the incredibly amazing night I would have missed out by staying in, but also because if I had taken home some random guy, which was highly likely, I wouldn't have had the energy to even starfish him at this point.

I laid there, visualising the absurdity of me splayed out on my bed, falling asleep as this random guy, who in my thoughts resembled either one of the Hemsworth brothers, went to town on me with no abandon or restraint. It took no time for me to drift peacefully off to sleep with the subtle smile on my face, overwhelming the throbbing in my temples.

It was a good night ... I think.

PART III
A Series of Unfortunate Events

CHAPTER 11

The next morning was rough ... very rough. To say I felt like shit would have been the understatement of the century. Lying in bed, I realised the folly of not closing my curtains before I slid into bed. The morning sun shining through my east-facing window illuminated every crevasse and corner of my room. Katie's clothes I'd borrowed, as well as my underwear, lay in a crumpled heap next to the bed and a subtle hint of the aroma of wine lingered ... or was it just seeping out of my pores?

My head pounded; I could feel an unnerving pulsing in my temples and my mouth told me I was obviously suffering from hangover dehydration. I needed a drink and I needed the bathroom, but I did not want to move from the cocoon I had created in my bed. Eventually, the desire to not wet the bed became dominant and I forced myself to stand, slowly, very slowly. Squinting to avoid the full effects of the accursed sun, the pressure built in my head and the speed of the pulses in my temples increased, making this exercise painful and somewhat embarrassing.

I was no stranger to hangovers, but as I dragged my naked self to the bathroom, all I could think of was my desire to crawl back into bed and sleep off the effects. Even the flush of the toilet hurt my head. Any noise seemed to penetrate into my brain like a hot drill. I made my way to the kitchen for a much-needed glass of water and as many Panadol I could safely stomach before slinking back to bed, feeling incredibly sorry for myself the whole time.

Re-entering the bed, the sheets still warm, provided me with a brief respite. Laying there, thoughts of last night swirled mercilessness through my conscious. A notification sent my phone into a state of, what seemed like, eternal vibration.

I didn't want to look, but after the state I was in last night it could very well be someone checking that I was still alive. Fuck! Collecting my phone from the bedside table, I came to the stark realisation that I hadn't connected the power cord before I'd passed out. Knowing the age of my phone, my battery was going to be in a similar state as my own person ... near dead. Even the brightness of the screen hurt my eyes and at a mere 15%, the battery level hurt my very soul.

'I can't do today,' I said to myself as I unlocked the phone and checked the message. It was from Katie. I could feel the pain emanating from her disjointed message, my instinct told me she was in as much pain as me.

K: Want to share an ambulance?

...

H: 🤢 😣

...

K: Lol ... all seriousness, how do u feel?

I was relieved to hear that I wasn't the only one suffering this morning. While it is somewhat perverse, it reinforces that my body has every right to shut down after the supposed pasting we gave it last night. The realisation from last night that Katie was not perfect should really have changed my perception of her. I'd already elevated her, placing her on this metaphorical pedestal when, in reality, I had just been unrealistic in doing so .. In many ways, that made this friendship so much more "real", the notion that her and I were both flawed in some way. That being said, I'm still not one hundred per cent sure I believe it.

H: TBH, I feel like shit!

...

K: Was a hell of a night though

...

H: Thanks for, you know … listening

I just wanted to put it out there early and awkwardly, but having that proverbial shoulder to cry on and unleash the emotional fury had felt good. The only issue with it was that this morning feels like the aftermath of drunken sex, but with someone you actually have feelings for.

That entailed trying to find something to say that didn't make me come across as desperate, needy, or crazy, trying to avoid filling the inevitable awkward silences with my attempts at comfortable conversation. I looked at the positives. At least I didn't have to worry about breakfast or trying to figure out if the sex was actually any good.

K: No trouble, that's what friends are for I guess

...

H: 😊

...

K: Thanks for also listening to my shit. I don't think I've spoken to anyone about that before

...

K: I'm not used to opening up

What the fuck do I say to that? I really wish I had more of a talent with words, but the pounding in my head, the increasing queasiness building in my stomach and my general social awkwardness, made this difficult. Wary of my ever-failing phone battery, I stumbled together some kind of response that conveyed the sincerity that I actually meant.

H: Thanks for telling

...

H: It means a lot that you trust me

...

H: Unless it was just the booze, that's fine too though

...

H: *LoL* 😊

I was hoping that would have illicit some kind of humorous response from her. My desire for acceptance from this girl I barely know was incredibly powerful. I really needed her and, I was hoping, that after last night the feeling was mutual.

K: 😁

...

K: Still keen 4 lunch?

...

K: Late?

Shit! I'd forgotten about lunch plans ... I really was a mess last night. It would have been very tempting to say no, due to my state of near death, but the "late" part appealed.

H: Definitely! 2 sound ok?

...

H: I need to pull myself together

...

H: Lol

...

I know two o'clock was certainly on the very back end of what was acceptable for lunch, but I really needed to recover. Unlike my younger self, a cup of coffee and some less than healthy breakfast fare didn't cure a hangover anymore. Katie responded with exactly what I wanted to hear:

K: Two sounds good

...

K: I'll call you later

...

K: Phone is dying

The fact she was in the same hangover situation as me brought a little smile to my face.

H: Seeya

😊

Feel better

I avoided the temptation to respond further and chose instead to put my phone on charge before I forgot and was totally fucked for the rest of the day. I set my alarm, giving myself a fair amount of time to shower and throw some clothes on before leaving. In the meantime, I snuggled into my bed feeling quite content ... despite the state of physical distress my body was suffering.

CHAPTER 12

seriously contemplated cancelling lunch. My body was pleading with me to stay horizontal and motionless, but the desire to not fuck up the friendship with Katie in world record time was stronger. I sat up slowly, my head pulsing; waves of hot, sharp pain reminding me of the true depth of self-inflicted hurt I was in. I didn't even bother putting clothes on as I gingerly made my way to the kitchen, phone in hand, trying to find some respite in a glass of water and aspirin. I laid myself down on the couch to give the medication time to work, but the hangover continued to get the better of me. All I could think of was self-pity and the impending challenge of getting dressed and functioning as an adult while in public.

My phone violently erupted in a cacophony of noise, seemingly penetrating every inch of space in my lounge room, bringing me unwillingly into reality. As expected, it was Katie who sounded, if possible, worse than me.

'Okay, don't be mad at me,' she said. That wasn't how I expected the call to begin but the sadist in me was slightly intrigued by the apparent distress in her voice.

'Please tell me you're still as sick as I am.' My response sounded desperate almost as if I was pleading with this girl to be in physical pain and discomfort.

'I'm really, really sorry but I'll take a rain check on lunch. I am physically unable to function! Hell, I've tried for an hour to get dressed and it still hasn't happened.' Her voice had an unusual tinniness to it, almost an echo.

'That's fine, trust me. My relationship with alcohol is far from cordial at this point. I haven't been this hungover since ... well, last time I guess.' There was a pause and a laugh in stereo that still sounded pained. 'By the way, where are you? You sound like you're in a shed or a tunnel.'

'I'm lying on the bathroom floor in the dark, naked with a bucket.'

I had to force myself to hold in a belly laugh to avoid the pain that would follow. 'Confession ... I'm lying on my couch and I wish I had thought of the bucket.'

The conversation was one of the most bizarre I have ever had outside of those from the occasional trips of my early 20s. Two supposedly grown women talking on the phone, naked in various parts of their house, trying to avoid vomiting and the impacts of what genuinely felt like alcohol poisoning. The surreal nature of the experience was broken only by the pain and nausea that came with any form of movement and a knock at the door.

'Shit!' I rarely get anyone visiting and it was even rarer that they appeared unannounced.

'Just ignore it, Hannah. Be really really quiet and they'll just go away.' I held back a giggle and held my breath hoping that whoever was out there would just fuck off and let me die in peace. You could only imagine then what went on in my head when I heard a fumble of keys, one being inserted into the lock and the terrifying 'click' that came with a successful unlock.

'Fuck ... I've got to go.'

I dropped my phone to the floor and turned my head just in time to see the door begin to open. A very unwelcome wall of natural light penetrated the room, creating an even sharper pain behind my eyes, blurring my vision. However, it was the even more unwelcome, and instantly recognisable figure causing the intrusion that led me to accept the inevitability of what was to come. In the brief seconds that followed, I made no substantial attempt to cover up or appear even remotely human; it was futile.

My clothes, my robe, a towel, anything, were what seemed like miles away in my bedroom.

There was only one person I knew that a) had a key to my place and b) would be insensitive enough to use it to let themselves in unannounced. The silhouette started to take the expected shape and form, a look of stunned surprise forming on the face of the unwanted interloper.

'What the hell, Mum? What are you doing just letting yourself in?'

CHAPTER 13

Your mum walking in on you naked and hungover is not ideal. What made it even worse was that it didn't seem to faze her. Closing the door, she proceeded to open the front curtain, to my disdain. She gave me a disturbingly long look told me that I looked bloated and dirty. Wow ... thanks mum, all I needed at this very moment in my life was criticism of my body and hygiene. And she wonders why I don't visit.

I sat up, covering myself as best I could, thinking her next target would be my breasts or thighs, as she prowled her way towards my bedroom. Like a woman possessed, with the focus of Schwarzenegger's Terminator, she found my bathrobe and threw it to me through the doorway in one swift motion that successfully terminated any remaining self-esteem.

'Cover yourself, please dear. And go and tidy yourself up. You look like an unkept streetwalker after a big night.'

Wow, that hurt, and was disturbingly specific. I contemplated asking her about her experience with unkept prostitutes but thought better of it. Mum just stood there in my bedroom doorway staring at me as I put my robe on, tying the cord as tight as possible.

'Mum, what the FUCK are you doing here? More importantly why are you letting yourself into my place?'

I was pretty sure I wasn't going to like the answer.

'I was in the area and thought I'd see if you wanted a late lunch. Kristin cancelled at the last minute and I have a reservation.'

I filled the kettle and turned it on, hoping that through some type of witchcraft it would boil rapidly. 'And what part of that scenario gave you the right to just let yourself in to my locked house? I'm not a fucking teenager mum, you don't need to check up on me. For all you know, could have been entertaining or ... ' I trailed off, not know how to finish that sentence.

'The only entertaining you'd be doing here is with a "gentleman" you'd staggered home with last night. It is more likely that you'd be hungover and trying to get yourself together after another bender. It seems the latter was spot on; or is there a naked man around here somewhere that I've missed?' The sarcasm, oh ... the sarcasm. She continued, 'Oh, that's *right*, your male visitors are usually gone first thing in the morning. I'm still not sure if you're going out of your way to avoid any relationship beyond some seedy tryst, or if you are just not relationship material.'

That last one really hurt and It broke me just a little more because I ask myself that same question every single day, but to hear it from my mum in such a condescending manner hurt.

'Mum, please get out. I need you to leave now before I fully lose it.' I still, to this day, don't know how I remained that calm.

She looked at me with a genuinely surprised look on her face ... she really was delusional.

'Please, just leave. We'll talk later when I've calmed down and don't feel like I'm going to throw up.' *Deep breaths, Hannah.*

'Well, if you didn't drink so ... '

I visibly sighed but I couldn't let her finish another sentence that was in anyway critical. Fuck, if only this woman knew ... wait, she probably still wouldn't care. 'Mum, please. I really want you to leave. No, I need you to leave.' She stared at me, dumbfounded. 'Please.'

'Okay. Sure. I'm ... I'm sorry. I'll be in touch later when you've had a chance to ... ' Here we go again, the inevitable insinuation that this was all my fault. Sensing my reaction, she stopped, picked up her bag, and made her way to the door. She kissed me on the cheek as she walked past, awkward to say the least. 'I'll give you a call.'

She walked out into the afternoon sunlight, closing the door behind her leaving nothing but silence. I stood there in the kitchen wearing nothing but a dirty bathrobe and a hangover. I could feel myself starting to shake, tears forming in my eyes ... that unexplainable burning in my head. To this day, I still can't explain the intensity and pain of that burn. My doctors kept telling me it wasn't a physical pain but a manifestation of 'blah blah blah' ... all I heard was 'broken, broken, broken'.

CHAPTER 14

I wasn't sure if I was straight up angry or just depressed. Why had Mum's comments hit so hard today? Nothing she said was new, these judgements of my life were right up there with death and taxes ... inevitable and unescapable. Was it simply the fact she had the nerve to just barge in, or was it the audacity of the woman to speak to me like that? Really, I think it was the fact that what she said about my relationships had an element of truth to it.

Not that I should have to, but I wish I had the self-control to have tried to explain the sight that greeted my conservative mother without losing my shit. To try and tell her that, despite looking and feeling as bad as I did, that I may have finally been on the right track after one bizarre night with a new friend. But I know Mum too well, she wouldn't have understood how that a night of drinking and talking with a friend could have made such a difference to how I felt. Even if I had been able to explain to my mother about my night out, her "traditional" mindset and perception of me would have probably led to her believe that Katie and I were secretly dating and that I was hiding it from her. My family, mum and her sisters at least, think that if you're single at my age the only explanation is that you must be gay or crazy. Some views are too deeply rooted to be entirely founded on logic, but I'm not sure which one of those would have surprised them the most, to be honest.

I'm not proud of what happened next. I didn't deal with this mind fuck in the most responsible, grown-up manner. Standing there in the kitchen after boiling the jug for the fourth time, all I could feel was a deep "pain", for lack of a better word and, strangely enough, attached to this was a raw, almost primal level of horniness I haven't felt in a long time. In my defence, my body was probably craving the natural endorphins ... well, that's what I am telling myself anyway. I picked up my phone, realising that I would probably regret what I was doing but ... fuck it! I drafted a quick text to Jarrad, trying to figure out a nice way to say 'I'm horny, come over!' without sounding desperate and sad.

Jarrad lived just down the road. I'd seen him around and casually said 'hi' a few times, but our relationship got a little more personal when I ran into at the local bar one night.

I need to clarify, I *literally* ran into him. I'd turned around from the bar to take an obscenely priced cocktail back to the table with my friends and we'd bumped into each other. He was trying to find his wallet and I was just pissed and not looking and the result was an Appletini spilled all over his shirt. He figured it was his fault, bought me a drink and we got talking.

He was a really sweet guy, single and quite socially awkward. He was supposed to meet a Tinder date, but she'd obviously stood him up ... no one is four hours late. He eventually asked me out, but he just wasn't my type. In other words, he was too nice and, overall, not an arsehole. I felt sorry for him. so I did the charitable thing, ditched the girls and took him back to mine for "coffee". Poor guy, he actually thought "Coffee" meant "Coffee" ... he got a very pleasant surprise.

Long story short, the sex was good. He wasn't overly attractive, he didn't have the most amazing body and he certainly wasn't well endowed, but he knew his way around a women's body which was a step up from a lot of other men I've been with. We went our separate ways in the morning, but we'd slept with each other a few times since then after random encounters or drunken text messages where either of us needed a quick release. I wouldn't say we were "Fuck Buddies" because that implies a closer relationship, so let's go with "Fuck Acquaintances". Now was one of those times I needed to call on Jarrad. Surely, he wouldn't let me down in my time of need.

'What the fuck! He has a girlfriend!' I could tell from his text that he felt bad, but I'm sure turning down casual sex made this awkward guy him feel good about himself.

H: Congrats mate

...

H: I hope you're happy ☺

...

H: Would love to meet her at some point

That was a straight up lie, but deep down I wanted to try and seem like I wasn't such a bad person for being disappointed that this nice guy had found someone. I wish it didn't hurt so much.

Fuck the tea! I grabbed a glass of red wine, two pain killers and locked myself in my bedroom. Almost as if I was making a "fuck you" statement to my mum. A "You can get into my house but not my room" kind of thing. I placed the pills on the bedside table, took a swig of wine which went down like a glass of needles and rifled around for my favourite toy.

I took my robe off, slipped under the covers and did what any self-respecting forty something year old single woman would do: I took care of myself with the marvels of modern, adult technology. It unfortunately didn't take long and turned out to be rather "meh" but it was better than nothing. Sitting up, I had another sip of wine, downed the pills and laid there, mid-afternoon on a Sunday waiting to be taken into a euphoric, pain free state … a prescription high when less than twenty-four hours ago I was the happiest I'd been in ages. As it all kicked in and life started to become a haze of bliss and confusion, a thought of impending regret came to mind. That was the last thing I remember …

Waking up to darkness is a surreal experience. I opened my eyes, still in a haze, to nothing. For a minute, I thought I was actually blind, or dead, or in a coma. As things started to clear up, I developed a vague memory of my last minutes of consciousness. I reached around trying desperately to find my phone, trying to get a sense of when I was existing. I found my phone face down on the floor, not plugged into the charger and sitting at a meagre eight per cent charge. The time read 3.15am, Monday morning, about three hours before my alarm was set to go off.

    I laid down and sighed, trying to contemplate exactually what I intended to achieve through a cocktail of red wine, pain killers and raw emotion. I have never experienced lethargy quite like it; my body felt limp, unable to physically function with relative ease. I hadn't eaten since Saturday night, which explained the discomfort in my stomach. I lay there, contemplating my next move. I was going to have to call in sick, I couldn't function at that shit hole of a workplace, with a bunch of people who made my life miserable. I drafted a message to Ryan who, since the conversation with Katie about his 'aesthetics', I actually hated more. As long as this encounter didn't end in intended or accidental self-harm, I was good.

> H: Hi Ryan, sorry to do this to you

I lie, I am so not sorry. In fact, I hope me not being there is a massive fucking inconvenience, you subtly handsome arsehole. Maybe I went a bit too far there.

> H: I won't be in today
> H: I have been up all night ill
> H: Both ends are destroying my toilet

Okay, that last line was probably a bit much, not to mention slightly embarrassing. Thank god I hadn't actually sent that because I'm fairly confident that if I had, Ryan's cronies around the office would definitely be privy to my articulate description of gastric distress. Ok, delete the last line.

H: Vomiting and Diarrhoea
H: I'm about to try and sleep it off
H: Sorry ... Hannah

I felt like writing, 'Sorry, not sorry, arsehole!' but I did kind of need a job to pay the bills and fund my nights out. Fuck it. I sent the message, realising that otherwise I could forget or pass out, resulting in another mid-morning phone call asking me to explain my absence. I put my phone on charge and lay back filled with that sense of relief that comes with sending in that 'I'm not coming today boss, here's a bullshit excuse' kind of message. Before attempting to fall asleep again, I checked my messages, realising that I had a few notifications when I unlocked my phone.

There were a dozen messages, all from Katie, including two missed calls. Fuck! She was concerned, worried that I hadn't been answering. Messages started around 5pm and continued through until 2am and seemed to be getting more frantic. One positive though: she didn't seem pissed off, just worried. I was too scared to even listen to her voice mail messages (Who leaves voice messages these days anyway?), instead I lay there feeling both anxious and somewhat happy as I'd never really known what it was like to have someone actually gave a shit about my welfare. I had to respond; I couldn't leave her hanging any longer, so I sent off a really quick message to at least calm her down.

H: Hey,
Sorry, it's been an interesting day
I'll explain later
I'm fine, I promise
I am really sorry
xOxO

I clicked send and decided that a movie might be a better way forget the last twenty-four hours than just laying alone in bed. After filling the kettle and typically forgetting to actually boil it I slid down into the couch and begun to scroll through my favourites list in Netflix.

You know, that thing people create to supposedly make selecting a film to watch easier and more efficient. Ten minutes later, still scrolling, trying to clear my mind, all I could think about were these movies, particularly the stereotypical romcoms or chick flicks that had populated my favourites. So many thumbnail covers and titles and they were all the same. It just hit me: Hollywood has been lying to me for years! Those bastards! They always tell this 'uplifting' story of the plain, ordinary girl with any number of issues and obstacles to overcome.

Usually they have the help of another protagonist, to find happiness in some kind of bullshit, artificial "happy ending". All I could think about was how, for a brief moment, that it might have been my time to be that girl. I had Katie. I'd finally admitted to someone I had a problem and that now I know had someone to help me. I'd thought that maybe, just maybe, I could be Bridgette Jones.

Could this just be one of those bumps along the road? Could it be one of the complications faced by the female protagonist along the road to the metaphorical "El Dorado"? Either of those was a nice thought, but I couldn't help focusing on the fact that I was possibly too fucked-up, too beyond saving, to fit into the Hollywood narrative. Realistically, my supposed abuse of alcohol and unhealthy reliance on pain killers brought me more in line with any number of b-list celebrities who were publicly dealing with the same kind of shit.

Great ... Maybe I'm becoming the less attractive, less famous version of Lindsay Lohan.

CHAPTER 15

My phone erupted, bringing me back to reality from my rested, dozing state. It felt like I had been laying there for hours, staring at the ceiling bathing in the afterglow of a drug and alcohol induced slumber. It was Ryan ... of course it was Ryan.

His response was surprisingly civil. To someone that didn't know him, you would be mistaken into thinking that he was a decent guy and a caring boss. He told me my absence was no problem and that I should rest up and focus on getting better. He also mentioned that I shouldn't rush to get back to work but to make sure I am one hundred per cent.

I was finding it hard to justify my feelings towards the guy at this point, he seemed to actually care and there wasn't even a hint of sarcasm or any guilt trip whatsoever. What the fuck was going on with him? As I contemplated how to respond, another message came through from him.

> R: I'll give you a call later, just to check in on how you are going
> Until then, I hope you feel better

What the fuck? My anxiety went from zero to "I'm freaking out" instantly. Why would he call me? This had to be a trick, a way to check up on me and see if I'm actually sick and not just galivanting around faking an illness. Or ... even worse, he did actually care and he was genuinely concerned for my wellbeing. At this point, I wasn't not really sure which one concerned me the most because the thought of this guy having a soul was fricken scary!

I sat up on the bed, breathing deeply, working myself into a state of panic and sheer dread. I didn't want to talk to him and have him catch me out in a lie, giving him another excuse to make my life miserable.

Wait..think, Hannah. What aren't you taking into consideration in this scenario? My subconscious was a real smart-arse sometimes.

The voice in my head was clearly attempting to calm me down. *Deep breaths and take your medication ... prescription medication* ... that I was supposed to be taking at this time.

I ran to the kitchen popped my pills, 300mg of bipolar numbing goodness, and stood there, trying to listen to my sarcastic, bitchy subconscious.

Deep breaths ... think Hannah!

Then, it hit me and I felt like an absolute moron ... it was so bloody obvious! I didn't have to worry about anything as, on this rare occasion, I was actually unwell!

CHAPTER 16

I sat there, more nervous than I should've been, waiting for a phone call from a man who had, in my mind, made my work life miserable. Considering the way my fucked-up brain is wired, that also carries over into my personal life. For some reason, I had convinced myself Ryan was a part of the reason I was so messed up.

Clammy and fighting a nervous twitch, I sat there, pondering the idea that I might have had it completely wrong about this guy. Ever since Katie got me to think about, and vividly describe, his frustratingly "not unattractive" self, I have found myself questioning my perceptions of Ryan on more than one occasion.

Don't get me wrong, there wasn't the stereotypical cinematic "Oh my god, the man of my dreams has been right under my nose all along!" or "I just worked out the feeling is actually sexual tension and I just want to sleep with you" moment, but Katie had me questioning my mindset. Was I that Hollywood office bitch that made everyone's life miserable through her undisclosed cynicism and pessimism? Was I the Joker to his Batman? Had I created a work nemesis to justify my sheer unhappiness, a scapegoat to justify how I felt about work and its role in how fucked-up I am? What the fuck was I actually doing with my life?

So many rhetorical questions floated through my mind, and only some of them relevant. I flung my head back, throwing my phone alongside me on the couch. After a slight, dainty bounce, a sudden, violent vibration erupted signalling an incoming call. It was Ryan.

Deep breaths, Hannah. It can't be as bad as you've been telling yourself... you've worked yourself up over nothing.

I took a deep breath as my finger worked the touch screen, answering the call. I could hear my heart through my chest and felt my temperature rise as I brought the phone up to my ear. *Deep breaths, Hannah!*

'Hello, Hannah speaking.' I hoped that my nervousness and its obvious physical signs would not register, but I wasn't holding my breath. Although maybe that would have been a good distraction or, if I did it long enough I could have passed out and fully skipped the unpleasantness.

'Hannah, Hi, its Ryan ... ' *No shit. I thought it was Chris fucking Hemsworth, you wanker!* Thinking of that witty retort calmed me a little. ' ... I just thought I'd check in to see how you're feeling. I've noticed ... Sorry, we've noticed that you've been unwell a fair bit recently, as well as distracted and not yourself.' Oh, here we go ... Insert metaphorical eyeroll here ... let's pretend to give a shit while actually passively aggressively telling me to work harder and be happy! 'To be honest, I'm worried about you. If there's anything at all I can do to help, in any way, please let me know. Email me, even, if you don't feel comfortable talking about it.'

Wait, he actually seemed concerned ... again ... and it seemed genuine. What does someone who is so fucked in head do, when someone who I thought was a total arse, offers to listen and to help? Well, anyone else might feel comfort in a potential new support network, but not me. I just started to get emotional.

Another breakdown on the way, lovely.

As I felt the familiar sensation of tears welling in my eyes and the almost incandescent hurt begin to radiate from my very core, I tried to think of something to say that would end this conversation. The silence was deafening with the only hint of sound being my increased breathing.

'Okay ... thanks. I'm fine sometimes I think. It's all good, thanks for the call and I'll see you tomorrow.' *Smooth, Hannah, very smooth, that sounded completely normal and grounded in fact.*

My sarcastic subconscious really irritated me sometime, making me regret my verbal choices even more. Ok, now think of something that is really pressing that will need me to hang up straight away … and make it good. 'Ummm … thanks for the call but I have to run. My cake is burning and my doctor is about to call. You know, telehealth and all. Thanks.'

With that, I hung up and contemplated how amazing poor my excuse was. A burning cake? That's a good one … moron! Trying to calm myself and fight back the tears I decided a hot shower and a cup of tea might help me work through one of the most awkward exchanges in the history of awkward telephone calls.

CHAPTER 17

I managed through sheer luck, to organise lunch with Katie that day. She happened to have not been rostered to work and I seriously needed a debrief. On another positive note, she didn't ask why I wasn't in the office as me "just not feeling it" would be a clear cover up for "I just can't face it". Despite that, I did, however, have a strange suspicion that she had just swapped shifts with someone so she could check in and make sure I wasn't about to have a complete breakdown and do something stupid after my unscheduled communication blackout the day before. It didn't matter to me at that point. I was just thankful for the contact, an element of positivity in my life that would, again, lift my mood and make me feel remotely like a functional, normal human animal. I'm also fairly confident that this was her way of ensuring that I avoid turning up to her place of work in an ambulance again. It becomes quite depressing when, as an ER nurse, you see your friend more frequently on-the-job than you do socially. Having to explain to your work mates how you know "that crazy woman" becomes exhausting after a while, I guess.

My walk to the café was peaceful, my earbuds in, Lily Allen playing, and a level of positivity reinforced by the sunlight shining brightly through the milky white whisps of cloud. Thoughts danced through my head from the completely inane: *I'm so glad I brought my sunglasses*, to the deeply profound. Of course, the deeply profound was centred on my rapid and frequent shift in moods and the underlying cause: *I thought the medication was supposed to keep my bipolar in check?, Am I really beyond help and I just need to accept it and learn to live with it?* and, most concerningly, *Was this all my fault? Does the way I live, and act and think bring all this on?*

Surprisingly, the final thought didn't hit me in the feels, it simply made me question that maybe the way I lived my fucked-up life, contributed to it all.

I could hear my psychologist's voice in my head begging me, in that ridiculously sexy English accent of hers, to accept that what was going on "upstairs" was not my fault and that IT IS in fact a chemical imbalance in my brain and that I shouldn't blame myself. Questioning otherwise was detrimental and dangerous, and I need to stop. Controlling this bizarre, internal monologue was exhausting and something I generally disregarded. I had been assured by multiple medical professionals that schizophrenia was not one of the problems with my head. That was, my dad would say, a good thing.

I turned the corner into the quiet back street, where this chic little café that Katie had told me about hopefully was. I couldn't see any café, but I immediately noticed the change in temperature as I left the warmth of the sunlight and entered the shadows of the narrow, unwelcoming street. However, I could smell the familiar, savoury aroma of freshly baked bread and pastries. Turns out the café was actually a quaint little French pātissier, and as I got closer, I already started to fear for my thighs; self-control around anything involving pastry and cream was not one of my strongest attributes. As I approached the bustling alfresco eating area, I was greeted by a sea of vibrant colour erupting from the plethora of dresses, hats, and accessories, most of which would have been well outside my price range.

The whole scene was in vast contrast to the grey urban neutrality of the alley and its complete lack of personality, but I think that's what added to its character and obvious appeal. I caught a welcome glimpse of Katie, nestled away in the corner; lucky enough to have secured a table for us. Her beige skirt and plain white halter neck blouse stood out through the sheer normality of the outfit, in stark contrast to the inordinate variety of colour and styles and display from the other, predominantly female, customers. I hadn't put a lot of thought into my choice of clothing, but I was happy with the simplicity of my navy, off the shoulder, floral dress. It was a $30 job I picked on sale somewhere and it was incredibly comfortable which provided me with a level of social confidence normally absent.

'Hannah, over here!' Taking in the surroundings made Katie's voice and exuberant wave stand out even more in the sea of kept women and socialites. I know, I shouldn't judge, but it was just so fucking obvious! I had no doubt at all they would be looking down on me and judging every aspect of who I was as soon as I sat down. It turned out, I gave them a great opportunity to kick off early because in my eagerness to acknowledge Katie's gesture I failed to notice the rather large crack in the pavement.

My toe somehow managed to get partially caught and I stumbled somewhat comically, arms flapping about in a futile attempt to maintain balance, before meeting the concrete with an almighty "thud". Pain shot through both knees, but it was the sheer embarrassment that concerned me the most. The silence was deafening as the attention of the café's patrons seemed to be solely directed at me, "that woman" trying to gracefully get herself upright and tidied up. I heard the whispers and snickers before I noticed the source: a group of stuck up forty-something women trying hard to avoid openly bursting into laughter.

Leaning down to brush the dust and grime on my knees, my hand was met with what I was hoping was blood and not random liquid from the alley, and a sharp pain that radiated outward from my kneecap. I wasn't sure what was redder, my face or the blood leaking from the graze on both knees. Katie pushed her way through the gawking onlookers with a mixed look of concern and disgust at the complete lack of humanity she'd just witnessed. Pushing her way through the crowd, she bumped into the sniggering lady, who was wearing an apricot dress of some type with a gorgeous black jacket that made me incredibly jealous. She was the obvious alpha female in her group and she gave of that air of arrogance and self-perceived perfection.

'Rude!' the woman said, scowling.

Katie's response, however, was a little more on the informal side. She stopped suddenly and took a menacing step towards the middle-aged lady, who was now standing. 'Seriously? You want to act the victim here? You just saw someone fall and potentially injury themselves and the best you could do was sit by with a smirk and smart-arse comment to your friends. Meanwhile, someone making an effort to help, in this a case a nurse,' – Some kind of guttural sound suggested doubt, and this just seemed to fire Katie up more –'Yeah, that's right I am a nurse. Do want to see my ID? A statutory declaration? A letter from the fucking queen? It shouldn't matter because someone happened to give a shit and actually try to help someone and you, poor Miss Gucci with the obvious botched nose job, has the nerve to act hard done by because your coffee was spilled! You are the very worst example of humanity!'

The woman stood there, speechless and in a state of obvious embarrassment. Katie turned to the other women at the table, the whole café in complete silence watching, listening, in what appeared to almost be a state of fear.

'I pity you,' Katie said, and pushed through the rest of the stunned patrons while me, a lone figure dishevelled, bloody and embarrassed watching from the background shocked at this sudden transformation. I had witnessed a side of Katie I would never have imagined as she morphed from this bubbly, grounded lady into an avenging Valkyrie, bringer of shame and misery. As she got closer, I could see a subtle smile on her face, and she gave me wink. The confidence she exuded as she strode towards me from the chaos she left behind her in that quaint little patisserie was obvious. The whole moment closely resembled the iconic 'hero walking slowly away from an explosion' scene from the movies.

Is it bad that at this point I was a little turned on?

CHAPTER 18

Katie grabbed me by my hand and tried to lead me away but I was still a little dazed and in awe of what I just witnessed. 'Are you good? Anything going on there other than your knees?' She said, looking down at my bloodied legs with a level of care I should have expected from her by now.

'Yeah, I'm good ... I think. A little shaken up, a little embarrassed. It's only a little blood, so I guess it could have been worse.'

Katie clearly saw through my rather poor attempt at a "it's really nothing" smile, put her arm around me and half dragged me into a sheltered alcove off the street which led to the vestibule of an apartment block.

'Nothing to be ashamed of or embarrassed about. Fuck them and their petty schoolyard bullshit. Did you enjoy the little verbal bitch slap I gave that cow? Because I certainly did!' Her genuine, yet incredibly cheeky, laugh brought me back to reality a little and, while Katie's assessment of the situation was spot on, I still couldn't drag myself aware from the utter sense of shame that I felt. Inside, I knew it was completely illogical to feel that way and that I would probably never see those women again anyway but my fucked-up brain immediately goes into the "this is your fault and this is why you can't have nice things" mode.

It must have looked like I was in my own little world as it took several harsh finger clicks and a 'You with me girl?' from Katie to bring me around. 'Wow, you really do have some issues going on in that pretty little head of yours, don't you?' Smiling, she expertly extracted some tissues from her handbag and kneeled down in front of me. With great care and attention, she dabbed away the blood, removing the dried, clotted sections with the touch of a mother caring to a child's scrapped knee and accompanying tears.

In many ways, I was the child in this situation in that I wasn't paying attention, hurt myself, got laughed at by the bullies and was now being comforted in the arms of someone wiser. Wow, this really was primary school all over again!

'Not stinging too much? Sorry about the spit, but it's the best I could do in a pinch.' The sting started to subside as she begun to clean up the impromptu medical waste of a dozen or so tissues. 'How's that? Feel better?'

Being typically Hannah, I couldn't turn up this opportunity to make a comment that, for many, skirted the boundaries of inappropriate. 'Wow, I could get used to this. Its normally me on my knees with the tissues cleaning up.'

Katie just looked up at me and there was that awkward gap while waiting for a laugh or, at the very least, a sign that she wasn't utterly repulsed. Waiting ... still waiting ... FINALLY! After what felt like in inordinate amount of time, Katie allowed herself a laugh and I breathed again. Standing up, she put her around me again and said the most poignant, poetic sentence that my messed up self yearns for ...

'Fuck it! There is a bar down the road, let's have a drink instead.' I hope I didn't look too enthusiastic but the idea of day drinking after that debacle was incredibly appealing.

'You had me at "fuck it"!' The sound and smells of that alley faded as we gingerly made our way out onto the street and into the sun. The main street, while not overly busy, bustled in comparison with the sounds and sights of urban chaos. As we made our way down the road, the physical pain slipped from my mind, but the burn of the shame and embarrassment remained, buried within the chaos of my mind.

Katie took my hand and squeezed ever so gently, but with the emotional force of an out-of-control freight train. It was the kind of physical contact that, right there and then, I needed. It had the "I've got you, girl!" vibe.

CHAPTER 19

The bar was one of those classy little inner city numbers that reeked of pretentiousness and overpriced drinks. The clientele that time of day was, surprisingly, quite classy and seemed to be made up of a good mix of middle-aged guys in suits and young-ish girls dressed in cute, vibrant pastel outfits and expensive sunglasses. We got a few looks as we sidled up next to a window overlooking a busy pedestrian crossing but nothing that seemed to say, "What do you think you're doing here?" The eyes of at least two of the gentlemen seemed to follow Katie as she made her way to the bar, their attention seemed particularly focused on her arse.

'You don't see enough arse men these days, too many focused solely on the breasts.' In my typical style, that profound statement was audible and not just a random musing in my head. There was a slight giggle from a table of girls and a look from one particular redhead that told me she completely agreed with the sentiment. This was, thankfully, the only reaction I received from a bar that was far busier than it should be at this time of day. Katie seemed to eat up the attention, no doubt encouraging some incredibly lewd thoughts from the men as she made her way back to me with two rather large glasses of red wine.

'There are plenty of arse guys out there you know,' she said with a wink as she sat, no doubt witnessing the blood rushing to my face creating a tomato like complexion. "You spoke louder than you thought." There was a slight giggle as she took a rather large mouthful while I, struggling to recover, enjoyed the rich, fruity aroma of the wine I expertly identified as "red".

'So ... ' I knew this was going to be one of those conversations I put no thought into, just blurting out a variety of words best left internalised. It was clearly a combination of what I just went through and what had been building in my head for ages. ' ... you know I'm pretty fucked-up in the head right? Like, in every aspect.' While worded as a question, it was definitely statement. 'To an extent, that doesn't bother me a great deal. What worries me is ... ' I stop, taking a rather large gulp, swallowing without savouring like some heathen, all the while noting the expression on Katie's face. ' ... bothers me is probably a better choice of words, now that I think of it. So, what bothers me is that I don't know If I care. I don't really know what I want.' Here we go ... another mouthful and the pace increased allowing for absolutely no thought of what I was excreting. 'I'm forty, I'm single. I feel completely unfulfilled in most aspects of my life and, to top it off, my socially awkward and now, my very plain looking safety fuck is now in a loving relationship!'

I was surprised by cheeky smirk forming on Katie's ruby lips.

'I don't know if it's the pressure from my mum, the "perfect" life of my friends or the bullshit social expectations, but it really is starting to seem like I have come to that point in my life where I need to actually grow up and make some choices. I think I might need to try and start to "bother".' I paused and took a breath, I needed to compose myself ... slightly. Taking another calming sip, I lowered my voice slightly. 'I had a crazy dream once you know, I actually wanted to be a writer. It sounds so immature and completely clueless and the only remnants of it is the symbolism of it all. It's a dream reflects most aspects of my life at the moment: cold and dead.' Another mouthful and a quick scan of the bar to see if my public outburst had gotten any reaction broke up my self-loathing diatribe. 'This is your fault! After you convinced me you aren't the perfect girl I originally thought, you've had me questioning so much ... and thinking! I hate thinking! Do you remember what you told me that night? That we can save each other.

'That one statement right there changed me, made me think I might actually need saving or changing. It wasn't until I met you that I actually registered.' *Slow down, Hannah ... deep breaths ... drink some more ... find some way to not scare this girl away.* 'I just fell flat on my face, embarrassing myself in front of a group of women who completely took the piss out of me while you went crazy psycho defending me; totally unexpected.' I needed to be careful at this point because I'd finished the glass in one swift motion and had become consciously aware of my desire to not cry. 'I don't know how I can save you or even what from but I sure as hell want you to help me. For Christ's sake, save me, and ... ' This next part was loud, overly forceful and embarrassing but, to be honest I didn't give a shit. ' ... get that gorgeous arse to the bar and get me another drink!'

CHAPTER 20

Katie did well to direct the conversation back to a semblance of sanity, or at least a conversation that one would be comfortable having in public with someone, such as myself who lacks a filter and volume control at times. She was genuinely such a dear, and could see continuing down this line of conversation or even something somewhat related, was best left to another time or she risked me creating a public spectacle worthy of song. Instead she inadvertently reawakened what I had so hoped to hide from her.

What she said next was so inane, an innocent attempt to change the conversation by trying to convince me that A) *Friends* is NOT the greatest sitcom of all time, despite some obvious flaws, and that B) *How to Lose a Guy in 10 Days* is the greatest rom-com in cinematic history!

I don't know whether It was the sheer emotion of this morning or just that I was overdue, but it just happened. It's impossible to describe as I'm assuming its different for everyone but, to me, in that moment, it was like a blue butterfly graciously landed on an already brittle branch. The minute pressure from that tiny little thing led to a loud, unexpected, snap!

In my head, I genuinely began to question this women's sanity. Even a fifteen-minute diatribe on how it was the absurdity of the "Ross & Rachel" dynamic that made the relationship so polarising and added to the show's longevity couldn't satisfy me. I tried to point out that Phoebe and Joey not ending up together was one of the single greatest swerves in television history as in so many ways, they were the perfect couple.

I could have gone on about the intricacies of the fringe characters and how it was, in fact, them that created and maintained this friendship group through providing external targets and distractions. But I had now clearly moved to the absurd, that relentless need to keep going, the inability to take stock, slow down and just stop talking. *Shit! Here we go again. It's been a while; welcome back old friend ... now kindly fuck off!*

While all this was rapidly being communicated with continued verbal vigour, accompanied by a series of obtuse hand gestures, all I could think about was how insane Katie must be for not acknowledging the genius of the show runners. Conversely, a tiny "normal" part of me registered how insanely obsessive I sounded. My seemingly defective wiring wouldn't allow me to pull back; it couldn't register that it was time to stop, take stock and acknowledge that this simply wasn't a big deal. That knife edge that I was always balancing on, that bipolar "fine line" was beginning to cut as time seemed to slow to a near standstill with my inner self continuing to follow this seemingly obsessive monologue. Hopefully Katie would register my lack of control, put two and two together, and take some element of pity on this comical presentation of my eccentricities.

Deep Breaths Hannah.

Try and come back.

It took an automated pause, a moment of self-preservation (AKA a drink), and a moment to organise my next argument, before I noticed the wry smile on Katie's face. Her smile beautifully accentuated her dimples, reeked of mischief, while all the while, showing subtle signs of empathy, understanding and care.

I suddenly stopped breathing all together as I registered my mania, the speed of the fall. It all came together as I somewhat returned to everyone else's reality, resuming normal breathing and service.

'You're messing with me, aren't you?' It was almost a plea

expressed with a confused melancholy, sprinkled with a dusting of hope. Hope and a realisation that I read her reactions correctly and that she'd registered what just happened.

'I'm messing with you.' She let out a small, uncomfortable sounding laugh.

I put my head on the table in embarrassment while, at the same time, enjoying a sense of relief. I could tell there was so much guilt that she was hiding behind those pearlescent eyes. She was trying to bring things back, to take the focus away from what she just saw happen to me and, in the process, she had set off a manic event ... a meaningless obsession. A semblance of "normal Katie" returned suddenly.

'Hannah, I love you, but you are so easy to wind up. So, for the record and your sanity, *Friends* IS the greatest sitcom of all time, closely followed by *Parks and Recreation* and *Schitt's Creek*. As for *How to Lose a Guy in 10 Days* ... it's one of the worst pieces of cinema I have every experienced, hands down. Turned me off Matthew McConaughey and made me hate Kate Hudson even more. You know, the sadist in me really wanted to hear you tear into that train wreck.' She seemed to pause for a reaction with her expression changing to one of regret and quiet remorse. The bar had become increasingly crowded as lunch approached acted as a sort of white noise. She put her hand on mine, squeezed and with all the grace and care whispered, 'I'm so very sorry.. I didn't know'

I wasn't sure really where to go after that but I had the common sense to not saddle up and order another drink. Surely, that's a step in the right direction ... surely! I did a big mental "fingers crossed" and tried with futility to fob off the little episode. 'Nothing to be sorry about, honestly. It's been a rough morning and I'm genuinely not sleeping.' I paused, contemplatively. 'From memory, that's the first time you've seen me like that.'

I let out an obviously fake laugh in the form of some high-pitched noise reminiscent of the nervous giggle normally seen on a first date. 'Just be thankful that it was manic and not the big time low. Anyway, thanks for your understanding, I guess you were going to see something like that eventually. Now you know what you've got to work with ... and the fun part is that is me fully medicated!' I said it like it was a good thing. I guess it was a good thing. Wasn't it?

Subconsciously, I reached for my wine glass which contained only the very dregs, which was very much a good thing. I also couldn't help but think that there was some element of literary or film symbolism there, a sign that the protagonist had reached their very lowest, thus signalling the climb to normality and that happy ending I'm quietly hoping for. I'm pretty sure that was wishful thinking.

'I think I'm going to go home, if that's all good with you? I'm not really feeling it, after that to be honest.' I didn't really want to abandon Katie but I figured it was the best course of action and I was confident she'd understand.

'Yeah, no worries, but we'll share a cab to yours and I'll go home from there ... that's non-negotiable. To be honest, I don't want to take public transport on my own. If I wanted to dodge crack heads and sit on smelly, urine-soaked seats, I would go and visit my cousin.'

We both had a genuine laugh as we made our way through the now crowded bar. The lunch time rush must have picked up as the man and woman standing by the window for the last twenty minutes with some obvious sexual tension pounced on our table. They were both very attractive ... like high-end store fashion model attractive ... and work colleagues but there was a clear spark. Dating someone at work, or even worse, just sleeping with a colleague, must be an absolute nightmare!

As we stood on the curb trying a hail a cab, passed by countless people seemingly unaware of the world around them, I continued to listen to Hannah's passionate disdain for public transport until I felt the need to interrupt: 'Did I tell you about the time I saw penis on the train?'

Katie looked at me with almost a perverse level of curiosity as a cab pulled up to the curb and ushered us in.

CHAPTER 21

I turned the latch and closed the door behind me, and proceeded to throw myself on the couch, and my handbag haphazardly on the floor. I felt terrible for not inviting Katie in, but I really needed some "me time", some time to transition back into normality.

I kicked my shoes off and enjoyed the comfort of my ageing couch, welcoming its embrace and accepting the fact that I was pretty much going to settle here for the rest of the afternoon. As I closed my eyes and tried to focus on a positive, like the fact it was Tuesday and I wasn't going to have to sit through a work meeting this afternoon (Yay!), I registered that I REALLY wasn't going to have to sit through said work meeting!

The purpose of the meeting was to try and organise the periodic "aren't we all a happy bunch" work party. It was organised and usurped by the preppy minions of the social committee coordinator, who I am positive is pure evil. I smiled to myself at the thought of what insidious plans they would come up with to improve morale, but it couldn't be worse than last quarter's minigolf followed by dinner and drinks. Now, I'm certainly not adverse to lunch or drinks, or even minigolf, but who genuinely wants to socialise with the people they work with? Like really, genuinely wants to socialise … outside of work-hours … with people I don't necessarily like or, in some cases, can't even tolerate?

The worst thing is that you always get the impression that its mandatory without actually being mandatory. Like, if you don't attend it will be "frowned upon" and that the rest of the gang will spend a large proportion of their time bitching about the girl that couldn't make it.

I chuckled as I remembered the joy of drinking far too much after minigolf, forgetting to eat lunch and spending a large amount of time trying to get in with the ridiculously cute guy at the bar. I'd failed miserably. Turned out that as well as being ridiculously cute, he was also ridiculously gay. I'd made it back to the work table in time for a dessert, a cocktail and few disapproving looks from upper management. Oh, the memories.

My peaceful daydream was rudely interrupted by a rather forceful knock on the door. I waited, ignoring it, hoping they'd promptly fuck off.

I suspected it to be my mother because only she had the ability to show up at such an inconvenient time. Another knock clearly reinforced that it couldn't be that easy. Countless expletives and violent tendencies (kidding, of course … or am I?) occupied my mind as I gingerly stood up and made my way to the door, rubbing my head.

If it was my mother, I contemplated feigning leprosy or some other infectious potential pandemic causing pathogen but knowing what my mother thought of me, the only infection she'd expect me to have couldn't be passed on in a platonic relationship.

I opened the door with vigour and was met with the petite figure of Katie, armed outstretched holding what appeared to be house keys.

'You left your key in the lock,' she said with a cheeky smile. 'I happened to notice them as I was about to hop in the cab and thought I should … you know, make sure you don't lose them.' I took them from her hand and thanked her profusely. 'Hey, do me a favour.' Katie asked with a level of confidence that I was used to from her. 'Keep this weekend open. I've got the weekend off and I've got an idea that I guarantee you'll love.' The look she gave me made it impossible to say no and, to be honest, my social calendar was nothing if not flexible, and rather devoid of life. 'Now, just to clarify, keep the whole weekend free from Friday night to Sunday afternoon … girls weekend!'

This saucy addendum intrigued and added to the strength of her offer. 'Well, I was planning on a rather exciting weekend of washing, movies, and booze, but I guess I could put it off.'

She smiled and turned at the rather impatient honk from the taxi driver. 'I'll fill you in later. Get some rest, order take out and treat yourself.' She is always so vibrant, even when trying to deal with me after bearing witness to her first Hannah manic episode. I waved and watched as Katie's cab moved off down the street, hoping that I could somehow become a little bit more like her.

My place seemed somewhat emptier than normal after my second farewell to Katie and I suddenly became aware of a pain in my knee. It didn't even strike me before that the fall may have angered the knee I had surgery on. I locked the door, threw my keys on the cabinet and made my way to the kitchen, chasing some pain relief.

Everyone seems to have that one cabinet in their kitchen that is an absolute clusterfuck. One so lacking in organisation that it makes the cities train network layout seem positively cutting edge and well thought out. Mine was the notorious cabinet above my microwave which contained so much of everything that in reality there is was fact nothing. Basically, it was so full of crap that I have no idea what is actually there other than my medication crammed into the bottom shelf of said cabinet. Today was actually a good day as I managed to open the cupboard without being bombarded by a downpour of random detritus, mainly batteries and out of date medication.

The first box of pills I saw was irrelevant, my bipolar meds, so I pushed them to one side and saw the holy grail, my Oxy! I actually exhibited a little self-control and avoided the temptation of a prescription high and searched for a box of over the counter relief. As it turned out, I was in luck. Three paracetamol and a good litre of water made me feel somewhat human again. I stood there, looking out over my mediocre living space which could quite easily have been mistaken for one belonging to a college student but, quite frankly, I wasn't vain enough to care. Besides, it had everything I needed and, more importantly, it irritated the crap out of my mother that I lived in what she deemed "brothel like".

Believe it or not, I did love mum, but I really did enjoy getting a rise out of her prudish self. In that moment of contemplating my kingdom, taking stock of "me" I realised I needed two things: music and a shower. Music always came first. I'd invested in this lovely, and rather unnecessary, Smart Home set-up. The network of Bluetooth controlled speakers, all controlled by the voice of a faceless company, gave me happiness.

Luckily, I discovered that I could change its "name", for lack of a better word and boy did I have fun coming up with a replacement. I'd narrowed the replacement name down to Hollywood legend Bill Murray or my favourite Bond Girl "Holly Goodhead". Upon closer examination, I think I'd gone with the more socially acceptable choice. So … 'Bill Murray, play my soundtrack.' My soundtrack started with an absolute banger by Sea Girls and, despite the somewhat depressing lyrics, it really lifted me … the sheer joy of music exhilarated me.

'Damn! Look at my heart
Damn! Falling apart
Damn! Driving so fast
Can't outrun your past
Damn! Beautiful skies
When there's rain in my eyes
But you're gone and I'm still holding on
I'm still holding on'

Kind of fitting really, so maybe, just maybe, Bill Murray can read my mind? I genuinely found a semblance of peace in that one moment, with that one song. Even after everything that had gone on in the last 24hrs. Even the thought of work tomorrow was pushed to the back of my mind as I stood there looking like an absolute idiot to anyone unlucky enough to be playing Peeping Tom.

I made my way gingerly to the bathroom, turned on a shower so insanely hot and purifying that I could have multi-tasked and steamed some dumplings in the process. Dumplings? Yeah, that did sound amazing … Uber Eats it was. Random thoughts aside, I stepped into the shower and tried to focus on the muted music from the lounge room but all I could get was a muffled mess. I did the next logical thing and turned off my brain as best as I could and allowed the water and the steam to absorb me. While trying to clear my mind, my thoughts drifted to mum. I knew that, at times, I was harsh on her but even as far back as high school our relationship had been strained. Part of me felt bad, but I wasn't sure if I was capable of having a traditional "mother\daughter" relationship right now.

I was in my happy place … I didn't need this philosophical reflection right now. I tried to redirect, to focus on the steam, the heat, but the moment had passed.

'Fuck it!'

Interlude: Clueless

I attended a relatively small High School outside the city. Mum and Dad were once country folk, or bourgeois bumpkins as my dad puts it, having moved to the city after I finished school and made that big move to university. My time in High School was served in a small-ish establishment of roughly 300 hormonal teenagers all trying to find their place in the many social niches of 1990s pop culture.

Believe it or not, I was one of the popular kids ... but only by proxy. My best friend, who I had known since year two was "the" popular girl, the one everyone wanted to be. She was the school captain; smart, sporty, fashionable, incredibly beautiful and, surprisingly, so caring and nice. To my eternal disdain, this girl didn't even have any pimples ... bitch! That was Bianca: blonde, tall, perfect figure and, by the time we had hit high school, breasts that could turn every head in the room ... not that it was hard to make teenage boys pay attention.

Movies have told us that the popular kids are innately horrible, shallow people at their core, who always get their comeuppance in the end. In the case of Bianca, there was no need. She was the very poster girl of perfection.

I was the girl the teachers asked to show her around and take her under my wing on her first day, which, like most kids, I absolutely despised! It turns out, that was one of the best things that happened to me in my school life. From that encounter, I developed this insanely close friendship with this girl who, from day one, became the alpha female and, more importantly to me, my only close friend.

Skip to high school and despite me being the somewhat unusual one, the girl that was into several of the less popular subcultures. Grunge, a love of all things cinema, and anything remotely related to creative expression, never really achieved mainstream popularity at my little old school. Despite this, Bianca continued to take me under her wing and I integrated into every group she was a part of. We were the very definition of "besties". What always differentiated us the most was my love of writing. On occasions, it tended to take me away from things that were almost seen as an expectation for a particular social niche.

Bianca was never mad at me about this, but she just wanted me to fit with her and other friends. The pressure that I felt from this subsided when I quietly confided in her over a coke and packet of chips that I wanted to be a writer.

I could see on her face she understood the challenges of "getting there" and the perceived futility of making it but she supported me ... as always. I can never remember us having a disagreement, let alone a fight, after that moment of understanding. If there was social media and smart phones back then we would have so many brainless, vain pics scattered all over Instagram, Facebook and whatever the hell else kids are using these days.

I still miss her, I genuinely do. We still speak over Facebook every now and then and she calls me every birthday, Christmas, Valentine's Day AND New Year's Day ... she is still, to this day, such a sweetie.

The last time we spoke she was living in London, married to a corporate banker, and was kind of living my dream ... she was writing. She had a few novellas published but, embarrassingly, I've yet to bring myself to read them. I just couldn't do it ... to engage with the life I wanted to live. Of course, I've told her I have and the internet allowed me to fumble my way through any conversation on the content, but to be honest I was just straight up jealous of her success. Once again, she has managed to take something I was good at and just take it that step further. I knew that reading her work would have reminded me how much she'd done and of the amazing woman she'd become while I had progressed about as far as the Neanderthal on the evolutionary scale.

I keep telling her that one day I'll make it to London for a visit and joked that her husband can set me up with some 1990s Hugh Grant-looking gentlemen, but money and confidence are holding me back in that area. I didn't even make it for her wedding, and I was her maid of honour. It hurt her a lot, I know that, but that girl ... that amazing girl. You know what, she couldn't even bring herself to appoint another girl in my place.

I kept the title, she sent me the dress, and I stood there in her Auntie's house, playing my role over the internet on the most significant day of her life. I must have looked silly standing there in front of a webcam and the few of her relatives that couldn't make it, but I didn't care. I cried that day because deep down, I think we both knew that, unless she came home, we'd never see each other again.

Outside of my relationship with Bianca I knew I wouldn't have held the same social standing in high school. Underneath my popular kid exterior, I was into grunge, science fiction and fantasy. I read, I listened to music and most of all, I was a movie buff. I actually used to go to films by myself sometimes, just to get that hit from my personal drug. In retrospect, that was the very definition of sad.

As we got into Year 11 and 12 and parties started to spring up on the weekends, I would quite often skip them, not always by choice, as my parents were quite strict, and vegetate with a movie, a book or music. They were always afraid their daughter would end up drugged out, with a boyfriend and pregnant. Ironically, what they feared back then is now what mum is pressuring me for ... except the drugged out part.

It wasn't that I missed out, as I usually made it to the best parties, but I also was never the drunk one, the high one or the whore-ish one. Now that I think of it, I only really had one boyfriend in school and, unfortunately for the poor guy ... I think his name was Ash or Allan ... I was never really into it. I dated the poor guy for appearances and I felt terrible because he was head over heels "in love" with me.

Thankfully, I never gave him "first prize", holding onto my virginity until first year of university. He did get a sympathy hand-job in the garden shed at one of Bianca's parties and I let him feel me up a few times, but other than that, and the occasional kiss (all terrible, by the way), high school was thankfully devoid of anything physical. I think the only person to see my teenage self naked before college was Bianca's mum, who walked in on my changing into my swimwear one summer. The poor lady was mortified and it took a few months for her to look me in the eyes again. I remember over hearing her telling her husband about it and she was genuinely concerned she would end up in prison or on a sex offender register for spying on girls.

'She didn't lock the door. It wasn't my fault. It wasn't my fault!' she repeated as she dissolved into a blubbering mess.

I did apologise profusely at the time, but I probably should have gone home afterwards rather than spend the afternoon with Bianca laying around the pool and listening to N-Sync. What a day ... except for N-Sync.

My friendship with Bianca was that one constant, it was an element of stability in my formative years. While mum and dad were busy with work, friends and the garden, I knew Bianca was pretty much always accessible and, unlike my mum and to a lesser extent my grandmother, didn't assume I was gay because I showed no real interest in boys. This was one of the many very good reasons I didn't tell them about Ace (or was it Aaron?) it would have resulted in a whole lot of awkward, frustrating conversations I didn't want or need.

Just to digress, I actually really feel bad that I can't remember the poor guy's name. Come to think of it, I think I fucked him up! I definitely led him on, showed him little or no affection and on numerous occasions referred to him around others as "Just Andrew". Andrew ... I want to say Andrew. I'm 85% sure it was Andrew ... good old Andrew, my first boyfriend who pretty much showcased the origins of my commitment and relationship issues. Thinking back on it ... It definitely wasn't Andrew either. I am a horrible, horrible person!

It does kind of highlight that dependency I had on Bianca and that other aspects of my social life really did revolve around her to some extent. At times I felt like the friendship was somewhat unhealthy, and maybe only a little somewhat quasi-stalker-ish, but she saved me. Not literally, but she did keep me out of the social basement that I would have been relegated to without her influence. I would have probably festered away in the recesses of the library with "the others" I shared interests with.

Bianca and I took pretty much all the same classes, except for maths. I was in what we called "potato maths", in that the teacher would have just as much luck teaching the content to a sack of potatoes. Bianca did top level maths and excelled, as she did in every subject. I sat there in every class and no matter how well I did, she was one or two steps better. That would stew and fester in a more petty person but while Bianca was excelling in grades, I was excelling in apathy and a quiet cynicism.

    Yes, I guess a sense of jealousy of her consistent brilliance that I feel today begun to form, but at no point did this cause any resentment or tension between us. My teachers always saw my apathy as a character flaw ...

    'You could do so much better if you actually tried Hannah.'

    'Put some more effort in, you're capable of so much more!'

    ... but I see it as a positive as it fertilised our friendship, leading to its depth and longevity. It also didn't lead to me feeling like shit for always coming up short or insanely insecure. As an adult, even being the immature specimen that I am, I can see now that this wasn't the best attitude to have and may very well have contributed to some of my eccentricities, for the sake of using a non-expletive, and hang ups. For the positive and negative influences, she had on me, Bianca played such a significant role in my teenage years, and despite the distance, continues to do so. Still to this day I occasionally ask myself 'what would Bianca do?' A product of a dependence that followed me until high school graduation, that brutal moment when a young person is thrust violently into the unforgiving and unstable world of university, freedom, and perceived independence.

PART IV
Office Space

CHAPTER 22

Despite the prospect of work the next day and today's lingering emotional trauma, I decided to brave bed without pain killers and liquor. This might not sound like much, but to someone who had become, let's just say, dependent on that cocktail at night, it was quite an achievement. I was quietly proud of myself as I slid into bed and was unceremoniously greeted by the trashy book I had been reading.

Lying there, trying to focus, I registered the haphazardly made bed and, even worse, the sensation of sheets that were well overdue for a wash. Is it really a bad thing when a grown woman can't remember the last time she changed her sheets? Who was I kidding, it wasn't only lacking in hygiene, but also a sad testament to my sex life. I always changed my sheets after bringing a guy home. Had it really been that long?

In typical obsessive behaviour, I got up, ripped the sheets off the bed, removed the pillow cases, and with great finesse bundled them together and threw the roughly ball shaped object into the corner. What happened next can only be described as a feat of supreme skill, speed and dexterity as I collected new sheets and made the bed in less than five minutes!

The sheer rapidity and flow of my movements was simply breathtaking ... that is, until my knee collided with the bed frame with all the grace of a drunken uncle at a wedding attempting the Macarena. This rather unfortunate turn of events reminded me of the residual pain from today's fall and of the fact that the pain killers I took earlier were obviously wearing off. Putting the pillows back and turning down the bed, I considered the conundrum I now faced. Did I go to bed with the sense of pride in not resorting to the Oxy or do I crumble and accept the release?

I knew the answer before I'd even fully considered it and began my shameful walk to the medicine cupboard. *It's fine. If I take this I will still have twenty left before I need a new script. Who can blame me for taking one tonight ... I fell on my injured knee, for fuck's sake!'* Every neuron in my brain fired, all trying to justify that taking that pill was totally ok.

This oh so familiar ritual was another of my many hidden shames, just another aspect of my personality I am embarrassed by. Every time I took one of these pills I lose one more excuse and my internal shame deepens. With a sigh and obvious comparisons to Cersei Lannister's "walk of shame" I crawled into bed and turned off the lights.

Depressingly, the last thing I thought before succumbing to the pull of the pills was, *At least I didn't down it with booze.*

CHAPTER 23

Wednesday morning, and I once again came to the conclusion that Britpop does not make a good alarm. It was far too preppy and upbeat for a work day and too much of an actual alarm for a weekend. As I rolled over, trying to avoid the piercing ray of sunlight violating my room I once again contemplated calling in sick. Surely Ryan would believe that I still had a sinus infection … or was it a virus? I genuinely couldn't remember what excuse I'd used this time so I reluctantly crawled out of bed like a big girl.

Sitting on the edge of the bed, I took a moment to study my room prompting me to remember to deal with the ball of sheets I had thrown in the corner last night. I wasn't planning on washing today, but I figured that while I was in the grown-up frame of mind, I might as well put on a load before work. One of the only disadvantages of a king sized bed was the sheer size of the sheets which I became particularly aware of as I lumbered towards the laundry room. I threw them in the machine with some detergent and promptly turned on the television. This morning I was greeted with black and white and the monologue of a what seemed to be 1950s court room drama. Not normally my thing but I was switched on enough to know that it wasn't "Tequila Mockingbird". Ignoring the monotone delivery of the protagonist, I switched on the coffee machine and proceeded to go through the morning motions: pick out an outfit, shower, coffee, medication, hair and make-up, contemplate life's regrets and fight through a subconscious self-loathing. Wow. I was a little ray of sunshine this morning, wasn't I?

I was impressed with my speed and efficiency this morning,

getting completely organised and ready to trudge off to work with time enough to spare to actually enjoy my coffee. Sitting, skimming through my phone I realised I had missed a message from Samantha last night. Samantha, never "Sam" (she hated that!), was one of my vacuous friends who saw me as their little project. To be honest, she wasn't an inherently bad person, but she was incredibly judgemental of my lack of a partner and direction in life. As a consequence, she was always trying to set me up with some guy she knew or try and deduce through a series of not-so-subtle questions if I was a lesbian. It was disconcerting to know that the question of one's sexuality immediately comes to mind when people meet someone still single at my age. Such a lovely ... detect the sarcasm ... commentary on societal expectations.

    I hadn't really had much contact with Samantha and "the girls" since my friendship with Katie had grown, and considering I was always the black sheep of the group, I'd never expected it to be too much of an issue for them. They must have finally registered my lack of a presence and drawn straws to see who would 'reach out'.

> S: Hannah where have you been lately?
> We've missed you!
> Drop me a line and I'll organise a girls night.

I really didn't want to respond, but if I ignored it too much longer Samantha would assume I was either dead, kidnapped, or cranky with them. There was this incredibly ingrained culture among this group that if you didn't respond to a message within a reasonable amount of time there was something wrong. Luckily, they'd come to know that my ability to respond to messages was severely limited by apathy as opposed to malice. I needed to respond though and it had to be thoughtful, satisfying and swift.

> H: Hi Samantha. I've been flat out and kinda sick.
> Would love to catch up though soon. Busy this weekend but maybe after that?

I don't know what went through my mind, but as I typed away and hit "send" I was immediately hit with this violent sense of *What the fuck have I done?*

H: When you organise something, I might bring someone along.

The colour drained out of my face and my regret was immediate. I had just committed, in their eyes, to introducing them to Katie and, knowing how vapid and judgemental the girls could be, I was certainly not ready for the two to mix. Fuck! I need to get out of this, somehow. My fingers moved with previously unknown speed as I tried desperately to beat any response from Samantha.

H: Scratch that last part as I'm not ...

Too late, the three blinking dots on my screen had materialised into her response and I could already hear the curious sense of glee in her voice, even though she was, at this time, just a series of words on a screen.

S: That's fantastic Hannah! I can't wait to meet him\her!

I'll be in touch!

Xoxo

I didn't bother responding. I'd probably just dig myself a deeper hole.

Frustrated, I tipped the dregs of my coffee in the sink, grabbed my handbag and my keys and made my way out the door, down the steps and proceeded towards my bus stop. Walking down the street, I gave my usual wave to Mrs Leece who was already fastidiously working in her small front garden. I became increasingly frustrated at these two different parts of my life colliding. I had to find a way to stop it happening without making it seem too obvious to the girls that I just really REALLY didn't want it to happen.

I made it to the bus stop with plenty of time for once and accepted that I needed to just relax and deal with this later. *Deep breaths, Hannah.* As the bus rounded the corner and I had reached a sense of Zen I realised that a) I hadn't turned the washing machine on and b) I hadn't turned the TV off. Fuck! Inner peace and Zen out I door, today was going to be shit!

CHAPTER 24

The twenty-minute commute was relatively painless with the bus being empty enough for me to actually get a seat to myself. I did discourage one potential occupant, a younger gentleman in his 20s at a guess, by pretending to be taking a call from my gynaecologist as soon as I noticed him making a b-line towards my seat. Luckily, I managed to get the phone up to my ear and start mumbling about my cervix before he noticed. I wasn't particularly proud of that, but I really didn't want to have anyone up in my personal space today. Yes ... I am very aware of how difficult that can be on the morning commute but I made my own luck this morning, regardless of how despicable it was. I wouldn't lose any sleep over it, but I would acknowledge that my actions were more than a little bitchy.

The other unusual thing about this particular bus ride was that I didn't retain that 'public transport stink' that managed to linger on your person after disembarking. It's a lovely mix of sweat, grime and sadness so, basically, it smelled of the city. While I knew that wasn't really something others would smell and blame on me personally, it always bothered me. Today though, felt (or smelled) slightly different. It might have been the new perfume or the fact I'd temporarily lost my sense of smell but I was happy with how inoffensive I was as I walked the final five minutes to the office.

The automatic doors to the building slid open as I approached and I was greeted, as always, by Herman the doorman. He checked my ID and ushered me through the employee entrance while I faked a smile and an interest in his morning. Herman was an okay guy, but lacked any personality, which made him perfect for this job.

The front of the office was grey, sterile, and lacking in any colour other than a vase of pink lilies and the pastel dress of the receptionist. I think her name is Anne, but I really wasn't 100% on that. In my defence, she probably couldn't tell me my name either, as we ran in completely different circles. In fact, I'm pretty sure she only got this job to keep her "daddy" happy. It is important to note that the rumour is "daddy" is relatively high up in the government but this is unconfirmed.

My job was as administrative assistant in a rather obscure government department. Obscure enough to not have a massive office building in the classy city centre, but important enough to not be thrown in a tiny office space in a suburban shopping centre. That would probably be where I ended up when I piss enough people off.

Administrative assistant was HR code for the bosses' bitch. I pretty much looked after Ryan's schedule, took his phone calls, and dealt with the paperwork. It wasn't a hard job, but it was mind numbingly boring to the point where I have quite frequently been caught Googling things such as "job openings near me", "changing jobs at 40" or "jobs that don't make you suicidal". The last one was a slight exaggeration but it added to my reputation as the office crazy, which I really didn't mind.

Unlike most people in the office, I made no attempt to suck up to the boss or make friends. It was perfectly clear to everyone that I was not an up and comer, I wasn't looking for a promotion. I did what I did well, but they knew that, to me, this wasn't a career, but a job. Every day as I trudged through the office trying to look somewhat alive, I was reminded that I really should have a had a little more ambition and follow through after I finished university.

As I sat down and logged in to my desktop I couldn't get Katie's last conversation with me out of my head. A girl's weekend. I had no idea where we were going or what we were doing. It sounded amazing, but unsettling at the same time. Me doing something like this, something completely unknown and unplanned, seemed like a good way to shake things up a little in my life. Something spontaneous and hopefully involving wine, cocktails, a place to swim and the prospect of single guys would be a preference. Surely a girl's weekend suggested that all of those would be available in copious amounts!

Maybe this was a part of Katies plans to "save me", a way to bring about some change in my life. These were some very deep and profound thoughts from a girl who had eight hours of monotonous and menial tasks ahead of her. Much coffee would be needed to bring me back to reality and give me the will to get through today.

I dumped my things and did my very best to sneak past Ryan's office, while at the same time being obvious enough that some of the honest workers knew that I was actually at work, and on time. From a distance, I noticed that his office lights were still turned off, meaning I probably had at least half an hour before I had to engage in forced pleasantries with him and get some on the spot updates to today's schedule.

As I entered the break room, I could smell the not-so-subtle aromas of cheap coffee bubbling away, telling me that someone had made my day by saving me the job of brewing. Unfortunately for me, it was Ryan.

'Hannah, I'm glad your back on deck. How are you feeling?' He sounded somewhat sincere and managed to avoid overwhelming me immediately with a tirade of jobs that were now overdue because of yesterday's absence.

'Much better, thanks. I'll catch up what I missed first thing this morning, if that's okay with you.' I managed to get my cup filled and sweetened up without too much eye contact, which was a good thing. Ever since Katie had pointed it out, I couldn't help but fixate on the fact that my boss wasn't bad looking. The thought sickened me.

How could I go from despising a guy to noticing, and almost fixating on, his cute arse and chiselled facial features. He'd grown his beard out a little recently, which wasn't normally my thing, but he managed to kept it meticulously manicured and well-kept. I shook myself back to reality as he handed me the milk, forcing some level of eye contact.

He really was quite "fuckable", as Katie put it, but he was at least ten years younger than me, my boss, and still somewhat of an arsehole. Still, didn't mean I couldn't look, I guess.

Ryan stood there for an uncomfortable amount of time before asking for a meeting at 10am in his office and then left, without even waiting for a response from me.

Yep, he really was still an arsehole, despite his somewhat improved attitude towards my wellbeing since "the incident" as Katie and I had continued to call it. It really was easier, and less embarrassing, to call it that then "self-inflicted head wound" or "fake fall".

I quickly forgot Ryan's redeeming features as I made my way back to my desk, trying not to spill my coffee. 'Fuck you too!' I mumbled to myself as I passed the door to his office wishing for some emergency to come up meaning we wouldn't be able to meet as directed.

I couldn't be so lucky. I sat down, opened my emails and was met with a wall of unread messages, many of which were tagged as 'URGENT'.

Fuck!

CHAPTER 25

Despite the fact that I really did give zero shits about my job, I was still somewhat concerned about what Ryan had to say. Afterall, I still needed to keep the fridge and medicine cupboard stocked ... and pay the bills of course.

Theoretically, if I got shown the door, I had very little skills that would be a viable income source. I guess I could always resort to selling feet pictures online or setting up an Only Fans. Who was I kidding, why would people pay to see my average body and lack of sexual creativity with the number of deviants and free porn online? Plus, I did actually have standards ... somewhat ... possibly ... but poverty would possibly lower them.

Hell, my standards in men had certainly lowered after an extended drought. However, I really shouldn't worry because other than diddling books or committing a crime, it was hard to get fired from a government job. It was one of the few perks of working for a group of arrogant, self-serving arseholes with the innate ability to suck the life out of even the most passionate and hard-working employee.

They sure as hell had some trouble with me because when I arrived, little did they know, I had no fucking passion to start with. Anyways, it was a long few hours. Frequent visits to the bathroom must have led people to think I had a serious issue with my bladder or a nasty urinary tract infection. I'm also positive I managed to earn a few looks of disdain from Ryan as I couldn't help a sly glare into his office each time I passed it. I noticed he hadn't put a box of tissues on his desk, so maybe I was all good.

It hit 10am and the bitch in me wanted to wait and see how long it would take for him to chase me down. There was certainly a self-destructive part of my personality that I managed, in this case, to supress. I promptly made my way to his office. I adjusted my skirt and contemplated undoing my top few buttons to show "the girls" but I was not really in the mood to set the women's rights movement back twenty years, all for the sake of staying out of trouble. I quickly filtered that thought. 10:01am and knocked on Ryan's door and patiently waited for the invitation to enter.

'Come in and grab a seat, Hannah. I'll be right with you.' He was smiling … fuck! I hated that smarmy, but somewhat ridiculously sexy, smile. I once again curse Katie for drawing my attention to it. I noted that he was actually finishing an email and not deliberately making me wait, which was a small relief. I sat down directly across from him with professional poise in a rather uncomfortable chair, and tried to maintain the appearance of calm.

The room seemed to be suddenly engulfed In a deathly chill, one of foreboding and dread. Once again, I was being dramatic. It was just his air conditioner cutting in to regulate the temperature in his lavish office at a rather pleasant 24 degrees. Finishing his email and turning to me just in time to catch me, phone in hand looking somewhat guilty. In my defence, I was just checking it was on silent and I'm pretty sure that he registered that even I wouldn't be blasé enough to be Instagram-ing a meeting with the boss. Fumbling to tuck my phone away in my jacket I tried my best to act cool, calm, collected and like I somewhat give a fuck.

'I'm going to get straight to the point because I don't want to make you more uncomfortable than you obviously are.' Was it really that obvious? I kept telling myself that I didn't give a shit but it was becoming obvious that, subconsciously, I must have. 'First, and I apologise because I should have mentioned this earlier, but would you like access to a support person for this meeting? I honestly don't think you'll need one … this isn't a "bad" conversation.' He even used the 'bunny ears' for bad … it was a nice little touch that settled me somewhat and I knew enough that he had to ask me that question.

'I'm good, honestly.' I was as nonchalant as possible, as a cool as a cucumber, I was calm and I was collected.

Ryan moved forward slightly, shuffled some papers and adjusted his keyboard. Was he … nervous?

'Look, to be completely frank, I'm worried about you. Not your performance, but you … personally. You've had a few days off recently unwell and there was the incident in the shower that, honestly, raised a few red flags.' I was genuinely shocked, stunned and in awe, mainly because he was fine with my job performance. 'I'm not asking you to go into details, as its none of my business, but I've spoken to HR and those above me and have advised them that as of Friday afternoon, you are on two weeks leave. It obviously has to come out of your allowance but it's been approved as 'special leave' meaning it won't impact your sick days or long service leave.'

I felt the colour drain out of my face and saw the last few months of my life flash before my eyes. I didn't know what to say, what to do and I certainly wasn't aware of how this must have made me look. 'This isn't negotiable, but you must speak to a professional in that time to get an "okay" to come back to work and we need it in writing. I'll say it again, we are not concerned about your performance. We … I … am concerned about you. For Christ's sake, Hannah, your sarcasm and cynicism has been more restrained! That is a massive red flag,' he said with a forced, yet strangely caring smile.

I managed to summon the awareness to respond. It was becoming obvious that I was exhibiting all the characteristics of a poorly put together scarecrow, albeit one that is slightly on the 'over stuffed' side.

'Thanks ... I guess. What do I do with my work flow in that time frame? We are coming up to funding applications, I think.' Look at me, looking like I plan ahead in the office. I'm looking positively professional.

'To be honest, we've already booked a temp and they start tomorrow to shadow you for a few days. However, if for some reason you can show her what's to be done by COB tomorrow then I have no reason to see you in the office Friday.' Wow, a temp, that literally means I won't have a mountain of work to return to when I get back. 'Let me be very clear ... ' Ryan continued with a smile. ' ... I WILL NOT see you Friday as you will be "working from home".' Once again the cute bunny ears.

This guy was either a) developing a sense of humanity or b) just trying to get me out of the office to break in a replacement. Either way, I didn't care ... two weeks off and all I had to do was see a doctor before I returned! I stood up and thanked him and he moved towards me to shake my hand which I, unfortunately, read as him going for a hug.

The confusion that followed as he tried to dodge what could be considered an "inappropriate workplace interaction", according to the code of conduct, would have been quite something to see as a casual observer. I backed away slowly with an obvious blush, thanked him and left. I closed the door behind me, aiming to go about getting as much done today as humanly possible. As I sat down and logged in again I registered that for the first time in ages I had a smile on my face at work ... and that my phone must have fallen out of my pocket in Ryan's office. Fuck!

CHAPTER 26

Leaving work that afternoon, I really did feel somewhat liberated. I hadn't taken two whole weeks off work in a few years as an extended break tended to be more work in the lead-up. It always meant being super organised and training up some temp straight out of university who had nothing going for them except a vapid personality and a perky set of tits. It probably sounds like I am stereotyping here but I was genuinely speaking from past experience. The oldest temp I'd seen in the office would be twenty-five at the most, and they all look like they have come straight from an open casting call for a Baywatch spin-off.

I kept telling myself it was just a massive coincidence, or that we had very few candidates, until I saw the guys from HR who employed the temporary staff for my department. It looked like a round table of everyone's drunk, creepy uncle who stalks your Facebook profile for a chance to ogle your friends from college. Of course, the positive of this was that they'd never hired anyone with a great deal of talent or skill, so everyone's jobs were pretty safe. Still, I'd love one of these lecherous old bastards to slip up just once so a progressive in the office can take them to the cleaners.

I still had to spend a day with a temp the next day but considering this was such short notice, I was hoping they'd just get Marg. Marg was an office legend! I'd actually filled her position when she retired, and Ryan tried to get her back whenever he could as she was super-efficient and took no crap from anyone. I'm sure Marg probably shared my negativity towards new and casual staff but, at that point I hadn't been down trodden by the daily grind and, without blowing my own horn, I was actually quite good at what I did .. If it was Marg filling in for me, it would be more her teaching me than the other way round, which I would be more than happy with. I'm not one to take offence to anything like that. I really don't give a shit if someone wants to tell me how to be more efficient in what I do. Plus, I loved Marg. We got along really well because at heart we're both cynical and hate dealing with idiots.

One of the many issues I had with work was the total lack of connection to the outside world that we had after passing through the main employee entrance. The staff only areas really were in stark contrast to the open foyer dominated by its street front glass windows and doors with the view only partially obscured by the government logo. It was quite frequently a nice surprise as we re-enter the real world to be greeted by a wall of obnoxious light and a convoluted explanation of the goings on from good old Herman. Sometimes it was a car breakdown or an ambulance, and there was that one time some guy was stabbed right outside our door. That was a big day, as the police wouldn't let us leave until they'd cleared the crime scene and taken statements from everyone. That was what we deemed an "unpleasant" surprise.

Mostly, it was just some unpredictable weather that had blown in after lunch. Today was one of those occasions. Herman, in all his wisdom, pointed out that there was a change blowing in and that rain was coming. Considering the sky that was not obscured by skyscrapers showed a dark, ominous wall of cloud building, and the fact large drops of cool rain were already starting to periodically strike the pavement I'd say that it wouldn't take a genius to make that prediction.

I nodded to Herman and gave him a smile as I exited the building and was greeted but a gust of cool air that still managed to reek of a back alley. I had a decision to make: did I attempt the dash to the unsheltered bus stop knowing that it was still twenty minutes away from its scheduled arrival? Or did I make a five minute dash into the covered shopping mall around the corner and wait until it cleared? I could get a later bus at the much busier, but covered, stop there. Fate made up my mind for me because the second I stepped out from cover the rain increased with the cool drops striking me at an ever-increasing rate.

I turned and made a hurried attempt to get to the shopping centre without breaking a heel or falling face first in a puddle. I had absolutely no intention of getting wet in this white blouse that was barely covered by my work jacket. Relatively dry, I made it inside just the heavens opened up. The rain became torrential, quickly filling the gutters and overloading the storm water drains. For once, I'd actually made the right choice.

Turning to survey the mall I realised I'd never actually stepped foot in here before. It was far too close to work for me to want to visit in my own time and I never really left the office during the day through fear that I might just run off, never to return. There were a few people around, which was to be expected considering the weather, but it was far from crowded. I was very careful walking on this tile floor in wet heels as I made my way to the open area of the centre. In typical Hannah style, I wasn't careful enough. While trying to check the bus schedule for the nearest stop on my phone, I walked right into a faux marble column. My phone, the harbinger of my misfortune, fumbled out of my hands landing with a meaty thud on the tiles. I dropped my handbag and stood there in the middle of the shopping centre looking like an absolute idiot. A couple of private school kids whispered and chuckled as they walked by but I was pretty sure I'd escaped too much public ridicule.

'Hey Miss, are you ok? No blood?' I blushed and nearly lost control of my bladder ... I had spoken too soon.

CHAPTER 27

The voice came from one of those new trendy bubble tea bars, the ones usually filled with high school girls and hipster university students. The twenty something girl working the counter was obviously closing up, but seemed to have a genuine interest in my wellbeing ... it also could have been just a morbid need to check out any wounds.

My phone was okay thankfully, but a few drops of crimson rested precariously just under my nostril. Rushing out, the girl handed me a napkin and ushered me into 'Tea Tao', a name so bad it was actually 'punny'. That poor attempt at humour really did reinforce why I'd never be the Chandler of any social group. She introduced herself as Liv, sat me down checked I was ok. Her caring nature really took me by surprise as it's not something you usually get in the city unless someone's chasing a light, a cigarette or trying to interest you in the sale of illicit substances. Not that I'd know that of course.

Liv rushed by the counter started to make-up me some kind drink that reminded me of what the 70s always looks like in bad films: colourful, over the top, and making no sense. Before she could finish, a young couple stuck their heads in asking if it was too late for a tea and this adorable, seemingly well-mannered girl replied with a 'CAN'T YOU READ THE SIGN? WE'RE CLOSED! READ THE SIGN!'

The couple retreated with haste, not even looking back at risk of further condemnation and humiliation. 'Sorry about that ... ' Liv's voice returned to the tranquil, well-spoken tone from before. ' ... but I hate those type of people. Walk in here, after closing, and assume that because I'm still here they can get in a sneaky order. I hate them so much!'

Wow, that was a lot of pent up malice from a petite, and, or so I thought, delicate young lady. 'How's your nose, miss?'

I wasn't sure whether to be offended that she'd automatically assumed I was a "Miss". She wasn't wrong, obviously, and the more observant of random tea store workers would notice my lack of wedding or engagement ring. Plus, I guess I kind of had that 'old crone' kind of look after being battered by the weather and a random column.

'It's fine, I guess. Blood didn't get on my work jacket or blouse, which is a positive.'

She handed me the concoction she'd been brewing, which despite being thrown together in haste, actually looked pretty good. Embarrassingly, I hadn't actually tried a bubble tea so I wasn't prepared for the overwhelming creamy sweetness and, of course, the tapioca pearl that I somehow managed to aggressively propel into the back of my throat. Apparently, as well as not being prepared for the taste, I was also unsure how to actually drink the thing properly. I must have looked like quite the Boba virgin, recovering from the projectile I'd just unceremoniously inhaled. I must have made her day, she had a massive and ridiculously cheeky smile on her face after seeing my reaction.

'That happens all the time and I love it. I especially love it when those prissy private school kids cop it. They seem to think this is their personal gossip place and some even had the nerve to ask me to reserve a table for them. Can you believe that? Spoiled little fucks! Too used to getting everything their own way I guess … silver spoon and all that.' She was a feisty one who obviously had a massive issue with the self-entitled and snobbish. That certainly explains both her willingness to help a stranger but also her aggression. My guess was that she has been burned in some way or another.

'So, what's the deal? Why the, you know, obvious hatred towards these people ... other than the obvious "dealing with them at work" kind of thing?' I didn't actually expect an answer, and rather expected to be told 'fuck off now, we're closed and your obviously fine!' but, no, the girl wanted to vent.

'I've worked my arse off my entire life, first job at fifteen in a bakery working 3hrs before school every morning and another 3 or 4 in the afternoon. All through high school just to put some money away for university but also to help out mum and dad.' This girl was angry at the world and needed to get this out and I'd just happened to hit my head and walk into her tea shop. 'I succeeded, I made it to university and now, just to pay the bills and keep up with tuition, I work two jobs. I've got a five hour shift tonight at a bar in the city, a 1-hour commute home and then a 9am class.' One simple conversation can go a long way to really put your life in perspective and remind you that shit isn't too bad. 'That's all fine, I can handle that, I genuinely can, because that's been my life. My whole family have worked hard and we always get by and we are happy. What drives me insane is that at both my jobs I have to deal with spoiled little *fucks*' – The emphasis she placed on 'fucks' brought a genuine shiver to my spine. I took a rather reserved mouthful of the tea to try and put on a façade of being comfortable – 'looking down on me, prancing around in their designer clothes with their phones and their ear buds and their vacuous friends. They have never worked for anything, never know what it is like to not know what you'll have left at the end of the week in your bank account.' Her tirade oozed passion and a subtle, yet present, undercurrent of sadness. 'They'll get into university and they'll probably end up knocked up or drugged out by the end of first year and waste an opportunity. They have no fucking idea what it is to earn something, to work for something and they come in here and speak down to me like I am the hired help. They make me so fucking angry!'

There was an awkward silence but I knew what she was on about, and I agreed. I was so "white, middle class" growing up, you'd probably find a picture of our family in a visual dictionary if you were looking it up. I had known girls though, and at school and university, who went through the same thing Liv was going through and it sucked. It simply reinforces the idea that life really wasn't fair and for every person that gets a free ride, there were two or three that get fucked over or start from 100m behind.

I didn't know what to say or do. I could see in her glassy eyes a vain attempt to hold back emotion, to fight back the tears. This girl was the very best in humanity and she was sitting here about to lock up and make her way to a second job to help stay in school and she would probably have to take my bubble tea out of her wages.

'What are you studying?'

She regained some composure and that spark that I saw in her when we first met returned. 'Law.' She stood up and moved to finish her lock up routine in an attempt to hurry me along.

'Oh, you're one of those people. Fuck you and your breed.' I really hoped she'd pick up on the smile and facial expression. I tended to make inappropriate statements as an attempt to find my way through difficult conversations and situations. Luckily, she laughed.

'I'll leave you my number,' she said. 'You might need my services in the future. You clearly have a law suit against the owners of the shopping centre. That column was clearly not correctly marked and it was so obscurely placed.'

There we go, sarcasm ... I'd known I liked this girl. I rifled through my bag and the only cash I had was a $20. I threw on the bench and made my way to the exit.

'Hey, miss ... It was only $7.50 and I really don't want your charity.' I turned back, still feeling the after effects of my embarrassing encounter.

'It's not charity, that's all I've got and you've shut the machine down. I only work around the corner so, next time I'm in the office, I'll come in and I'll have some store credit. Just make it happen yeah?' She hastily scribbled a note and attached it to the note with a paper clip. 'I'm Hannah by the way. Thanks for the help, it really is appreciated.'

We exchanged a smile as I closed the door and I made my way to try and find the bus stop. Here I was just about to head off for a weekend away with Katie followed by two full weeks of paid leave. Liv probably would've appreciated one or two days off and here I was, getting two weeks, PAID. I kind of felt guilty ... kind of ... but it did give me a kick start and helped me to remember that I did have things pretty good. Despite the fucked-up head, the pills, the being alone, I still had a pretty smooth run compared to some. There, that was my "feel-good moment" for the week with the only negative being that I now had credit at "Tea Tao" and I fucking hate bubble tea!

CHAPTER 28

The bus was late, giving me plenty of time to ponder the shit mood I was suddenly in as I'd gone from feeling like one of the lucky ones to "pissed off at the world" in support of Liv. At times like this, I was never sure if it was those mismatched chemicals in my brain or something else less embarrassing. That's the thing I find with bipolar, you are constantly doubting yourself; is what people are seeing the real you or is it the BP? There is always the question of, do these people know enough to know that this doesn't mean I'm psychotic? Those kinds of thoughts weigh heavily on me a lot of the time, I've just become pretty decent at not letting it show; smiles, jokes, my incredibly gifted sarcasm are the tools of my trade.

The medication, also known as the sweetest substance known to humankind, other than whatever the hell was in that bubble tea, only keeps things in check. There was always that feeling of inevitability but, to an extent, isn't that just life in a nutshell? *Fuck! I really need this bus to arrive, I am getting far too profound for my liking.* Force of habit kicked in and I checked my phone, looking for that digital distraction. I'd missed two messages, one from Katie and one from Mum. Completely disregarding my mother for the time being, I read the text from Katie which turned out was a response to one I sent her earlier.

    K: Two weeks paid leave! You've won the lottery right there!
    How crazy do they think you actually are? Lol
    Soz, will talk 2morror, am on night shift.
    Xoxo

My fingers started busily, almost robotically, generating a response that I had no doubt in my mind would be too long and unnecessary. I was so proud of myself because, at that point, I stopped, took a breath, moved away from the creepy guy trying to look at what I was typing and cleared the message. For the very first time in my life, I kept it simple.

H: No problems. Have fun. ☺

I put my phone in my jacket pocket, discretely zipped up my handbag and shuffled even further away from the guy. Turned out he was not only creepy, but he stank, and I'm pretty sure he was also rather high. Another situation that highlighted just how fucking terrible travelling on public transport can be. The positive at this point was that he hadn't appeared to have left any bodily fluids anywhere at the stop and he still had his pants on. If only it could stay this way for the next thirty minutes or so, I'd be home free without needing the eye bleach.

Five minutes or so later, my bus showed up. As it pulled to a stop inches from the curb, still coated in a film of rain from the previous storm, a pungent wall of petrol fumes from the shitty exhaust greeted us. The door opened and as I stepped up, I noticed the hypnotic path of the water dripping down the windows, how it almost gave the impression of sweat rolling off the arms of a runner. A beautiful metaphor, reflective of the smell I was met with as I scanned my transport card and moved to a seat half way along the bus next to an old lady and her bags of shopping.

Either my senses were getting more sensitive or someone, or something, on this bus had a serious medical condition. No one healthy could produce enough body odour to create the miasma I was faced with. The old lady must have noticed me trying to supress my gag reflex, something I've been told countless times I'm not very good at, because, in one concise sentence she answered my many questions.

'About a dozen sixteen-year-old boys just got off the bus at the last stop.'

We shared a glance of understanding and of shared repulsion. The rest of the trip passed in silence, with me coming to grips with the fact that tomorrow would be my last day at work for two weeks! Two weeks of no meetings, no shitty coffee, and, most importantly, no work. At heart, and I hated to admit it, I really was a lazy fuck. I just didn't get these people who worked more than they absolutely had to or take on extra for the sheer sake of it. That girl, Liv, I can understand that. She works her arse off for a reason ... she had an end game. Others who just work hard for the sheer enjoyment ... fucking bonkers, really.

Don't get me wrong, I do my job and I do it pretty well to be fair, but if I didn't have to do it there is no way in the world I would be in that office day in day out, slowly dying. Drinks, music, some remotely attractive guy with low standards, and a chair, would be my life if I didn't have to work ... and wouldn't it be sweet?

I didn't so much as *forget* the message from mum, as deliberately disregarded it. But she clearly wasn't standing for it. Just as I was stepping off the bus, my phone rang and the thoughts of that unread message instilled a sense of dread to the point that I actually hoped this would be a telemarketer or a scam caller.

I wasn't so lucky. As I fumbled for my phone it became immediately apparent that it was mum. I contemplated not answering it, but knowing her she would probably get in the car and come over to "check in".

'Sorry, Mum. Just getting off the bus. What's up?'. I moved my phone slightly away from my ear and prepared for a verbal tirade.

'So, not responding to my messages at all anymore then?' The struggle between disappointment and repressed anger was evident in her otherwise surprisingly calm voice.

'Jesus, I'm sorry, Mum. I didn't even see it. Today has been batshit crazy and I got stuck in that storm as I was coming out of the office and missed the bus.'

Most of that was true, but I didn't want to provide too many details or that would just give her more things to probe me on. I sure as hell wasn't going to tell her I'd been given two weeks mandatory leave or I would have to either outright lie or have a massive deep and meaningful with her to explain the whole thing. Plus, if she knew I wasn't working she'd try and catch up, which is code for meddle, far too many times over the course of those two weeks. Instead, I'd just pray that she wouldn't find out. It was a big city, surely I could keep it on the down low.

'Well, have you even read the message?' This was not going to end well. Now, I love my mum, I really do, but she is just so full on.

'No Mum, I haven't, please save the whips for dad.' Fuck, what did I just say? I'm pretty sure I just insinuated my mum and dad were into BDSM. I really hoped she didn't get it ... I really, really hoped she didn't get. The rather lengthy, awkward silence didn't help. If there was a pit I could have thrown myself in at that very moment, I would have thrown my phone in and ran.

'Hannah, I don't know what you're getting at, but you have such a filthy mind. What your father and I do in our time is none of your business.'

What the hell did she just say? I blushed so much I'm sure mum saw me through the phone. 'Um ... okay, sorry ... I guess.' What else do you say after your mum seems to confirm she's into that sort of thing? This is all my fault, I somehow need to erase my memory or move away and never see my parents again, because I sure as hell won't be able to look at them the same way ever again.

I could hear the dread in her voice as she tried to somehow dig her way out of this while I just wanted this conversation to end. 'Ahh, I'm certainly not saying we do that kind of thing, not at all, but ... what I am saying is ... well, if we did, whatever we do, is none of your business.' Worst ... cover up ... ever! 'Besides, I'd hate to think about all the debaucheries you've been involved with in the past. That's probably why you aren't married yet.'

There we go, that old chestnut. Only my mother could turn a few unintended statements about BDSM and her sex life into another story about how disappointed she is I'm not married. Apparently, it was now because I'm obsessed with all sorts of weird sex kinks. Surely, it has nothing to do with the fact I'm not in a relationship or simply that I don't even know whether I want to get married. I avoided verbalising that last point because she'd probably exclude me from the will and I do have my eye on grandma's diamond necklace that she'd inherited.

'Mum, get to the point because currently, the only positive about this phone call is that it distracted me for the walk home and gave me an excuse not to talk to the guy from across the road.' Realistically, that wasn't a big problem because he was a really nice guy and so ridiculously ... eatable. I could think of some more vivid, descriptive words but it's probably for the best that I don't. The fact was, he was married, and way out of my league (but mainly because he was married) that I avoided conversations with him when possible. Also, his wife was an absolute nut job.

She was obviously very aware of how attractive her husband was and very self-conscious, because the second he starts talking to me or any other female, she just appears. It's almost like witchcraft ... another female starts talking to hubby and she just materialises out of nowhere with a look that burns through your very soul. I think her name is Bella and she is a fucking bitch! She called me a whore once, just because I had the nerve to cross the street to have a conversation with her husband – that he'd initiated. That conversation, that I'd was secretly hoped would be along the lines of 'my wife isn't home ... come inside', had literally been, 'Do you know the name of the guy up the road that is an electrician?' Apparently, me answering that question made me a whore. The thought of what she would have called me if she knew what I'd actually been thinking still makes me smile every time I see the blonde bimbo.

It was obvious from Mum's tone that this conversation certainly hadn't gone the direction she'd expected. 'I just wanted to catch up for lunch and a coffee on the weekend if you were free. I was going into the city with some friends and thought you might like to meet but judging by your attitude today I—'

I straight up cut her off which, while a risky move, would save an extended argument and I just wanted to get inside and have a shower and a drink. 'Can't do it, Mum. I'm actually out of town on a girls' weekend and won't be home until some time Sunday afternoon.'

'Oh, who with and where are you going?' Here come the probing questions, looking for any fragment of information she could push me on. *Be short, concise and to the point, Hannah.*

'A girl I know, Katie. And I have no idea where we are going. I'll give you a call when I get home though and we'll sort something for soon.'

I thought mum was actually a little lost for words until ... 'Is this your way of "coming out" dear? If you're a lesbian it's—'

Once again, I cut her off with razor sharp certainty. 'Bye mum, I'll call you when I get home. Love you.' I hung up, feeling a combination of anger and just being straight up deflated. I was thankful though that I was home and as that key clicked and the door swung open I finally breathed a sigh of relief.

CHAPTER 29

not only locked the door but latched it as well. I really needed to guarantee no unwanted visitors and, after today's conversation, definitely no unexpected visits from Mum. I dumped my bag and keys in their usual spot and made my way to my supposedly decorative, and nearly always empty, wine rack. Being the civilised woman of the world that I am, I opened, what I hoped was a nice shiraz to let it breath. I still really don't know what the hell it does, or if it even matters with the quality of wine I buy, but every now and then I am patient enough to let it sit for a bit.

I put my phone on charge and on silent and opted for a hot shower and some music which, unfortunately created a huge problem as it forced me to make the most difficult decision of the day … what to listen to. I needed something really chill, non-confrontational and especially nothing that would encourage me to go out, get drunk and make some bad life choices. Yes, I'm talking men … it'd been a while and I could almost guarantee that if I went out I would do, or try to do, something (and/or someone) that was both embarrassing and something I'd regret. Plus, I was holding out for a classy, non-trashy, Keanu Reeves-like, gentlemen hook-up this weekend. Surely Katie would have catered for the desperation of a forty year old crazy woman?

It struck me like the good old proverbial truck: was I limited by my age, looks and personality to base level, mediocre, inner city pub hook-ups? Was I forever going to be the one the guys settle for at the end of a night just to get their rocks off?

When you're average looking, average performing casual fling screw settles down before you do it really does raise some red flags.

The whole question of 'what do I want?' was kind of moot at this point because I barely even felt like one-night stand material, let alone someone you'd want to take home to meet your mum. Wow, what amazing thoughts that occupy my fucked-up mind when trying to regulate an already "up and down" mood. I'm really glad I opened that wine now and seriously started considering just taking the bottle, with a straw into the shower with me. Self-control and respect for myself kicked in and I decided to do the classy thing and just take a "portion" in instead. I really took this tasteful experience to the next level by putting said portion of wine into a travel mug designed for hot drinks just to avoid water ruining the flavour profile and depth of my $10 bottle of wine. *Stay classy, Hannah.*

On a positive, my melancholic thoughts had led to an appealing music choice. 'Bill Murray, play soundtrack to *The Secret Life of Walter Mitty*. I'm talking about the Ben Stiller remake, a film that really got far too much hate. It is genuinely one of the few movies that made me laugh out loud, cry, and come out of it feeling hopeful and uplifted. To me, "emotional rollercoaster" is Walter Mitty and the soundtrack is more than solid.

The disembodied voice eventually acknowledged ... damn NBN speeds ... and the guitar of José Gonzįlez began to fill the silence of the living space. I closed the curtains and made my way through my room, into the bathroom with my 'coffee' in hand. As usual, the bathroom had an uncomfortable chill, unworldly at times, but it always warmed up quickly as a piping hot stream of water created an ever expanding bubble of joy.

I rested my mug on the shelf in the shower, having to move my shampoo out of the way to do so. I turned on the hot water and let it run hard and fast as I went back into my room to find a clean towel and robe. I know its wasteful but it takes a while for the water to get to the temperatures I enjoy. I strip off with relative haste exposing my naked self to the full-length mirror.

Catching a glimpse of myself with all my imperfections meant that I once again tried to reinforce to myself that I'm not that bad looking and my body isn't terrible … surely.

On this occasion I was actually quite happy with that casual glimpse of my reflection as it also reminded me I needed to do a little "lawn care" before the weekend. That being said, ignoring or forgetting things like that is usually a good way to guarantee that someone will see you naked.

I grabbed a clean towel from a pile of clean washing and my robe off the bed and made way into the bathroom, now engulfed in a bubble of welcoming steam. I adjusted the temperature after every so elegantly dumping the towel and robe on the vanity and stepped into the torrent. The music faded to just a subtle hint of a distant melody and I took a gulp of my not-horrible wine. The water surrounded me and this space became safe, it became mine. I tried to clear my head of the negative and focus on what's coming up … a weekend away, two weeks paid leave and, what was currently the most exciting, shower wine!

CHAPTER 31

I went to bed that night in typical Hannah fashion: drunk, unsatisfied and, on this occasion, more than a little hungry. Despite what the delivery girl had said, the meal I'd opted for turned out to be thoroughly disappointing to the point I was unable to actually finish it. As for the wine, let's just say there was none left and maybe a little bit less in the whiskey bottle as well. I really had no idea why I had the need to once again end up on the northern side of acceptable midweek drinking but I ended up justifying it in my head with the vague notion of being upset by bubble tea lady. I had to think twice to actually register her name was Liv. So fucking disrespectful of me to forget the poor girl's name but I blamed that on the wine and the general instability of this afternoon.

I just couldn't shut my brain down and it took all my self-control to not give in and just pop a pain killer. I'd moved past the relief and joy of the enforced holiday and couldn't get past the fact that it had taken something like this and a weekend away to give me something to look forward to and inject a little happiness into my mediocre routine. This was probably the right occasion to note that I was not inherently "sad", as such, but there were times that, because of my fucked-up brain, I really couldn't see a way out of this rut of a life I'd put myself in, regardless of the pact Katie and I'd made.

The sad truth was at this point, that part of me felt pressured by everything and everyone to just bite the proverbial bullet, find a man, get knocked up, and settle down. There were such things as a mail-order bride, but do they do mail-order husbands? I could browse an online catalogue and find myself a nice Eastern-European

Hemsworth-ish gentleman to bring over and marry. Oh the joy I could experience as he walks off the plane with a giant Toblerone bar only to be revealed to be a short, balding fifty year old turnip farmer with an uncanny resemblance to a hairier Danny DeVito. Mummy would be so very proud.

All sarcasm aside, it would almost be worth it just to see the look on Mum's face as I showed up to a family BBQ with my new boyfriend. I'd tell her, 'I think he's a keeper'. The hilarity of that thought took me to the very edge of consciousness and eventually the darkness caught up with me. I drifted off into a sleep that was, unfortunately, occupied by dreams of my mail-order husband and I playing the proverbial "beast with two backs". The one advantage of this nightmarish experience was that it reminded me that there were worse things than going through a dry streak.

For once, I woke up before my alarm, dehydrated and still haunted by visions of running my fingers through my mail-order husband's luscious locks ... of back hair. Things were so vivid that I could almost feel the subtle greasiness of one of the fuzziest backs I'd encountered, in reality or in dreams, as I'd passionately embraced what I hoped wasn't a potential future.

Eventually my old friend, the red wine headache, kicked in exacerbating the dry unpleasantness of my throat. It did bring me down off my high horse a little and made me aware of how shallow I was being and that my mail-order bride, let's call him Dimitri, was probably a really nice, genuine guy ... one who had to lie about his appearance to get a wife from overseas.

Holy shit! This was a new level of absurdity, I was feeling sorry for an ugly man from my dreams who was an obvious con artist. That really was a new experience for me and one that I hoped to completely banish from my memory. *Sorry, Dimitri, it's over. Our very brief dream wedding and night of unfulfilling dream sex is in the past. It's not you, it's me. I'm just not in the right place at the moment. Etc. etc. blah blah.* There. It was over, now I could move on with my day, one that should be filled with the joy and anticipation of a time off and a weekend away with Katie.

Fuck ... it was Thursday! That meant staff morning tea. Another social event where I was forced to socialise and share some shitty homemade slice or crackers and dip hastily purchased from the supermarket in a mad dash, ten minutes before work after forgetting it was your turn to provide for this important team bonding event. That sparked a genuinely terrifying thought: was I rostered on today? Because if I was and I forgot ... the death stares and not-so-subtle jibes I would receive would be brutal.

Our social committee are brutally serious, almost mafia-like. From my limited viewing of gangster movies, I'm pretty sure I've seen contracts put out on people for less. If I forgot, it would be yet another black mark on my name in the face of god (the social committee) and men (the boss) and, despite being away for a few weeks after, I would still have to face the eternal wrath of the morning tea commandant, Jenny ... or is it Jane ... and her social stormtroopers. To think this is all in the name of morale and esprit de corps. I grab my phone and in a state of sheer panic and fear, I text Ryan.

H: Hey. Sorry to bother but I'm in a pickle.
Do you happen to have or know the morning tea roster?
Now to wait, hope, and pray that it's not me. I think what makes this weekly hell even more vulgar is the fact that people actually judge your value as an employee for the food you provide. I remember a few years ago a new girl brought in two packets of Tim Tams, a dip, and some water crackers and they talked about her for months, giving her the stink eye every time she took something from one of the share plates at subsequent morning teas. It was brutal, but they eventually forgave her and even welcomed her onto the social committee when she showed up with a New York style cheesecake, with a raspberry coulis AND a salted caramel slice! Her position

in the office social hierarchy rose significantly after what we later referred to as "Cheesecake-gate".
My phone vibrated …

> R: Hey, it's you … sorry.

Fuck! This always happened when my kitchen was barer than a supermarket toilet paper aisle in 2020.

> H: Thanks … I guess.
> Bakery visit on the way to work.
> ☹

I dumped my phone on the bench and did what I call 'the superman'; stripping off any item of clothing in a haphazard, yet rapid manner while speedily making my way to somewhere important. In this case, the shower.

I have never showered, gotten dressed, and done my hair in such a short amount of time. It was so rushed and rapid that Bill Murray or the news guys didn't get any attention this morning. I know it's strange that someone who appears to give so few fucks about work should be worried about a morning tea, but forgetting things like this doesn't sit well with my anxiety. I adjusted my bra, realising I had reached for the most uncomfortable, yet sexiest, one that I own and I reached for my phone. Three messages from Ryan and one from Katie.

> R: I'm guessing that's going to ruin your morning.
> Don't stress too much
> The girls can get what they get

We both knew that kind of attitude would crash and burn, but credit to him for trying to dispel any fear of social club reprisal.

> R: Don't worry about morning tea … its sorted.
> I just ducked into a bakery on the way and grabbed a few things for you.
> You owe me $20

Great, now I have to stop into the ATM as well. This morning keeps getting better. Wait. 'Don't worry about morning tea … it's sorted.'

Films Have Given Me Trust Issues

That amazing, annoying, somewhat handsome man! If he keeps up giving me holidays and saving me from social club commitments I'll have to stop hating him as much.

> R: I'm guessing you're in the shower
> Please don't fall ☺
> See you at work ... last day!

There we go, smart-arse Ryan was back and no inclusion of a smiley face emoji can convince me this wasn't a sly dig at my 'unfortunate accident'. I repressed my anger for a few moments, thinking I should actually thank the guy.

> H: Thanks heaps. #Lifesaver
> I'll sort you out when I get to work

I made the cardinal sin of clicking send before actually reading what I wrote. Upon reading the message, I was mortified. First, and possibly most embarrassingly, I'd actually used a hashtag. This wasn't Instagram, or Facebook and I wasn't vapid millennial wannabe. Now, somewhat more concerningly was that I told him I'd 'sort him out' at work.

The amount of unintentional sexual innuendo there was staggering. I just hoped that he didn't take it as me offering to provide him with one of many possible sexual favours in his office as a 'thank you'. I certainly didn't watch those type of movies ... generally. I hoped he wouldn't reply and would just ignore my idiotic response ... I wasn't that lucky.

> R: ☺

Must I remind you of the sexual misconduct section of the CoC? CoC of course being 'Code of Conduct'. I let an audible and less than subtle groan. Just when my opinion of the guy was slightly improving.

Katie's message was less uncomfortable. Despite being rostered off, she'd been called into work and was obviously in a mad rush.

> K: Stupid bitch at work "sprained her ankle"
> Now I have to work ☹

Will drop by yours about 7 tonight with a pizza
C U then
X

I'd certainly welcome the company as, hopefully, Katie's company would prevent another night of excessive wine consumption. Besides, I hadn't had a chance to really talk to her about the last few days and my "leave". She'd obviously been so busy with work and, with this weekend coming up, I didn't want to be that clingy, insecure friend who won't give you ten minutes peace.

H: Great, c u then.
Plenty to chat about

All I had to do before work now was find an ATM, meaning I wasn't in such a rush. I put my phone in my handbag and went for my keys, deciding I'd treat myself to a coffee at that hipster place near the bus stop. I had forty minutes until it was scheduled to leave so I had plenty of time to dodge the neighbours, beat the rush of bohemian students and grab a flat white before battling the stank and sadness of public transport. Now that I thought of it, there was actually an ATM next door to the café ... #winning! Fuck. Hashtags again ... twice in one day! I needed to have a long hard look at what might be influencing my vocabulary making me sound vapid and "young".

I double checked I had everything, locked the door, and stepped into the crisp morning sunlight into what was, hopefully, going to be a great day.

CHAPTER 32

The café was buzzing which generally indicated decent brew, but the look and feel of this place nearly made a shitty vending machine Iced Mocha seem like a decent alternative. This place exuded hipster vibes but I could actually smell the pretentiousness and self-righteousness, with a subtle hint of weed, from fifty metres away. The name of the place, Jam and Bread: Roastery and Talkhouse, reeked of hipster and youth culture. Apparently, the name had a little duality of meaning with the owners, both priding themselves on "Fresh, homemade, organic, local Jam" and live music, in the form of an open mic on a Saturday afternoon.

One big question came to mind as I stood there, entranced by the sheer number of beards, curled moustaches and visible tattoos … how the fuck could jam in an inner city café be "local"? Did they have berries growing in their window boxes and back alleys? Did they get weekly airdrops from the berry farms of rural Australia? I really wanted to ask, but the thought of having to listen to a long-winded answer, designed to make me feel bad for buying "commercial" jam made the thought of that self-inflected head wound sound more appealing. And hashtags, hashtags everywhere … these things are invading every aspect of life at the moment. #jamlife, #artisan, #openmic … they were literally everywhere!

All that being said, the coffee smelled amazing and despite how busy the place was, there were only two people lining up, and a barista with an insanely colourful solar system tattoo was pumping out coffees at an alarming pace. I lined up and was pleasantly met with a smile from the guy in front of me. He obviously worked a desk job, but was incredibly cute. He was one of those guys that made you immediately blush and curse yourself for not taking more time getting ready. His chiselled jaw and obvious six pack spoke of a guy that ate healthy and went to the gym while his crystal blue eyes exuded a caring, loving nature.

I tried to avoid looking at his crotch area, but the hopefully subtle peek revealed another highlight of this random coffee shop guy. I learned a lot about random coffee shop guy in the next ten minutes or so; he had oat milk in his latte, his name was Hunter, and he had a boyfriend called Steve who, together with Hunter, made the most amazingly hot pair of men I'd ever seen. I wish I could say I was disappointed but "out of my league" was a massive understatement … oh, and the fact that they were gay.

It didn't hurt to look, I guess.

'Miss, what can I get you?' The barista behind the faux hardwood counter was obviously flustered at the lack of attention I was paying to her efforts to take my order, but it certainly didn't justify the calling me "miss". Was it really that obvious that I was a girl who was obviously over ripening and still single? I really need to stop being so sensitive about that because, according to Katie, it turns out a lot of people just refer to women in general as "miss".

'Large flat white on skim, two sugar, double shot please.' I looked at the price board and was a little taken aback by what I thought was an overly inflated price. $7.50.

'I'm sorry miss, we don't stock skim milk,' she said with a smug, self-righteous expression while tapping the sign, drawn in chalk with a sad cow face, conveying that very point. I really didn't get what was so bad about skim but, okay, when in Rome, do as the hipsters do.

'Okay, regular milk is fine.' She took my name and I tapped my card and waited next to Hunter and Steve, anxious of the time. I genuinely couldn't be late. At least there was an ATM outside. I had to walk past it to get back to the bus stop, so that made one chore this morning much harder to forget. I was also okay for time, assuming solar system tattoo girl, whose name tag read "Lizbeth", didn't slow down to regular inner city speeds for a barista at peak hour.

I collected my coffee from Lizbeth, getting a welcoming smile and wink. Certainly not something I'd excepted but, then again, I could just be one of those cynical folk that think the worst of everyone. Up close, if you looked past that hipster façade and the tattoos, she was quite an attractive girl. And not as young as I'd originally expected. She had the most amazing olive skin, completely free of blemishes and accentuated by her eyes of deep green.

I suddenly became incredibly self-aware of how uncomfortably long I must have been staring at this girl as she continued to brew and froth at an impressive rate.

'Are you local?'

I was brought back into reality upon the realisation she was actually talking to me.

'Yeah, I guess. I'm a short-ish walk up the road. I'm not a normally a café kind of girl, so I haven't been in here yet. How long have you been open for?' I was aware of the time but considering how rare a polite barista was these days I didn't want to be rude.

'Going on five years, I think. I'm guessing you don't pay a great deal of attention to anything past the bus stop generally?' she said.

'Pretty much. Plus, I'm usually in a mad rush. Disorganisation and I are true kindred spirits.' I hope that wasn't misinterpreted as a sarcastic crack at hipster slang but the damage was already done. 'Thanks for the coffee, I've got to get to the ATM next door before my bus.' Steam erupted from the coffee machine with a somewhat poetic 'hiss' as I smiled and started to turn towards the door to fight my way through the growing throng of people.

'Hey, you should drop by more often. I work most days until about five. Word of advice, don't come for open mic unless your fond of aural torture.' She gave me a glowing smile that radiated the positivity of someone south of middle age and I waved and exited.

As I stood at the ATM waiting for the machine to process my transaction, hoping that I haven't been scammed or overspent in a late-night, drunken shopping spree, I became aware of what just happened. I think that girl was hitting on me. In fact, I'm positive that girl was hitting on me. I wasn't sure how to feel to be honest. Knowing a girl that beautiful was interested in me felt amazing, despite my heterosexual persuasion. However, it also got me thinking that as well as giving out the single vibe, was I now giving out a lesbian aura as well?

It didn't inherently bother me, it just raised a few questions. No, it didn't awaken repressed sexual feelings but it did get me thinking about what parts of my appearance or personality gave away my status as spinster, while alluding to some that I was gay? Something to ponder over a drink or seven with Katie over the weekend, after all, we were saving each other supposedly.

I contemplated going back in to see Lizbeth and put the hard word on her ... wait ... *interrogate* her maybe? I was really quite curious but apparently it proverbially killed the cat and made people like me miss the bus. My money was ejected from the hole in the wall and was disappointed to note that the one hundred dollars I withdrew came out in a single crisp, clean note which, I'm positive, would be quite difficult to break. I just had to hope that Ryan was as wealthy as he dressed and that he carried around the equivalent of a small mutual bank in his wallet so I could get some change.

As I turned, I caught a glimpse of good old Bus 352 turn the corner and I made my way to the bus shelter in a comfortable amount of time with a hipster coffee, the most I've had in my purse in at least twelve months and and some light-flirtation from a younger girl. All that and the relief of knowing that Ryan had sorted morning tea for me resulted in me stepping up into that cesspit on wheels in a somewhat positive mood. I even managed to score a takeaway coffee where the disposable lid was properly secured and unlikely to pop off as I was taking a sip. To be fair, that'd only ever happened to me once but it managed to occur on a day that I was wearing the only white blouse I own and was about to make my way into a mandatory end of year review with the big boss. I'm sure the massive brown stain and the aroma of coffee made it pretty clear what had happened, but he'd still looked far from impressed.

On this particular day though, the Thursday before my extended break, everything was coming up Hannah! Except ... as I took a seat, I came to the numbing realisation that I hadn't taken my bipolar medication.

Fuck! 'Fuck!' I think I made my expletive a little too loud and emotive as I got an unapproving look from the elderly gentlemen on the seat opposite me. Oh well, this will be interesting because generally, when I miss my meds, I end up either manic or on a downer. Roll the dice people and look out ... which one was it going to be today? Fuck!

CHAPTER 33

The foyer to office felt oppressively hot, which I thought I was imagining until young Herman appeared, forehead glistening with beads of sweat. It certainly wasn't the most attractive sight – or smell – to be greeted with first thing in the morning, but it set my mind at ease knowing I wasn't flushing.

'Air conditioner is on the fritz, sorry about the heat.'

Herman's explanation made perfect sense, the thing had been stuffing up for months now but don't worry, 'It's all good, people; the contractors will be here tomorrow to fix it up.'

We'd heard that statement from management at least once or twice a week since the AC had started playing up but alas we were yet to actually see any kind of action other than that motivating 'carry on and all that' government attitude. I guarantee you the air conditioners in their offices wouldn't be on the fritz for long. They'd probably fly in contractors from overseas if required, just to make sure they got to frolic in a consistently pleasant ambient temperature.

The system servicing the main office space was thankfully still functional, which meant stepping into there was reminiscent of that first swim of the summer or the first cocktail on Christmas morning. As I approached my desk, I was greeted with the most amazing gift I could have hoped for. Sitting at my desk, working away busily, was Marg.

They had managed to con, I mean *hire*, that delightful old crone into doing my job for two weeks. With Marg on board, I knew The day would be a breeze, probably an hour or so of going through what was scheduled, an hour or so of policy documents I needed to update, and the rest she should pick up by osmosis.

'Marg, I see they were desperate enough to beg the home to let you out for a few weeks?' My hand on her shoulder and my smile exuded more affection than the statement suggested.

'Funny … you know I couldn't afford to go into a home on what the government paid me. Ryan just wanted someone with a better arse to look at for a few weeks … and to sort out these new form letters. What were they thinking?'

'I'm glad they got you, Marg. It makes the hand over so much less stressful and I just don't need that today.'

Marg squinted at me over the top of her rather trendy glasses, probing, what felt like, the depths of my soul. 'Who else would they have got? Have you seen the rest of the temp pool for this department? It looks like a line-up of Playboy mansion dropouts. All boobs and legs, no brains or personality.'

We shared a laugh as I stowed my handbag under the desk and wheeled the spare chair from the next desk over. Sharon wouldn't even notice, she spent most of her day upstairs having been given a partial transfer up to management, which just happened to have her now working out of the office of the married man she was sleeping with. Worst kept secret in the office and that bitch thinks we are all oblivious.

As I adjusted the seat and opened up Ryan's calendar for the next week, Marg leaned in and subtly rested her hand on mine. 'Hannah, forget your meds again hun?'

I hung my head slightly and became very self-aware of any signs I may been giving off. 'Is it that obvious?' I said.

'You've just got a subtle shake to you and you feel a bit clammy. I've seen this happen a few times now. I know what to look out for.' I hadn't even registered that tremor at all, but I knew by the end of the day it would be quite pronounced. 'I'll have you out of here by the end of lunch, you'll be fine. If Ryan causes any trouble, I'll either threaten to walk out or seduce him,' she said with dry, comedic delivery.

'He couldn't handle you, Marg. You'd ruin him for other women.'

Marg was so incredibly caring, in many ways more than my own mother, but she did it in such a bitchy, inappropriate manner. We didn't see each other a lot or outside of work, but when we did, we always got along really well.

'Come on, let's get a coffee. A trick of the trade, always wait until it ticks over to 9am to make your first coffee … that way you're drinking on their time,' Marg said.

As we got up and walked to coffee room, Marg gave my arm a little squeeze. It was subtle, but it was enough to let me know that she had my back and that she actually gave a shit. I really did love Marg.

As expected, the main table in the lunch room was stacked with treats, both sweet and savoury, to satisfy the hungry masses and to be scrutinised by the social committee enforcers. As requested, everyone who was rostered on had to identify what they provided for no fucking reason whatsoever other than to provide people with an opportunity to "name and shame". Realistically, if this much effort, time and scrutiny was put into everything we did in this building, we'd be solving all the departments issues in record time.

Marg sorted us out a coffee; she always had hers black, strong, and in as large a cup as humanly possible. I enjoyed mine sweet and with just enough strength to get me through a stretch until I need another break. I could take the moral high ground and not make the old joke and compare how I take my coffee to how I like my men … I could. However, I wasn't that mature and the similarities between the two really were uncanny. So, here we go … weak and sweet, I like my coffee just like my men.

I heard footsteps outside and thought this was an opportune time to test a theory. I ushered Marg to the side behind the door and waited covertly as possible for a forty year old women in an unpractical work outfit. I'd always suspected that Jenny, or Jane, or both, made it their duty to inspect the morning tea offerings before break time just to ensure quality and to black mark the name of any that they feel haven't provided to an acceptable level. Low and behold, I was correct.

The door edged open and Jenny ... I was pretty sure it was Jenny ... walked in, chin up, with the gravitas of Margaret Thatcher and the self-righteousness of Gwyneth Paltrow. Luckily, she closed the door enough to conceal Marg and I. Until she left that was. She stood at the end of the table, back to us, thankfully, going through the names one by one and comparing it to what I was assumed was the roster she carried with her on a vibrant piece of canary yellow, A4 paper. The bitch even had the nerve to be ticking off names as she went around the table with a judgemental glare worthy of the best court room drama. She appeared to stop at a rather large cake, lots of chocolate, cream and strawberries covered in white chocolate.

I could vaguely make out the name on the post-it ... Hannah. On top of the cake, written in white frosting were the words: *Thank you all for your support* in cursive with a lovely little heart underneath.

'Isn't that lovely,' Jenny muttered with what appeared to be a satisfied smile. Her judgement ended and she begun to turn to, hopefully, return to her actually paid job. She wasn't wearing her glasses today which, to be fair, made her look a lot younger and a lot less grizzled. With some luck, not having those on her head would mean she would miss the two grown women hiding behind the door. I really didn't like our chances. Best I could do was to try and find a compliment to distract her from the fact we were obviously spying on her. Her knee length beige skirt, plain white blouse and black jacket didn't give me much to work with, but she'd obviously just had her hair trimmed and dyed.

I decided to strike pre-emptively, to make that first move.

'Jenny, hi ... sorry to startle you. We just didn't want to interrupt whatever it was you were doing. Your hair looks amazing, by the way.' That sounded somewhat plausible, if not rather insincere. It sure beat the truth of, 'we were spying on you, Jenny ... spying at you being a judgemental, controlling bitch!' Yep, I definitely took the better option.

'Hannah, Marg ... I didn't expect you both.' She was obviously shocked, but she reacted somewhat positively to the compliment as she reached for her hair and gave it a gentle, proud caress. 'I assumed everyone would be at work by now getting everything ship-shape before the ministers visit next week.'

Two thoughts came to mind: *why aren't you at work, Jenny?* and *Fuck, I'm missing a visit from the minister!* I couldn't control the smile at the thought of avoiding that extra stress.

'Coffee. Plus, Marg and I were on our way to the conference room to go over the schedule for next week.' On a whim, I actually came up with a decent idea. I could bring up the calendar on the big screen and wouldn't have to deal with idiots walking past, gawking.

'I heard about your "enforced leave". I do hope everything is well.' It really must have hurt her to say that because there really was the undertone of contempt in her voice. 'You did however, save me a walk as I was just on my way to see you.' Fuck ... here we go. What had I done now? I felt Marg's hand on my arm again with a tight, comforting grip. She must have sensed something: the speed of my voice, the tremors, or just a suspicion my brain wasn't working on all cylinders. *Deep breaths Hannah.*

'I just wanted to thank you for the beautiful cake you provided for morning tea, despite not even being rostered on. It's a lovely gift to the staff before you go off for a few weeks.' Marg squeezed harder and I caught the expression on her face out of the corner of my eye, it was the very definition of 'resting bitch face'. It took me a few seconds to comprehend what had happened, but this filled the gap nicely as Jenny walked past me giving me a fake smile as a nice farewell. I could tell what she was thinking: this woman usually either forgets or provides utter shit to the morning tea and now, here she is, offering up a cake, worth a solid $50, voluntarily. I started to shake at the thought of this ridiculous stitch up.

Fuck Ryan and the horse he rode in on. He knew I hated morning teas, he knew I hated the roster, and he knew I had no idea of when I was on. He was probably sitting in his office right now, having a right old laugh at my expense. And me ... thinking this guy had somewhat changed, that deep down, he was actually a remotely decent guy, who was somewhat attractive.

'That could have been worse,' I said.

Marg smiled and she did something she had never done before; she pulled me in for a very gentle, uncomfortable hug. One that showed a clear awareness of the fact we were both holding a cup of steaming hot coffee. I could now feel myself shaking and my face must have been the colour of an undercooked beetroot.

'You should just sleep with him and take all the batteries from his remote controls on the way out. That's a nice added "fuck you".' That cheeky smile of hers calmed me a little, brought me back to reality and focused my thoughts ... fuck Ryan!

CHAPTER 34

The conference room I managed to hijack was not scheduled for use today and to be honest, I wasn't planning on being here past lunch time anyway. I didn't even feel bad about this anymore after Ryan's bullshit this morning and Marg's insistence on me going home whenever we finished was the icing on the proverbial cake. This room, the main conference area on this floor, was named in memorial to some guy I've never heard of. No doubt another government stooge who spent his life making other people's lives miserable ... probably in this very office.

I was obviously on the down and the signs were becoming easily recognisable, even for me. The problem was anyone that didn't know me particularly well would just think I was harbouring an intense negative emotion which I called "sad-hate". Now, sad-hate was a lovely mix for these two incredibly intense emotions that were constantly locked in an internal back and forth, fighting over who was going to show themselves at any given time. Think of it as being a battle royale on *Herman's Head*; a bloodbath of medically subdued emotions beating the shit out of each other to assert dominance. This was the downers my meds sort to eradicate from my day to day, and they generally did a pretty good job.

Anyway, sitting in this room, trying to hook-up a laptop to the big screen while repressing sad-hate, I bitched to Marg about how typical it was of a government agency to name a conference room after a lifelong servant. How apt it was that a room used for meetings that were pretty much lectures from the boss that could have been as effective if sent in an email, was named after someone who probably dished this exact punishment for fifty years and then died, fulfilled, knowing he'd inflicted this on low paid workers under the context of "making a difference". I was getting worked up and my hands weren't doing what the brain was wanting them to do, I was befuddled and becoming a mess.

Marg settled me a little by reminding me that the room was actually named after a guy who used to visit local schools in the 50s and help provide education and resources to First Nations students who were largely neglected by all government agencies. In fact, he was somewhat of a local hero. I had no idea who he was, to the point that I'd just assumed he was another bastard working for the government. I felt like an absolute moron but at least it settled me down a little and made me really, REALLY regret forgetting my medication today.

The thought of having to face this morning tea which, because of my "kind donation", I would definitely have to attend with no medication and after already having a sad-hate adventure made me feel nauseous. I stopped and gave Marg some type of glare that I'm sure would have been hard to define.

'Do we have to go?'

She knew exactly what I was talking about and I'm almost positive she'd expected the exact question because her response was immediate and emotionless. She had a point though: I still had to come here after two weeks leave. I probably needed to maintain some level of control and forced pleasantries ... you know, paying the bills and all that actually required a job.

Seeing that smug look on Ryan's face and trying to avoid giving him a mouthful would take immense levels of self-control, even if was medicated. I didn't know if he'd actually misread the roster, a possibility, or if he thought this was his version of an hilarious practical joke. Either way, he wasn't getting his fucking money!

So, strap in and enjoy my wild ride. This would be the show of the century.

The term "kicking and screaming" is thrown around too frequently these days, but Marg trying to get me to leave the conference room and go to the staff morning tea was the very definition of both those things. I kicked the recycling bin over, spilling crumpled up generic, white A4 paper all over the floor. Now, by all over the floor, I mean there was three pieces occupying the bin at the time of my outburst, but I still refused to pick them up. That would show them!

The screaming was a lot more dramatic. It involved many "fucks", "arseholes" and "pricks" but I avoided the c-bomb which, despite my disdain for the word, tended to pop out when I was agitated, and agitated was the perfect assessment of my mindset at this point on a "no medication" day.

Marg picked up what gear we had, grabbed me by the arm and proceeded to drag me across the conference floor, to the door and out into the hallway, which was starting to show signs of increased foot traffic because of the aforementioned "social event of a lifetime".

I like to think I maintained a level of decorum and grace once I had the satisfaction of slamming the door in what was, retrospectively, overly dramatic.

'Hannah, look on the bright side. We are done and once you smile and fake your way through cake and a coffee you can go home and you don't have step foot in this place for another two weeks.' Marg led me down the corridor towards the tea room and I could already hear the inane babble coming from inside. 'Deep breaths. Just smile, have a coffee and say "hi" to a few people. If you're lucky, Ryan might not even be there … ' She started to say something else but trailed off suddenly and I could see in her ageing eyes overflowing with the wisdom, cynicism and sarcasm of a life time public servant, that something had changed.

You know those horror films where the main character is walking through a dark basement for some reason and all of a sudden there is a visual temperature drop? There is an obvious chill that the filmmaker so expertly conveys to the audience to let us know something is going to go down. Then the ghost thing appears, there is the inevitable jump scare, and the character flees in terror? That was almost exactly what this was like, except I played the role of the creepy ghost thing. Appropriate, considering how pale and clammy I appeared, and Ryan who had just rounded the corner was the helpless victim.

'You!' My hand raised in an accusatory gesture, just like a star witness would do in a courtroom, pointing out the guilty party to the jury. I sped up and pursued him with what I thought was a nice mix of the singlemindedness of a predator chasing its prey, and ladylike focus and intensity. He knew ... oh he knew! He turned on a die and backtracked towards the apparent safety of his office, obviously aware of my agitated state and the reason behind it.

Good old Marg, gave up. She got as far as the door to the tea room and accepted the possibility of workplace homicide and instead opted for a cake and some coffee. Actually, what I knew about Marg led me to believe that she would probably make a b-line for the caramel slice before Helen from HR started pocketing it for later.

I rounded the corner and spotted Ryan ducking into his office as expected. Coward. He could have at least had the decency to usher me into a storage closet, lock the door, and call the authorities to take me to the looney bin because, at this point, I had no doubt I would have looked the part of a crazy woman. I could feel my body and my brain reacting to the chemicals in my pills not actually being there and doing their thing.

There was almost a burning in my head and a feeling of intense fogginess. The doctor constantly reinforced me not to ditch these pills cold turkey, like I have with other medications in the past, and to make sure I took them religiously every morning and every night. When I first started on them, I honestly believed that withdrawals couldn't happen so quickly and that missing one dose wouldn't hurt. Until it happened for the first time, about six months in, I had no idea just how wrong I was. It physically and emotionally hurt.

I didn't even knock, I opened Ryan's door, expecting to be met with a smug, arsehole like smile and an "It was just a joke" throwaway statement. The kind of response you got from some heartless, narcissistic sociopath who gets their rocks off from publicly humiliating other people in the name of humour. What I got from Ryan was the exact opposite.

He stood there, waiting for me, looking like a contrite boy who knew he fucked-up and was waiting for that dressing down from mum and dad. I closed the door and took a step towards him, somewhat calmed by his almost miserable expression. He raised his hands in a symbolic act of self-defence, moved around me gingerly and closed the door.

'I'm so sorry. I misread the roster, honestly.' I sat down and tried to follow Marg's advice … deep breaths. 'This was not a prank, I was not messing with you. I genuinely fucked-up.'
He sat down on one of the chairs he had in his office for guests and made a subtle move towards me in, what I think, was an attempt to calm me. *Deep breaths Hannah.*

'I was ready to fucking murder you, Ryan. Today was definitely not the day for bullshit like that.' I started to calm myself. The guy had obviously made a mistake. He moved forward a little and our eyes met. I'd never realised it before, but he had the most beautiful crystal blue eyes that were almost hypnotic. My breathing slowed as I became lost in the simple, calming peace of his eyes. I almost didn't register his hand on my knee, not in an inappropriate or sexual way, but comforting and warm.

'Are you okay? Don't take this the wrong way … but you look terrible.' Despite the fact he was probably right, that kind of statement to a woman from anyone, in any situation, was a good way to bring them back to reality. Did I really want to tell? I didn't have to be specific I guess like, 'Hey, guess what? I forgot my crazy meds, boss man'. Ryan sat back in his chair and crossed his legs and placed his hands on his lap in a pose reminiscent of that favoured by a psychologist.

'Honestly, I forgot my medication this morning and the withdrawals kick in really quick. And no, I'm not going to tell you what they are for.'

His mannerism didn't change at all, but those eyes, they continued to draw my focus. I had no idea why I hadn't registered earlier how amazing they were, especially when I was talking about his redeeming features with Katie. There was a hint of care and 'I really do give a shit' in his stare which I never, ever expected.

'I was never going to ask and, to be honest, you'd have an amazing formal complaint to make against me if I did. Why did you come in? You should have just called in sick.'

I paused to contemplate the stupidity of his statement and quietly pat myself on the back for picking it up so quickly. Gold star to Hannah right there. Really? Wouldn't he think that if I'd registered that I hadn't taken my meds before I left home that I just would have taken them to avoid the unpleasant withdrawals? What a dumb arse statement. He hung his head a little as he registered his stupidity.

'I figured with me being on leave and "working from home" tomorrow that it wouldn't be a good look. Besides, I'd already left my place.' I smiled at him, or at least I tried to smile. I was hoping that my body moved the right muscles so as to avoid a look of subtle discomfort or constipation.

'You and Marg are done, right?' I nodded. 'I'm calling you a cab and you're going home. I don't want you battling public transport in this state.'

Could it be that he'd detected my passionate hatred of the filth and depravity of public transport? 'Ryan, I don't have cab money to pay from here to my place. Do you know how much that would be? I'll just catch a bus.' I really, really wanted to go home and I really didn't want to take a bus feeling like I did, so there were two options: listen to Ryan and treat myself to a fifty-ish dollars magical carpet ride in a cab, slightly cleaner and less meth heads than a bus, or call my mum to come and get me which she would absolutely love! If I actually asked her for help to get home from work, it would be like all her Christmases had come at once. It would be one of those things she would remind me of at every opportunity or, just for fun. Both options were really, really detestable but Ryan saved me from needing to decide.

'No, we'll pay for the cab. We actually have money built into the budget for things like this, it was kind of a COVID measure to get people off site if they were sick. However, please ... please do not make this public knowledge or Helen from HR will be "sick" every time it storms or she doesn't feel like walking the two blocks to the train station.'

Wow ... free taxi ride it was. I sure as hell wasn't going to argue with him because at that point that nothing in the world short of a large sum of cash or week alone with Ryan Reynolds on a private island in a world where he wasn't married and refused to wear clothes would change my mind. See, I did have some morals and standards ... I draw the line at sleeping with married men, even celebrities.

'Thanks Ryan ... ' I was definitely talking to work Ryan here, not some imaginary, withdrawal induced hallucination of Mr Reynolds. ' ... I really appreciate it.'

Ten minutes later, Ryan and I were standing on the curb waiting for the cab. As it pulled up, he opened the door for me and put my handbag on the passenger's side floor. I had no idea why he was holding it, but if I were feeling better I would have made a somewhat humorous comment about how that particular handbag didn't suit him. I'm really good at clichéd, unfunny jokes like that.

It turned out the government must have access to some special cabs because this one was super clean and it smelled like mango! More importantly, as I would later find out, the driver was polite but not talkative, and the radio was at an acceptable volume set to a contemporary, main stream radio station! Before the door closed, Ryan leaned in put his hand on my shoulder and said with great delight, 'Enjoy your break. And, by the way, you can keep the money for the cake.' He winked and smiled, once again became that arrogant man-child that had pissed me off for such a long time. Those eyes though ... wow! The taxi pulled out into traffic and I took one final glance over my shoulder at the building and Ryan standing out the front. I didn't have to see or deal with anything or anyone for two whole weeks. I sighed and settled in for the drive in what was quite a comfortable seat with extra padding from a special seat cover I think. Unfortunately for me, all I could think of at that moment was my arsehole bosses' eyes.

CHAPTER 35

I was always enthusiastic to close my front door after a day at work but today, it was even more a sense of relief. I should have been happy to be home early and excited at the next few weeks but I just couldn't get past the burning in my head and a growing feeling of just not being right. I dumped everything, fumbled manically for my medication; I must have looked so desperate. Some would probably say it was psychosomatic, but within ten minutes I was starting to feel somewhat more like myself. Katie was coming by later and despite the fact she was probably the least judgemental person I know, I still wanted to not be looking like someone turning after a dramatic zombie bite. Thank you *The Walking Dead* for awakening a fear of the apocalypse, and television programs that are dragged well past their use-by date.

I boiled the jug and made myself a cup of tea, extra sweet, extra milky, to wash down a few over the counter pain killers to try and get me past wanting to just go to sleep. I kicked off my shoes, took off my jacket, and parked myself on the couch in front of the TV to catch up on some shows I've been streaming. I was excited! Some free time, no need to cook dinner and I had several hours before Katie would be here. I sat my cup of tea on the coffee table and started up the latest episode of *Severance*, a show I really only started watching because of Adam Scott but, here I was, six episodes in and depressed because I was running out of episodes.

The meds did their job pretty quickly as I gradually became entranced with this state of pure peace and relaxation. The burning in my head was now just a remnant, a fading memory of intense discomfort that reminded me of the self-loathing I once held. I was feeling more normal, for lack of a better word. I was also now totally over the moon in knowing that enjoying this show justified the subscription I paid to the streaming service offered by a large, multinational corporation named after a fruit that I constantly bitched about, despite owning every gadget under the sun with their branding.

Hypocritical, I know, but I was too unstable to really give a shit. Sitting there, enjoying every aspect of Adam Scott's bizarrely sexy appearance, I started to fixate on the fact that I hadn't actually spoken to Katie in a few days. The character of Helly somehow led me to this. Her subtle intelligence and willingness to speak her mind bore a stark similarity to the characteristics I admired so much in Katie. This feeling that came with having not spoken to her led me to how I hadn't really thought about just how emotionally invested I was in her and this whirlwind friendship. In retrospect, if people could see inside my head, it could be interpreted as somewhat obsessive.

I really do overthink things and become my own worst enemy. The last thing I needed to do was talk myself into thinking I was the protagonist of that film *Roommate*, the one where the girl becomes obsessed with her new roommate. It really was a pretty terrible movie, but it made for a standard, half-decent date when it was first released. Pretty ordinary movie followed by a pretty ordinary meal and, typical of me, the coup de grace ... ordinary sex. Those were the good old days; early 2010s, me still being the only single friend in my group and still making a bunch of bad choices. So, really, nothing had changed except I think I was a dress size smaller and a little perkier.

The tea hit me with a sweet fruitiness which I can unfortunately say was predominantly the two teaspoons of raw sugar I added, but it refocused me. I'm surely not the obsessive\stalker type, am I? I lacked the focus and commitment to follow through or even pursue that kind of creepy behaviour. What I was, however, was a little scarier and a lot sadder ... I was lonely.

I looked around my house. There was nothing that suggested any deep connections or relationships. Hell, I didn't even have any family photos hanging around the place other than the last Christmas photo with my grandma hanging in my bedroom. The lounge room was getting darker as the afternoon progressed, adding to the gloom and the negativity I felt, which was almost certainly a product of my medication fuck up.

I got like this every now and then. It generally followed a very predictable formula: first, I get down about being on my own, then I go out with the girls, if they can, I get drunk and either end up sleeping with someone and wake up with a hangover, a severe case of dehydration and a longing sense of regret or going home alone, drunk and horny. Unfortunately, white wine tended to get me in the mood. Then, I generally felt better because if there was an encounter with that guy, frequently an unsatisfyingly brief encounter, which was usually enough to remind of the liability that is "man". I move on and I'm happy except for a constant internal struggle, a fight to the death so to speak, between two opposing ideological behemoths. Spoiler, every bout has ended in a draw.

Do I want to meet a man and settle down or do I want to ride solo for a while longer and see how things pan out? Getting married for the first time at sixty was still the thing to do, right? I'd pretty much given up on the thought of having kids, which was fine, because I'd never been an overly maternal woman. When my friends were swooning over each other's newborn babies all I could think about was how inconvenient and parasitical those things were. Sure, they were cute and fun to play with, but I'd always considered my relationship with babies to be like the zoo: fun to go and spend a few hours looking at the cute animals but when they give you the shits and you get sick of the smell you just leave. Or, in the case of babies, give them back to their parents. So it generally doesn't bother me to not have children.

In the past, during each of my three historic pregnancy scares I had seriously fallen to pieces and started to plan how I could get my mum to adopted said child. I know, that made me sound like a horrible person but I had no desire to try and squeeze something the size of a watermelon out of my vagina to then have to care for it for eighteen years. I was the last person who should be raising a child, except maybe for those random naked people and meth heads you find on the bus, and I was accepting of that.

I guess what I really needed to do was think about trying to figure out what I wanted to do but the thought of trying to "find yourself" (I really hated that expression) at forty was not something I was overly keen on. Every episode of every television show that deals with this shit is just straight up depressing and just really reinforces who clueless and all over the place I was.

It was a good time to maybe make myself look somewhat respectable before Katie arrived, so I finished my tea, which I'm now positive had three sugars and not two, turned off the television, and opted for some music. Before going too far, I sent Katie a message telling her that if she arrived earlier, I would just be in shower. I didn't expect a response, but I also didn't want her to show up unexpectedly early and have me not hear her knocking.

'Bill Murray, play some music.'

As soon as Bill, in his numbing, artificial approximation of a voice, had finished telling me what he was going to do, despite me being the one that gave him the direction, the speakers filled the room with the upbeat rhythm of "The 1975". The burning in my head had finally, completely receded and I felt like medicated me again.

CHAPTER 36

The steam and piping hot water cleared my head and purged my body of the day. Standing there, hands on the wall of the shower, head directly under the flow I was hypnotised by the vortex of water draining down into the darkness of the grate in my shower floor, no doubt, meeting up with the few clumps of hair that has managed to work its way down. A more "emo" me would probably try and compare this to my own life fading away into the inevitable pit of darkness that is old age and death but, instead, all I could focus on was how proud I was at my lack of shower wine.

Congratulations Hannah, you've achieved not drinking a glass of wine in your afternoon\evening shower. I smiled at the dark absurdity of it all, the fact I was internally celebrating something minor that, if it became habit, would no doubt raise a few red flags. However, I knew deep down that I could never be an alcoholic, simply because as I'd once heard in a bar (ironically), alcoholics go to meetings whereas I go to parties. The excitement of observing the drain and contemplating a minor step towards a future of alcohol dependency was pleasantly interrupted with a faint knock. As it turned out, Katie had unexpectedly finished early and was now knocking on my front door with all the power of Zeus.

Stepping out onto a rather unpleasant bathmat, one in obvious need of a wash, I hastily attempted to dry my hair to the extent that it would minimise the trail of drips from here to the front door, and wrapped myself in a fluffy, clean towel. One of those giant, man sized towels big enough to comfortably wrap a medium sized pig.

'Hold up, I'm coming.'

I made my way to the door at a pace that tried to balance speed and safety. Unlocking the door, I was met with the welcome sight of Katie, obviously straight from work as she was still in her uniform, carrying a pizza and a six pack of what appeared to be pre-mixed cocktails. She had that adorably cute, cheeky look on her face, which could mean any one of many ideas, statements or images was occupying her thoughts.

'Jesus, I haven't heard anyone yell that out in a while. It's not normally something I say to myself.' She had me, I had no idea what was so funny. She must have registered the look of confusion on my face because she proceeded to explain the joke which, which in all honestly, was clichéd and somewhat immature ... my type of humour. 'You know, you said, "I'm coming" ... I haven't heard that in a while ... get it? Come on, join those dots.' She gently pushed past me and headed to the kitchen, surely to dump the pizza and put her drinks in my Mother Hubbard fridge.

'Close the door, Hannah, for Christ's sake, the only thing between the outside world and your naked body is a towel. Also, maybe take this opportunity to put some clothes on.'

Everything Katie said made complete sense and the group of teenage boys that just come into my periphery certainly hastened my actions. I closed and locked the door and, following Katie's advice, went to get dressed.

'Thanks for coming over, I really need it after today.'

'No problem, besides I needed to organise you for tomorrow. Considering you're technically working from home tomorrow, I figured we could leave early so I shuffled a few things around at work. I hope you don't mind.'

Jeans and a sensible sleeveless floral shirt seemed like a good option, if only I could find a bra. 'That sounds good. Hey, there are some clothes in the dryer in the laundry room. Can you rifle around and try and find me a bra?' My clean ones seemed to have all gone missing or teleported to another dimension by the same mystical force that removes one single sock or your favourite underwear.

'Do you want practical or sexy? Because there is a vast selection in this dryer.'

Shit ... that was where they'd all gone. It probably helped to actually empty the clothes dryer at some point.

'Surprise me, but my preference is definitely with comfort and practicality.' I didn't want to close my door but standing topless in a room knowing my female friend was in the room next door made me quite anxious. I'd never been one of those girls who were completely comfortable with being naked around others.

'You know you shouldn't put bras in the dryer. Not good for them,' Katie said. I could hear the dryer door close and her footsteps getting closer. Anxiety building, I quickly grabbed the damp towel and covered up my ladies in case Katie came in.

Deep breaths Hannah, its nothing she hasn't seen before. My anxiety was abruptly ceded as I got hit in the face with my bra, expertly thrown around the corner of the door by Katie.

'Hurray up and get dressed. I'm not a fan of having a conversation with a disembodied voice.'

I heard the fridge open and I knew she was going for one of the drinks she'd brought. Judging by the brief look I had at the label and brand, I'd probably have more of a chance of getting diabetes from having two or three of them than getting drunk.

'Wow, very mature.' I walked out of the room, now comfortably clothed and, as expected, was immediately handed some kind of drink which literally tasted like a mildly alcoholic, artificially fruity soft drink. I'm sure teenage girls would swoon over this obvious attempt to sweeten – pun intended – the Australian tradition of writing oneself off.

As it turned out, the drinks Katie brought were a gift from another nurse which was a good thing as, otherwise, I'd have to start questioning her taste. Luckily, there were only three each and we both poured three-quarters of the last drink down the drain which, realistically, was probably the best place for it. The pizza was "meh", as with most takeaway places in this area, but it certainly filled a gap and was far superior to the dumpster fire that was that protein bowl I'd ordered in previously. Besides, pizza really is just like sex, even when its bad, it's still okay.

"Bill Murray" and his random selection of music provided a great soundtrack for a night of much-needed conversation. I had missed this girl, even after such a small span of time … I really had. I did have to make-up a few excuses on the spot to justify a few random nineties hip-hop songs, as they really didn't reflect what most people saw as an appropriate music choice for someone matching my description. I had what I call an "eclectic" taste in music. Alternative rock, mainstream pop, hip-hop, classic rock and a plethora of other subgenres make-up my playlists as I am partial to many sounds and styles … except country. I fucking hate country! I never really expected to offend as many people as I did with that statement. The anger and vitriol for merely suggesting the music was "subpar" genuinely shocked me. Despite their preciousness, I stand by it, I fucking hate country music!

Yes, I have a soft spot for a particular Icelandic band and yes, I was a Triple J girl, back in the day when it was actually good. Once again, my internal monologue distracted from the actual conversation that was going on around me. Katie seemed to have registered that I wasn't firing on all cylinders because she stopped mid-sentence to check in.

'Hey, are you with me or are you distracted by something in your own little world? Purple elephants maybe?' She smiled, somewhat hesitantly, probably because she registered making statements about seeing purple elephants to a woman with mental health issues might not have been the greatest idea.

'I fucking hate country music!' Here we go, completely random comments in the middle of a completely normal conversation; this day just keeps getting worse.

'Random but, yeah, it's not my thing. Where did that come from?' she said with a rather puzzled look on her face as she gracefully frisbeed the crust of her last slice of pizza back into the box.

'That was what was going through my head. For some reason my unnatural hatred of country music distracted me. I'm really sorry, back to you … what were you saying again?'

In almost synchronised perfection we both sat back in our respective couches and she started on the plans for the weekend. 'So, leaving early tomorrow yeah? I've organised to pick up the car anywhere from 10am. It should take us a few hours to get there, but the earlier we leave the more we see, do and drink.'

We were taking a car? That added a whole new level of amazingness to this trip; I loved road trips! 'So, where are we going?' I asked, hoping against hope that this wasn't going to be one of those surprise weekends.

'It's a surprise' – *Fuck, my worst nightmare* – 'but I can tell you to pack a going out outfit, a swimsuit, and whatever the hell else you want to wear. Take a jacket just in case, always play it safe when on a road trip with me because bad weather seems to follow me.'

I kept telling myself that Katie knew me well enough to not throw anything too "out there" for me in an effort to avoid any unwanted melt downs. 'Okay, ummm … no more details? Nothing? You sure you don't want to tell me?'

She registered the change in tone and did her best to reassure me. 'It's fine, you'll love it and if you don't, I'll let you drag me away on a weekend to the most bizarre, unpleasant destination that you can think of … like a visit to a postcard museum, or a nature hike, or even to watch a weekend of professional golf.' She faked a shudder; all of those options sounded absolutely terrifying. Who in their right mind would actually voluntarily travel to watch a game of golf in person? Whenever I happened to see it on television

I always took a few minutes to look through the gallery, as they called it, to see if there were any women holding up "help me" signs.

'Okay, fine ... but I'm not packing tonight. After the day I've had its probably best I do it fresh in morning after sleep and a brain of full of medication.' I'm normally a "night before" packer but I genuinely think that, in this case, holding off until tomorrow would be the best option.

'I've already packed, I'm that damn keen.' She started to get up, struggling because of the depth of the chair that she'd sat in. It made me feel heaps better to know that it wasn't just my fitness levels that slowed me down when standing up from that couch. 'I'm going to make a move and head home, I think. I've got to put on some washing and try and make the house somewhat tidy before I go away. I wouldn't want people to break in while I'm gone and think I'm a slob.'

I laughed, not necessarily because it was funny, but because my mum had said pretty much the exact same thing once before we'd gone away on a family holiday. 'I probably should get to bed as well, I didn't realise how late it was.' And boy, was it late ... 8:30! At least we both had excuses for turning in so early.

'I ordered an Uber. They should be here in a few minutes.' I walked her to the door and turned on the external light. She leaned in and gave me that bizarre half hug that some girls tend to give each other sometimes. As I opened the door, a car, which I am assuming was the Uber, pulled up. I'd never been a massive fan of booking an Uber but this one didn't look too sketchy. I could see the guy driving's face illuminated by the internal light in the car and, good news, he didn't look like a serial killer!

'Try and to get to mine by about 9.30 and we can go from there but anytime is fine. You can even have breakfast with me if you want ... if you enjoy week old bread and off brand weet-bix.' She opened the door of the Uber, which upon closer inspection, turned out to be a Tesla. I hope he's fully charged and doesn't run out before he gets her there ... unlike some "items" found in my bedroom. 'I'll see what I can do.' She waved goodbye and the car pulled out into traffic, cutting off a taxi in the process. Surprise, surprise another driver in the city with no clue or care. As I closed and locked the door, double checking of course, and turned off the external light all I could think about was the girl who just left my house in an Uber with, what appeared to be, a really sketchy driver. I couldn't help but begin to compare her to other influential friends that have played an important part in my life.

Katie was amazing, in many ways she was the perfect friend who shared so many qualities with friends from my past, but at the same time she was so unique. That single idiotic move, that I compared to something from an old *Carry On* movie had resulted in a serendipitous meeting in a hospital emergency ward. I just hoped that I didn't fuck it up and that she didn't end up like Bianca or one of those others who I was so close with but are now just a fond memory and a phone call, email, or text every now and then. Those people, were now in many ways just a remnant of my past life, a mere memory.

CHAPTER 37

I slept restlessly, tossing and turning, thinking about everything I needed to do, pack, or organise before I left in the morning. There was also that excitement that I could only compare to that felt by a child on Christmas Eve, a blushing bride the night before her wedding, or the strapping groom the night before his buck's party. I ended ticking one item off the list in my head at about 2am, forcing myself to get up and pack my medication in the suitcase that I was definitely, definitely going to be using for the weekend. Just to be one hundred per cent sure I wouldn't stuff it up, I picked the bright baby blue suitcase and even placed my beach towel, sunscreen and make-up bag in it just so would safely identify the right bag.

I contemplated putting in a bottle of wine or the gin I have gathering dust in the cupboard, but Katie had been adamant: do not bring alcohol. I hoped this was not a sign of a dry weekend, but merely a less than subtle hint that there would be plenty to be found where we were going. After a few hours of what somewhat passed as sleep, I got out of bed about 5am and finished packing my suitcase making sure, first of all, to pack what Katie had asked. I packed both my one-piece swimsuit and bikini – I hoped one of them would fit – a nice set of heels and a dress for going out. I actually went with the little apricot number I brought for the night out Katie that ended up just turning into a drunken night at home ... good times.

I had the common sense to make sure to pack a strapless bra, which I had to extract from the dryer with its forgotten brethren, and some remotely sexy underwear, on the off chance I scored a man. Let's be honest here, I could pretty much guarantee I would score a man as we all know the average guy wouldn't turn down the opportunity for no strings attached sex after a few too many. I really shouldn't be happy about the fact that I was often willing to settle for any kind of physical contact after a night out, but the drinking and people all crowded together had a bizarre tendency to really turn me on. Besides, if I was honest with myself, I had been going through a dry spell and sometimes dealing with yourself just didn't cut it.

The rest of my suitcase filled with the essentials: everyday but really cute outfits which, for me, consisted mostly of floral spaghetti strap dresses and sleeveless tops. I had a thing for the light and vibrant colours and they vibe they exuded. I was lucky because, generally, they looked pretty good on me. I added a pair of jeans and a few cute little skirts to match the tops. I took a risk and packed no nightwear other than my robe, as I generally slept with nothing on. I'd never been able to get used to being restricted by any clothing while trying to sleep. There were, of course, some times when it was absolutely essential ... for obvious reasons.

I hoped for Katie's sake that we weren't sharing room because otherwise she'd have to cope with my naked body at night and in the morning ... not really something either of us would appreciate, I guessed. A normal person would have packed something comfortable to sleep in just in case but, as we've ascertained, I'm not normal so I decided to run the proverbial gauntlet. Besides, I'd have my robe and I'm pretty sure I could MacGyver my way into it and cover my lady parts before Katie had an opportunity to cop an extended eyeful.

The thought of others seeing me naked reminded of the need for some serious lawncare before leaving. I wasn't exhibiting the hairiness of the missing link or of a 70s porn star, but a tidy was certainly long overdue. Surprise, surprise, I opted for a shower but this was predominantly to shave my legs and a few other delicate places. Standing there under the steaming hot torrent I was met with a dilemma of how much to take off the bottom. I was always one to avoid getting too carried away and conforming to the unreasonable standards that seem to be set by celebrities and society in general. Plus, I was always worried I'd end up doing a Sweeny Todd on my lady bits, ending up in ER with an embarrassing story.

After doing a pretty decent job on my legs, I decided to risk it for the big weekend and go all out. I'd never been so nervous in my life, not even while being breath tested in college with a car full of drunks after having only half a glass of wine. Now, by wine, I mean goon, because can you really call it wine if it comes out of a silver bag? However, there were no cuts and everything came out silky smooth ... except for my opinion of myself. I should have just left something there, just something so I could avoid looking like an anatomically incorrect Barbie doll.

I dried myself, making sure to clean my teeth there and then so I could ensure my toiletries made their way straight to my suitcase. I was not going to make any packing faux pas or forget anything this time! *Be positive, Hannah.* I slipped into a baby blue dress, which was possibly the most comfortable thing I owned, and committed to battling with my hair and finding some practical, yet remotely fashionable, flats for the trip. I spotted some black Colorado sandals in my open closet through the clutter and decided they'd be a decent option.

As far as my mornings went, it was relatively stress free and smooth sailing. I even managed to find the motivation to take the remaining bras out of the dryer. Admittedly, I did just dump them on my haphazardly made bed, but they were at least in my bedroom ... winning!

I checked everything was turned off and double and, somewhat obsessively, triple checked that I had everything. I tried to avoid taking any oxy with me, but that part of my brain riddled with the beginnings of a possible addiction wouldn't let me. I compromised and left the packet at home opting instead to take one pill, wrapped in a little baggie and tucked in my suitcase for safety. I promised myself I wouldn't use it, but if shit went south, these little things give you a hell of a buzz after a few drinks. It was depressing that the buzz was so appealing to me and I knew that it was far from safe ... I just wished I had the self-control and strength to say no.

Confident I had everything, I called a cab, locked my door and waited with ever growing anticipation on the curb hoping for a cab ride that wouldn't be too unpleasant. I wasn't not asking for a repeat of yesterday's positively glowing example of a taxi experience, but something short of loud music, a foul stench of booze and sweat from the night shift, or constant inane chatter would be a win for me. I didn't really have high standards, as you have probably noted.

As I stood there, edgy and eager for the weekend to start I contemplated two things of note: One, I was probably going to be arriving at Katie's house around 8.30 because I didn't take into account just how early I had gotten up and ready, and, more importantly, two ... the fact that I hadn't been on a girls' weekend away since college. It was a weekend that I had almost entirely forgotten about but the stark reminder that I hadn't done anything like this in a long time, brought back the somewhat supressed memory of a trip that, in all honesty, was okay. It was just that the people I went with no longer meant anything too me ... they were just faces, and memories and I felt terrible about that. So much of my life had been bouncing from person, (or people) to person, looking for a connection and I haven't really found that since university. I guess that made me a little sad, but also very unsure about what type of friend I actually was.

The cab rounded the corner and, somewhat inappropriately loud, I remarked to the world, 'I really am a paranoid bitch at times.'

INTERLUDE: PITCH (IM)-PERFECT

University was the freedom I'd thought I wanted and needed to thrive and "find myself". That expression really did bother me, it was one of those terms you see thrown around in feel-good movies where the protagonist has to go on this clichéd journey in order to discover who she really was. Like most Hollywood movies, as we've established, it usually ends in a "happily ever after" with some incredibly attractive man as they either a) ride off into the sunset together to further explore themselves and their relationship, or b) they settle down to a life of mediocrity. Fortunately for these characters, a mediocre life in the films is as far removed from real-life mediocrity as wine is from grape juice. That being said, I am a bit of a sucker for films like that. I've always wondered how these star-crossed lovers would function with a real-life nine to five, real-life public transport, and real-life costs of living. Seeing middle class characters in these types of movies own a gigantic, two story, white picket fence house with a pool and immaculate lawn, was about as realistic as the most obscure b-grade science fiction film ... no, even worse, that one about the sentient car tyre that murders people. You'd be surprised how many people refused to believe that film actually exists, and they challenged me, accusing me of a poor sense of humour when they could have quite easily Googled it.

I think I'd gone to college trying to find a little bit of independence, to do things that I couldn't do previously. I went into o-week with this check list of things to achieve in my first year. The list was pretty much all related to boys, booze, and being impulsive and unpredictable. One even included all three ... go on an impulsive, unplanned weekend away, get incredibly drunk, and have sex with the most attractive boy that would have me – I want to note though that this was pretty low down the list, as a lot had to happen before I got to that point. My top three were pretty much: lose my virginity in a tasteful fashion, if there were such a thing, have a drunken o-week that would result in me being labelled one of "the cool/fun ones" and make a new friend and/or boyfriend. I'd ticked off all these things within five days.

Mum and Dad always wanted me to do something practical at university, considering they were paying for it. In typical mum style, she believed thought that gave her licence to not only 'encourage me' but to actually force me to do something she deemed valuable. She wanted me to be a teacher, so it was pretty much out of spite and a developing sense of teenage rebellion that I enrolled in a criminology degree. Now, I didn't do it just on a whim as it was genuinely something I was interested in, but I knew there was no way mum would condone, tolerate or accept me doing something I wanted. She kept saying I was only there because of her dollars. So, I was going to study criminology, despite having no intention of working in that field, which I just know would piss off Mum and Dad even more. There was a degree in writing I could have done, but not even I was spiteful enough to do that to Mum … she would have disowned me. But the fantasy of studying writing, which was so close to becoming a reality, once again became a dream.

I guess you could say that I started out on the wrong track from day one, and I genuinely blame my mother. It took her ten years, ten whole years to apologise for essentially holding a financial gun to my head and trying to force me to do something she'd deemed "practical".

'I just thought it would make you more employable, dear. It's a tough job market and there were plenty of teaching jobs.' It took her actually talking to a teacher, one of the many men she'd tried to set me up with over the years, to convince her that you can't force teaching on someone. It is such a different ball game where, if you're not passionate and you don't want to be there, you are potentially fucking up the futures of young people. In retrospect, the millennials did a pretty good job of fucking up their own futures, but still, it was an argument that convinced my mum that maybe, just maybe, she was actually wrong.

I met Sally and her boyfriend Cameron on day one. Ironically, they were both studying teaching and you could tell from how they spoke about their futures in the profession that they were born for it, that they lived for it and were up for the challenge. Sally was even employed at a local school as a teacher's aide, so she was lucky to already have her foot in the door. Their future was bright, with the very real outcome of walking out of university into a permanent job doing what they love.

As a sad testament to the profession, I found out last year that both aren't teaching anymore. Cameron became despondent, though I didn't get specific details, and took a job at some big company working HR and Sally, poor Sally, had a complete breakdown.

Part of me wished we'd stayed in touch. I considered reaching out, but what do you say to someone you hadn't spoken to in nearly twenty years who was, essentially, broken and trying to put herself back together? I was the last person that should be speaking to someone who had fallen apart. I am brittle, but not quite broken.

I clicked with both of them immediately, but very rarely did the three of us all hang out together for some reason. The very first night we went out to the university bar to see a few bands, one of which I actually knew, which was a positive. In a grand feat of deception and subterfuge I managed to somehow sneak into the bar and get through the whole night without being hit up for ID or, miraculously, paying for a single drink. It turned out college guys were quite happy to ply a girl with booze as a way to "get to know them" and I am not ashamed to say that I took advantage of this male weakness.

For some reason, in a sea of beautiful college girls out to impress in their miniskirts and tight tops, this average looking girl got a lot of attention. My jeans and simple black tank top stood out at the bar for being ordinary and run of the mill but, as I later came to realise, my top was also quite tight.

All the vodka and sodas, which became my college drink of choice after that night, gave me an inflated sense of confidence and I started to become a little infatuated with the dark haired, freshman boy straight out of private school and we became quite touchy feely too after he managed to actually find us a place near the pool tables to sit down and talk.

I can't remember the guy's name, or even what he was studying, but the new-found freedom that not living with your mum and dad provided saw yet another internal battle going on within my vodka impaired brain. The newly independent, rebellious me just wanted to break the ice, crack the egg, take a running leap out of the plane and just sleep with him.

The other, more reasonable, sensible side was very much of the opinion that it was my first night out of o-week … o-week! You could count the amount of time I'd actually spent at university in hours. There was plenty of time and I really was quite drunk.

Deep breaths, Hannah.

Which side of my psyche would win in the eternal struggle of good vs bad decisions? The fact was, that after that moment my common sense gave in and my immature mind surrendered to my raging hormones and free vodka. I didn't see another song that night.

He walked me back to college and, as you could guess, I lost my virginity in what could possibly be the most embarrassing sexual experience that, at that point, I could imagine. I was coherent enough to understand that this wasn't going to be "magical" but, then again, whose first time really was? One of the girls that I went to school with lost hers in the gymnastics equipment store room at school … now that was classy.

The guy, let's call him Max, did a really good job of getting me back to his room, one that was thankfully enough located in the college right next to mine, and didn't contain any body parts of previous victims. I don't remember many specific conversational details, other than me telling him in a rather slurred fashion that this was going to be my first time.

The guy, Max, was quite gentlemanly, because upon hearing the truth bomb I just dropped and seeing that, in the light of the college corridor, I was actually a lot drunker than he thought, became nervous and reluctant. He offered to give me his bed to sleep it off and that he'd take the common room couch. He offered to walk me back to my room, hell, he even said he would go and wake up his sister who was, apparently, a few doors down and was the floor tutor, to look after me. I declined and insisted that I was ready and that this was going to happen. My eagerness may have come across as forcefulness because I remember a sudden look of terror as the colour drained out of his face and, suddenly, it was him who seemed like the virgin.

Long story short, there was lots of kissing, clumsy fumbling with clothes, condoms and body parts and, eventually, everything went into where it needed to be.

The positive about being drunk was that I didn't register any pain because, looking back on it as a grown woman, he was quite gifted in that region and I was thankful that he was not your typical college Neanderthal. Looking into his eyes, I simply couldn't comprehend this was happening. Time seemed to stop and all these thoughts and questions starting running through my head at a million miles an hour.

I remember trying to focus on the little things, the feelings; was it good? Was I doing the right thing? Where was my handbag? Was it the room or me that is spinning? What was that gurgling sensation?

And that was it. The beginning of the end of my first three minutes or so of "maturity". The sudden need to vomit overcame me and I pushed the poor boy off me with such force and purpose, he rolled onto the floor. Like a deer in headlights, he lay there, limbs strewn at obviously uncomfortable angles, on a surface often considered to be the hardest known to man. I dashed out of the room into the blinding light of the corridor which was, thankfully, deserted trying to figure out which direction the bathroom would be.

'Left, go left!' I caught a glimpse in my periphery of naked, and now quite flaccid, Max fumbling with his underwear, trying to cover his shame.

I made it to the bathroom in time but unfortunately, my aim was impaired and a large portion of what came out ended up on the toilet and the floor surrounding it. Stark naked, at some ungodly hour in an unfamiliar college, I was kneeling in a locked cubicle, mopping up vomit with toilet paper. Oh what a magical night.

Max snuck in about five minutes later, fully clothed and as pale as I had ever seen a living person. It seemed that this shit show of an experience had sucked the very life out of him, because he looked like he'd had his soul forcibly removed.

He handed me one of his robes and escorted me back to his room. By escorted I mean he held me up as I tried to avoid falling in a heap ... he basically carried me.

I remembered hearing voices from the far end of the corridor as he closed the door. Sitting next to his bed, was a huge two litre water bottle and some paracetamol. He pulled down the covers of the bed and essentially dropped me in his bed, covered me up and turned the lights off. I'm assuming he spent the night on couch or in someone else's room because he never came back. Mind you, I was out of there as soon as there was the tiniest slither of sunlight peeling over the horizon.

I left him two things before doing the dash: a post-it note that said 'I'm sorry' and another post-it note that said 'Thank you'.

I had another first that morning, this one more successful than the night prior's miserable example of how not to have sex ... I completed my first, of many, walk of shame. As I dashed across the common lawn dividing his college from mine, a cool morning breeze whipping at my untidy hair and I realised two things: 1) that couldn't have possible gone worse and 2) I still had no fucking idea where my bag was!

As it turned out Sally had my bag, and I never saw that poor guy again, both of which were a relief. Sally and I did however, become close friends and I spent a significant amount of my time with or around her during first year. As with the friends I usually acquire, I deemed her far superior to myself in regards to looks, grades, motivation, future prospects, and access to money.

This girl was loaded! Her mum and dad were accountants and regularly sent her "care packages" of home baked cookies and cakes from her grandma and great wads of disposable cash. Which, in her defence, she did use relatively sparingly and treated her friends quite regularly. I felt kind of bad because I knew that if I had access to that amount money during first year, I would have been living the highlife with new outfits, every CD and DVD my heart desired, an actual entertainment set-up for my college room and, oh maybe tuition fees, so mum didn't have me bent over the proverbial barrel. Speaking of being bent over the barrel, I met an amazing guy at the Criminology "meet and greet" BBQ for new students and we hit it off straight away.

We actually ended up in a huge argument in our very first conversation because he had the gall to insist that *National Lampoon's Christmas Vacation* was NOT the best Christmas of all time. The nerve of the guy to think *Home Alone* was the superior comedy\ Christmas combo. Anyway, we dated for about twelve months and, despite my desire, he wouldn't sleep with me until I turned eighteen. He wouldn't even let me stay over, but he was the very definition of the perfect guy: cute, but not to the point that I had to worry about girls who looked like Sally taking him away from me. He had great taste in music and films and he wasn't a footy head arsehole. He also dressed very similar to me, but obviously in a more masculine style. Simple outfits that usually revolved around jeans and sensible shoes.

After I turned eighteen, it still took him a few weeks to get physical and I actually consider that night my first time. I have made a lot of really bad sexual choices over my life, but Jack was not one of those. He was gentle, considerate and caring, and he constantly made me feel safe and comfortable while at the same time providing sex that was constantly amazing and, let's just call it, innovative.

We broke up when I changed degrees at the end of first year because, for some reason, he couldn't cope with the fact that we literally seemed to spend no time together other than when we were fucking, which he felt didn't make for a positive relationship. He certainly didn't harp over the downfall of our relationship for too long, because apparently he was dating someone else within a fortnight. Me on the other hand, decided that I didn't want to be tied down anymore by a college relationship that, in the grand scheme of my life, would go nowhere.

In other words, I was too lazy to commit to anything so I became a three date or one-night stand girl, and that was enough because I actually enjoyed my studies and, due to the faculties neighbouring each other, I got to spend more time with Sally.

My new degree was in writing, something that my mother would detest because employment opportunities for writers are quite scarce. I didn't tell my parents, and I stand by that decision, as I had the support I needed from Sally and her almost sickening sense of positivity and ability to deliver uplifting motivational speeches. My results were always above average, but when comparing them to Sally's constant high distinctions, it was incredibly deflating to know that my best was never as good as hers. I know that I should never let things like that bother me but it was incredibly damaging to my self-esteem to know that regardless of how good

I did, she was always that little bit better. It didn't impact our friendship too much, but there was always that understanding that I had a massive inferiority complex festering in the background and what hurt was that I knew, she knew.

Three years and I graduated with a Bachelor of Arts with a major in Creative Writing and my lecturer insisted that I continued to study as a post-grad. Sally had gone off to take up a position in a school and I didn't know whether I could a) afford it or b) have the motivation to actually do the post-grad because all I wanted to do at that point was write and try and get something out there that reached other people. So, I declined and I moved into a little flat, knowing that I had a mother who was furious at me for changing degrees without letting her know.

I took up a job at a small local school working admin in the main office and decided to write the great Australian novel in my free time. Considering I ended up working for the government in some shitty department, never having finished the novel, it was obvious that "shit happened".

Basically, I kept picking up extra days at the school and the extra money meant more disposal income, which meant more nights out. The constant weekend hangovers and excesses meant that the novel I'd always wanted to produce got pushed aside like those chocolates in the box's grandma used to have lying about that were remarkably similar in taste to cough medicine. I think they were going for cherry, but they certainly fucked that up!

I lost all motivation and my dream died in that tiny little flat. My novel was dead in the water, three chapters in after six months and I told myself that I was "just taking a break". I was planning on rekindling my creative juices when in fact the only juices I was rekindling were mixed with vodka. After eight months with the same three chapters complete, I gave up, telling myself I would come back to it when I had settled down with a more stable lifestyle and had more time.

I think I knew even then that the "hiatus" was going to be permanent. In a tiny little study, converted from a spare bedroom, on a cheap desk I brought from a garage sale, in that cold, dingy flat with shitty neighbours, in a shitty part of town, I gave up. Instead, I opted to find that solace I was after in that buzz I got from a night out and a belly full of booze. I gave up on the one thing in life I really wanted to do and, at the time, I couldn't have given two fucks because I was a grown-up with independence, a decent wage coming in, and social life that involved acquaintances, as opposed to friends. No attachments, no commitments and no worries.

In retrospect, life was pretty sad and, deep down, I think I was pretty sad as well. Give me some credit though because I did a hell of a good job of hiding it. I could have won an Oscar for my performances. I deeply regretted not reaching out to Sally, my most recent friend and the cornerstone of my support network but I couldn't bring myself to share what I have achieved or, more accurately, not achieved. This was my existence until one fateful night that I fell down the stairs of the pub onto the stickiest, most vomit inducing carpet I have had the unfortunate pleasure of being in contact with. It wasn't just the smell or feel but the colour and the patterns, it was enough to make the world spin. For the record, no, I hadn't even been drinking … Yet. I had been on my way to the bar, after just showing up to a work function. I was helped up by Will and, once again, a placeholder of a partner entered my life and changed me … and not for the better.

PART V

The Hangover (Parts I, II and III)

CHAPTER 38

I got out of the cab at Katie's to find a maroon Ford Focus sedan in Katie's drive, and I'm not talking a recent model. My knowledge of cars was about as well developed as my understanding of art house cinema but, at a guess, I would say a mid-2000s model. I assumed that either that was the car we were taking and she had somehow acquired it early, or that she had a visitor. My filthy mind immediately went to a "Magic Mike" like male visitor who either had or was helping her play the proverbial "beast with two backs". The door was open, which intrigued me even more, was I going to walk in on something I really didn't want to see ... or did I?

I was a little conflicted because the "me" part of my brain immediately went to "ewwww" while another more curious, voyeuristic element of my psyche was incredibly curious. Maybe next time I was at my psychologist I needed to mention this. Nothing like a good Freudian psychoanalysis.

The presence of a figure half tripping out of Katie's door, spilling a handful of what looked like bags of lollies onto the stoop, appeared from the dark nowhere of a house with all the curtains obviously drawn. The question of who the hell owned this car was answered there and then. The figure erupting out of the house was, in fact, Katie carrying far too much baggage for her petite figure. She was taking her suitcases, emphasise the plural here, to the car to start to pack which didn't make sense as we weren't picking the car up until later on.

'Hey! Michelle dropped the car over early and caught a cab from here, so it looks like we can leave earlier than expected.' The smile on her face was contagious, as she fumbled around grunting and moaning, trying to collect the bags of sweets she had dropped, and it quickly spread to me.

'So, two things. You know there is such a thing as making two trips … ' I said, knowing quite well that I would have done the exact same thing. ' … and also, what the fuck are taking with you? We are only going for the weekend, you know.'

She managed to collect everything, haphazardly holding it in any bodily crevice she could that would hold something: under her arms, under her neck and was proceeding to make her way down the stairs … very gingerly.

'What, you only have one bag? Don't you know a girl has to pack for all occasions? Plus, for all you know in one of these suitcases there is the body of some jilted lover I'm planning on disposing of.' The boot of the car opened, allaying my fears of there being no room because, unexpectedly, it was quite spacious.

'Well, is it? Because I wouldn't cope in prison, not enough access to booze and men,' I said with forced sarcasm.

'Second bag is Michelle's, I have to leave it at the cabin we are staying at.'

My heart sank at the thought of staying in a cabin. All I could picture was rustic (dilapidated), quiet location (no basic amenities) and most importantly, nowhere near a place to go out, get unnecessarily stupid and find a man or, at this point, subhuman may even cut it.

'Relax Hannah. By cabin, I mean pool, hot tub, new refurbed bathroom, and living area and a kitchen and master bedroom that is "a work in progress". Michelle's family owns this cabin a few hours out of the city that they spending an absolute fortune to do up and she offered it to me anytime I wanted a weekend away.' This was starting to sound a lot more appealing than the simple cabin that in my head closely resembled something from a slasher film. 'It's not fully refurbished on the outside but, from the pictures I saw what has been done is amazing! I figured we won't be 'cooking' as such, so space for meal prep won't be high on requirements but the hot tub and pool are fully functional ... and there are beds AND we won't need to share a room. Not that I mind, but I figured your anxious self may have an issue with something like that.'

As the description of this little piece of weekend away heaven developed – a haven in the semi-rural backwoods – my excitement levels continued to rise. 'We are five minutes out of town and right next to a winery and restaurant. And here's the real kicker ... apparently, the guy that used to own the cabin worked at the winery so there is a path from the property through to essentially the cellar door, which the owners have no problem with us using!'

At this point, I nearly collapsed from anticipation at that joyous feeling of knowing I would be a short walk from wine and a restaurant. 'There is a caveat though. Don't freak out too much, but they won't allow boys. They are pretty religious and there are security cameras everywhere. Basically, no hook-ups.' The disappointment must have been visible on my face as I could feel my eyes droop and my face go from peachy keen to hazy shades of winter. The look on Katie's face was one of instant remorse, clearly terrified that I would pull out. 'Hannah ... I'm kidding. Sleep with as many men as you want, just don't make a mess of the hot tub as I intend to pretty much spend every hour away from the vineyard in that thing.'

She'd kept an incredibly straight face through all of that and I was impressed ... very impressed. I love how this woman can manage to somehow create a practical joke that played into my fears and turn it into something that had the possibility of resulting in some kind of melt down. All of this, of course, is simply due to the fact that I was promised men. Normally, that kind of simple thing, a change of routine at the last possible minute, and I go to water, I literally fall to pieces.

Part of me wonders why if this was why I couldn't have a normal relationship because in normal relationships, shit happens, things change, and most others can deal with it. Since a certain significant event in my life, which my head doctor labelled PTSD, I haven't been able to cope with anything that is even a subtle, miniscule change that may not even impact me directly. I couldn't imagine how dealing with someone having a breakdown over something like, let's say needing to work late, would be. I can't possibly comprehend how a person could deal with my instability, knowing that anything could cause an anxiety driven melt down reminiscent of the Mount St. Helens eruption.

Whenever I think about the physical pain it causes, even with just 'me' I really do wonder if no ties, no commitments and no one to upset or trouble is the best way of life for me. How could I expect anyone remotely normal to settle down and commit long-term to someone like that? It actually turns out to be a happy coincidence really considering my life direction and luck with relationships. *Deep breaths Hannah ... don't think about it and it might go away.*

'You worried me for a brief minute there, I thought I was going to have to unpack my sexy dress and replace it with a cardigan or a pants suit.'

Katie picked up my suitcase, threw it in the boot with the robust force reminiscent of a post man handling a 'Caution: Breakable' package. 'Relax, I wouldn't take you anywhere where neither of us could drink and/or have a night of regretful, yet strangely fulfilling sex. Now, get in the car, I've just to finish up inside.'

It was kind of sad how the prospect of no sex actually made me feel. A girls weekend of fun, celibacy and a few drinks should have been enough but when I say I needed some, I mean I REALLY need some. Katie locked the door to her house and made her way down the steps into the vibrant sunlight, carrying two travel mugs and sporting a smile that just made me feel all warm and happy. This girl had a gift. With just a casual smile and coffee I hadn't even asked for, she had created a sense of positivity within someone so naturally negative. I had to be careful though, because if this kept up I could actually lose my ingrained cynical attitude and aura of scepticism.

CHAPTER 39

The drive out of the city was as peaceful as it could be, considering the general fuckery that was motorway traffic. Living in the inner suburbs meant that my version of driving was taking the occasional cab which, as I have frequently emphasised, was best described as an experience that needed to end with a cleansing shower and a wine. Those nightmarish experiences, coupled with family road trips when I was younger, being forced to listen to inane conversation and the mentally debilitating music favoured by mother, scarred me for life. People talk about eye bleach, but I ever hear Amy Grant or Rod Stewart again I will need ear bleach.

Thankfully, Katie's music was a decent mix of 2000s Britpop and contemporary, with the occasional alternative anthem thrown in for good measure. I was in my happy place when a realised there was even a spattering of Lilly Allen mixed in with everything. At one point I was met with glorious harmonies of Toto's "Africa" and I couldn't help but belt it out, serenading the very heavens themselves. Afterall, it is physically impossible and obscenely rude to not power out your karaoke jam, regardless of where you are.

As we left the confines of the concrete and steel of the city I genuinely begun to enjoy the drive. Katie's discussion of an attractive new doctor was one that I actually took an interest in, especially in the description of his apparently firm abs and chiselled jaw line. Apparently, she'd accidentally walked in on him changing shirts after shift, but I really doubted the "accidental" nature of this encounter.

Someone once told me "journey before destination" but I was

always just a "fuck the journey" kind of girl ... just get me there! This was different, the drive was somewhat cathartic and as the scenery became gradually clean, crisp and semi-rural, I achieved a rather inflated sense of total bliss. After about three hours the highway narrowed to single lane and I spotted a sign that read: Winery: 5km on the left.

'Is that us?'

Katie checked the GPS directions on her phone and from her confused look, was still trying to figure it out. After what must have been at least two kilometres of thinking, studying, and comprehending, she acknowledged our approaching turn off. I was actually a little torn, I really wanted this drive to continue but the thought of wine and that cabin, that glorious cabin, an anticipated haven in the mess that was my day to day existence, overruled it and old Hannah resurfaced. Fuck the journey, when the destination is wine.

There is something inherently different about wine and grape country in that I can almost smell the pretentiousness and aura of perceived superiority that it contains. Now, I am by no means a frequenter of such establishments and I am certainly not a wine connoisseur, but I've seen enough movies and television programs to see just how such venues tend to be for the beautiful, affluent and educated ... unless of course it was one of those raucous college road trip comedies. That atmosphere of snobbery would be even more exaggerated in those films but would just be torn down by a series of drunken, debaucherously hormonal young adults. Katie and I were possibly capable of doing the exact same thing, just maybe without the "hormonal" and "young" element.

What I always did like about the winery experience was that, suddenly, everyone was a wine expert and the basest of booze enthusiasts could miraculous go from swilling home brew in the back shed with Steve-o from over the fence, to being able to spot the difference between a two regional Merlots. I tended to just keep my mouth shut and, only when directly asked would I mumble a few things like 'that's different', 'interesting body' and 'I loved the texture'.

I was generally pretty good at faking things, a talent I acquired after countless disappointing partners. If you look pensive, take your time swirling it around your mouth, and smile, you can generally hide your lack of knowledge. One thing I will never do when doing a tasting, and there is most definitely no joke intended, is spit. I outright refuse to expel expensive wine out of my body voluntarily as, let's be honest, even the worst wine at a cellar door still carries an exaggerated price. I find my time at a winery is best served sipping on a "rich, full-bodied shiraz" while trying to look sexy and spot any attractive, or even average, bachelor in the wild.

While the idea was definitely to find some temporary male company this weekend, I also was aware of the need to stress to Katie the idea at this was not the sole purpose of the weekend for me, nor was it how I would evaluate the trip as success or failure.

In typical Hannah style, I was torn, another internal fight club. I really didn't want her to think that I was hopelessly and shamefully desperate. I needed her to know that I mainly wanted to be here for her and for the experience. However, fighting out of the blue corner, weighing in at (insert mumbled approximation of weight) is, to be brutally honest, my base, animalistic need for sex … with an actual person. One thing that many don't associate with bipolar in particular is, as my doctor so expertly put it "hypersexuality".

When it reared its ugly head, it could be messy, and unfortunately the signs had been there that things were about to peak. This manifested itself in very different ways and I was in many ways blessed that I was away from my own abode to so any potentially bad decisions wouldn't result in people knowing where I live. Katie was a smart girl and I was positive that she'd be aware of that element of my personality that, in all honesty, was nowhere near as fun as it sounds. This was what ultimately helped me to make the decision to have a somewhat awkward conversation with her, knowing quite well that we were only about five minutes away from the cabin. *Deep breaths Hannah.*

'So, completely randomly … you know I want to be here this weekend to spend time with you, right?' A somewhat quizzical look developed and I decided to continue to talk without even waiting for her to answer. 'So, I'm going to try very hard to not focus on men this weekend, but I really need some attention.' She smiled but somehow managed to maintained a 'what the fuck are you talking about?' look. 'Now, I have to reinforce this … I do mean REALLY. So, if it looks like I am become obsessed with that goal, I apologise in advance but please always know I am here for you.' My breathing sped up and I could tell I was developing a lovely shine to my face and the glassy eyed appearance of a seasoned stoner. 'I love you and you are the best thing that has happened to me and if I go somewhat crazy, I am so sorry.'

Seriously Hannah, deep, slow breaths … you control this thing in your head … keep telling yourself that because one of these days, maybe, it might actually fucking work.

I tried to hold the tears, but even in doing so, my breathing sped up to the point where an outsider might predict an imminent medical emergency. I couldn't control it and once I got myself worked up, in this case over nothing, I lost who I was and I became this other thing that was nothing but an embarrassment. Stupidly, and to my credit, I can recognise how genuinely stupid it is. This started with me wanting to express something relatively minor and evolved into me falling apart.

I felt the car slow and registered it stop just off one of the most beautiful roads I'd ever driven on. Katie undid her seatbelt and I was met by an awkward but welcomed physical contact.

My breathing slowed somewhat at her reassuring, caring voice.

'It's okay, relax. Easy for me to say, I know, but I've got you. Remember, the whole "saving" thing? We have got this together … every step of the fucking way! I know the complete bipolar thing, I did my homework after the last little incident. I won't judge, even if you get with every guy there, but I will sure as hell protect you make sure you don't do anything silly.' I smiled a little, breaking through that broken expression that I got sick of seeing and feeling. 'Just don't hit me if I have to drag you away from some seedy wine snob.' I laughed, my breathing started to return to normal and, as usual, I felt like an idiot. 'You're not broken … I promise.'

Her ability to read my expression was exceptional because at the very moment, that's exactly what I needed to hear. I did the very best I could to straighten myself up and try to have my face return to a semi-normal state.

'Come on, let's get going … I need a hot tub,' she said. She did up her seat belt, pulled back out onto the road and proceeded to finish the journey, in more ways than one.

'Thank you.' I left it at that, nothing more needed to be said.

Out my window, I could see the winery, flanked by field after field of immaculately maintained vines and bordered by an impressive stone fence and wrought iron gate. A Romanesque driveway snaked its way from the main road up to the large cellar door, restaurant area and bar. This place was, even by winery standards, massive and contained its own accommodation to the west, with what would have been glorious mountain views, in the form of a rather impressive looking wing of modern suites.

A rather less conspicuous gravel track turned off into a sparsely wooded area leading up to what I assumed were our accommodations. Katie was right, the outside of the cabin was certainly "rustic" but thankfully it looked intact and free of any haunted summer camps or serial killer vibes.

More importantly, I noted an area fenced off to the side of the cabin facing the winery which, even from this distance, I could see featured an impressively new entertaining area with a pool, hot tub and outdoor kitchen area. That final part however, was irrelevant, as considering I avoided cooking at home I had no intention at all of poisoning us on a weekend away with my subpar excuse for meal preparation. To the side of the fenced off area was a section of lawn and a path that led through the boundary fence into the vineyard ending up at the carpark of the cellar door. Now, that was damn impressive and a much-welcomed feature for those inclined to wanting to avoid an extended walk home.

It didn't take us long to get our suitcases inside and unpack to the minimal acceptable standards for a weekend away. For me, this essentially meant hanging up anything that needed to be hung, and taking my make-up and toiletries to the bathroom. The interior of the cabin was so much more modern and refurbished than Katie gave it credit for but, judging from the look on her face as she took in our weekend surrounds, she was fairly taken aback as well. As it turned out we both had our own freshly painted, well-lit bedrooms with gorgeous king sized beds and an amazing view of ... well, nothing really, but it was still better than what the urban grey and smog I was faced with out my own window.

The only real negative comment we both had was that there was only one working bathroom. I could cope with this because there were three working toilets, two inside and one outside accessed through the entertaining area, which alleviated my innate fear of sharing a toilet with someone I actually liked. For some completely illogical reason, I had always been deeply terrified of embarrassing myself in that area, so having a toilet to myself certainly came as a relief.

Katie's room was nearly identical to mine, sharing a wall and the same view of the fields.

'Swimming or hot tub? What's the plan? I can't see any point in getting dressed up and going across to the winery yet.' Katies' voice projection was impressive as I could hear her quite clearly despite their being a rather solid wall between the two of us.

I was sprawled, spread eagle on my bed contemplating this challenging conundrum when Katie showed up at my door wearing nothing but a navy blue, front tie bikini that highlighted every amazing feature her body had going for her. She was tying her hair back into a simple ponytail, with a befuddled, almost confused look that said 'why the fuck aren't you in your swimsuit'. I adjusted my position on the bed rather quickly to one more ladylike and befitting of the refined lady that I was.

'Just testing the bed out … I'm very particular.' Sitting up, I reached over and started to nervously rifle through my suitcase that was sitting precariously on the end of the bed, looking for my swimmers. I'd ended up bringing a conservative canary yellow one-piece and a slightly less conservative longline bikini, in a classic black. I'd never really considered the pressure I would feel and the comparisons I would make between her and I in our respective swimsuits. I could never compete with her and even knowing it would be just the two of us in the pool, I couldn't help feeling ridiculously self-conscious and somewhat embarrassed. Copping another quick glance at Katie's figure I opted for the one-piece.

'Nope, don't you even dare! Girls weekend, so go with the two-piece number that I have no doubt you put away in there "just in case". Flaunt it, you've certainly got the figure for it.'

With a confident smile Katie turned and left, closing the door on the way and I could hear her in the next room walking around, pacing, probably a combination of checking the place out and just simply waiting for me. *Okay, I can I do this … deep breaths.*

I found the bikini and considered that, despite its more conservative top, the bottoms revealed the same amount as Katie's and that made me feel a little anxious. I took my time in getting naked, carefully folding my clothes and placing them on the bed in a nice, neat pile, something that was definitely not me. As I shimmied into the bottoms two things came to mind: was glad I shaved, and would I really care as much about how I looked in this thing if it was anyone else? Was I this self-conscious simply because that it was Katie, the one person in my life, who at this point in time, whose opinion I actually have a shit about?

I put my top on and, because there was no mirror in the room, looked down to get some idea as to how I looked. I moved my hands up, down and around my body trying to identify any obvious flaws or faults. I kept telling myself that I really didn't look that bad, that my body would be considered 'normal or better' on the Hannah scale.

My opinion of myself is always in a state of flux, changing with my mood and outfits but today, despite all the anxiety, fear and sheer perfection of what Katie was wearing, I thought I looked okay which, for me, was a pretty big compliment. Except for my boobs … because they looked amazing in this top!

I grabbed my towel and made my way outside to the pool area. Katie was sitting on the edge of the pool, dangling her feet over the edge looking absolutely transcendent. I stood there, almost waiting for some kind of compliment to allay my insecurities.

'I love that swimsuit! It looks amazing on you. I would kill for breasts like yours.'

Just like that, I felt better and that sense of relief, coupled with the kiss of the sun and the overpowering smell of the chlorine told me it was definitely time for a swim. I need a brain cleanse, I need that combination of the warmth of the sun and the cool kiss of the water to wash away the overthinking and the, at times, outright negativity that lives rent free in my head. If only I had Bill Murray to offer up some music!

CHAPTER 40

The afternoon was a balance of swimming and lying face down on a brand-new, white sun lounge. The contrast between the sun and the water made me tingle all over, offering up two very different sensations: one, a sudden reawakening, and the other a warm, welcoming embrace. Generally, I enjoyed the latter as it was not only incredibly relaxing, but I needed a tan and the rapid increase in body temperature was almost like a warm, sensual hug. That last part was probably a massive exaggeration due to the simple fact I hadn't had a sensual hug in a very long time, and I didn't think being carried to a bed in a drunken state by your friend counted. Besides, I equated "sensual" with relationships, something with feeling, emotion and all that stuff that clouds your thoughts and messes with your perception of the world, not seedy one-night stands. Most of my gentlemen callers probably couldn't even spell sensual, let alone provide a definition or an example.

As I lay there, slowly baking myself into a lethargic trance, I came to the sudden realisation that I was, in fact baking myself into a lethargic trance without having applied sunscreen. I was upright and moving quicker than a college guy after hearing "last drinks".

'Fuck! Katie, I forgot to put on sunscreen and I know, I just know, in a few hours I'll closely resemble a steamed lobster!' All I could think about was how I was going to look in my outfit with a back that could have doubled as the backdrop for the Chinese flag.

'I've got some Aloe Vera spray in my suitcase, let's get that on and we'll see if we can control the damage. We need to start to get ready soon anyway, so we might as well use this as an excuse.' I could tell she was holding back that cheeky, playful smile, knowing full well that I was stressing the fuck out!

Katie dried herself off and led me into the house and I was immediately hit by the artificial, regulated temperature of the reverse cycle. I really wished I had one of those at home that actually worked properly. Each year I told myself I was going to upgrade with my tax return, and ended up blowing it on something unnecessary like a series of Bluetooth speakers that I named Bill Murray or, believe it or not, a PlayStation – one of those fancy new ones that were near impossible to find. I'd found one and I bought and I had no idea why.

So far, I'd used it to watch DVDs, stream a variety of services (which my TV could already do) and play Crash Bandicoot for a total of about six hours. You had to love those manic, bipolar impulse buys.

'Take your top off and get in here so I can put this spray on. Wait, scratch that ... shower first.'

I was taken back by the 'take your top off' until I registered the actual purpose behind it. I hurried to the bathroom, stripped off and had possibly the most rapid, unsatisfying and, frankly, terrifying shower ever. Why? Because I had to use unfamiliar shampoo because I'd left mine at home, the water pressure was so different to mine and, most importantly, I forgot to close the door. At least three times, Katie came in to get things while I used a combination of steam and my hands to hide my lady bits.

'I'm not looking, I promise. Besides, it's nothing I haven't seen before ... on me of course, I haven't been spying on you, I promise ... or have I?' She was screwing with me, I knew it and it brought a smile to my face, but it was still slightly unnerving. You always see and hear of women running around comfortably naked or near naked, complimenting each other on their body, underwear etc., in films but these were obviously made by a group of men living in this amazing fantasy world. While I was sure this did happen, it was not something I'd personally ever heard of or experienced, nor had any desire to do so.

I was stressing, trying to work up the confidence to have Katie apply the aloe vera spray she had that I would only be covering my front with a towel. What if she sees my ladies, the ones that would obviously have a little more sag than hers and laughs?

Okay, let's get this over with.

I turned off the water, dried myself and wrapped a gigantic towel, which was amazingly soft and retained a lingering floral aroma of the softener, around as much of my body as I possibly could. 'Aright, let's do this.'

Katie came in, still in her bikini looking absolutely stunning. I know I need to stop comparing myself to people, but it's hard when you have a gorgeous friend standing in front of you, in a swimsuit you couldn't even dream of wearing confidently and a figure to die for. I turned around and lowered the towel enough to give her access to the slow roasted shoulders and sections of my back, trying immensely hard to avoid showing my backside or exposing my breasts. I know she wouldn't care, but I would be mortified.

'Just relax, this would be quicker and easier if you weren't shaking.' I hadn't even registered how nervous I was until she pointed out my involuntary tremble. 'I know there is absolutely no point me saying this and that it will do no good at all but you need to know that you are really attractive. Try to stop being so self-conscious about your body and hard on yourself.' She continued to rub spray and it was both refreshing and relaxing.

'Thanks.' That's all I could mutter, I guess I just wanted this over with.

'Alright, we're done. Let's get ready because I think we need a drink.' Out of nowhere, she handed me a glass of champagne and ushered me back to my room. 'We have to be out of here in one hour ... be ready!'

I didn't need more of an invitation than that. I closed my door, dropped the towel and, in a very unladylike manner, downed my champagne in two mouthfuls.

I was planning my schedule for getting ready in my head when I was rudely interrupted by what I could only describe as the worst song I have ever heard. Katie had obviously found the speakers and was playing something you'd find at an inner city college rave … not that I'd ever been to one.

'WHAT IS THIS SHIT?' I raised my voice in a vain attempt to overwhelm what I could only loosely describe as music. Her response was equally as loud but not as obnoxious as the "music".

'FRED AGAIN. I WAS TOLD IT IS IN.' Really? If this was "in", than I wanted out. We both regretted her music choice because about thirty seconds later, the music changed and the sexy voice of Mr Jack Harlow soothed the pain. I could tell, at that point, that despite Katie's supposed miracle spray, my back was developing the nice luminescent red tinge of the lobster I mentioned earlier. There is a lovely pun there about being "buttered up" but I'll leave that alone in favour of the distress I was now in, picturing how I was going to look with a glowing, iridescent back and shoulders.

At least I wouldn't get lost in the dark on the walk home I guess. So many "what ifs" scuttled about in my brain but I had to take a moment to breathe. I let the music envelop me and I took the first step to getting ready. Underwear.

At the risk of sounding like an 80s action hero I uttered the immortal words, 'Let's do this!' My level of positivity really did surprise me as it was so ridiculously out of character for me, but I put it down to knowledge of the fact that I'd snuck in one of those amazing pain killers. It was kind of sad, but knowing that if it all went to shit I still had a nice little "out" waiting for me before bed made me feel strangely upbeat.

CHAPTER 41

knew immediately that the sunburn was pretty bad when even the subtle, delicate spaghetti straps of my apricot dress elicited a response that, while not numbingly painful, certainly registered enough to make me think about the stupidity of my lack of skin care this afternoon. *Deep breaths Hannah, suck it up and move on. You will not let a few little burns ruin your night As a rule, men are not going to be paying attention to your back – at least at this point of the evening.* What felt like first-degree burns could be a little off putting while in the throes of love making, if I ever managed to get that far, but at this point it was mainly the discomfort of the strings rubbing on my shoulders.

Katie assured me that it didn't look as bad as it felt and with a few strategically placed mirrors she managed to convince me of, not only that, but that I actually looked pretty decent from the back in this dress. That was a lovely little boost to the self-esteem which, after seeing how incredible Katie looked, I needed. In less than an hour, she had managed to present herself in a manner reminiscent of the red carpet at some televised awards ceremony. I could see it all play out in my head like I was one of the star struck spectators ... I could almost hear the parasites of the paparazzi probing her as she elegantly made her way down the runway, waving at her adoring fans.

'Katie, Katie, who are you wearing tonight?' 'Katie, is there any truth to the rumours of your affair with Jason Momoa?' 'Your hair is amazing!' 'Whatever happened to your old friend Hannah? 'I don't even know if it was the last question that bothered me the most, because if either of us was going to have an affair with Jason Momoa, it would be me or I would die trying!

Revisiting reality, Katie wore the most figure hugging little black dress I have ever seen. It accentuated every part of her body and, importantly, it didn't give away the proverbial goose for free in that it was not overly revealing or sexual. In fact, in many ways, my dress showed more flesh than hers. She wore a pair of black, block heel shoes that looked incredibly comfortable and make-up that was simple, elegant and almost undetectable to the undiscerning eye. Her hair was almost identical to how I'd done mine, in a kind of organised blowout style, with the main difference being hers looked professionally done.

I was planning on wearing heels, but considering the rather uneven path we'd be navigating, I went with some simple black elevated flats that were insanely comfortable and still managed to complement the dress.

'You look amazing. And I promise, you wouldn't pick up on the sunburn unless you were looking for it. Trust me ... I'm a nurse.' There it was again, that cute, cheeky smile that accentuated her near perfect cheek line. I don't normally take compliments well, or seriously for that matter, but this one felt different because I actually believed who presented me with it and I actually gave a shit about what she thought.

'I guess you're passable as well. You might find some guy willing to settle at the end of the night.' I took a gamble and won on her knowing me well enough to register my love of sarcasm and poor humour.

'Thanks, Hannah. I know that's high praise coming from you.'

As Katie tottered around looking for her clutch, coincidently finding mine in the process, and making some obvious preparations to leave (lights on, doors locked, music off, no incriminating items lying around in case we brought someone home), I registered a level of nerves I haven't felt before a night out. Why the fuck was

I nervous? Why was I so worked up, so set on this night being amazing? There were the obvious reasons, but the only thing really different between this and a regular Friday night was the location ... and the company I guess.

I was with someone I was comfortable calling my best friend, I looked remotely acceptable and I was going to an incredible winery which was hopefully loaded with attractive men and relatively cheap drinks. Who was I kidding, there was no way there would be cheap drinks. I was pretty sure places like this didn't do happy hour ... or girl's night ... or two for one offers. Wow, my taste in places to go out back in the city were at an obvious low after considering they all featured one or more of those incentives.

'Alright, you ready?' I nodded in Katie's direction. She grabbed my hand and we made our way to the side door. I double checked I had my phone, and, in typical Hannah style, it was sitting at a cool 45% charge and we made our way out the side door which locked with a comforting 'click'. Katie exhibited an amazing sense of awareness by checking that she had the keys after the door had locked, which gave me a small coronary, but as it happened, she did in fact have the keys in her clutch.

She gave me a cheeky smile and a typical "calm down" kind of look.

As we got to the gate and begun to navigate the far from illuminated path, I registered one possibly significant fact. 'Fuck! I left dirty clothes and underwear scattered all over my bed!' I turned to go back but Katie was insistent in bravely pushing on, forcing me to deal with the fact that I might have to deal with this embarrassing personality trait if I managed to bring a guy home with me. She just smiled at me and forcibly dragged me through the gravel and dead grass.

CHAPTER 42

The sensation of finally stepping foot on the smooth perfection of the concrete carpark was positively orgasmic. It was a surreal experience because there was this sudden rush of relief and decrease in adrenaline and anxiety having reached the safety of the flat surface However, this pretty quickly became heightened again at the realisation that I was only a few minutes away from this unique and incredibly exciting social experience, which, to me, was somewhat of an experiment. How the fuck was I, "Hot Mess Hannah" (my new anti-hero name for the inevitable Oscar award winning film about my life) going to respond and react to the looming "undiscovered country" of this classy establishment?

I could already hear what sounded like polite conversation issuing from the entryway to the main cellar door. I could hear a crowd of more people than I'd expected. I'd had in my head that the majority of the people would be in the bar\restaurant area, but there seemed to be quite a few still here for tastings and civilised conversation. Retrospectively, I really should have brushed up on what civilised conversation actually was, so I didn't start harping on about some person, place or thing that was now hopelessly outdated. I was, however, prepared in one regard: I was the queen of fake until you make it! Now, by "queen" I meant that I had some skills in the area thanks to the, at times, crippling anxiety (insert sarcastic laughing out loud emoji hear to hide the sheer state of embarrassment I have in these situations of no control). State of the economy … blah blah, have you seen the new Christopher Nolan film? … blah blah, the human rights abuses in _____(sadly you could insert any number of countries here) is horrendous ... blah blah and, if all else fails, do you watch *The Block*? Better yet, just comment on their outfit, hair, or choice of wine and go with the flow.

Deep breaths, Hannah ... you've got this!

The exterior of the winery's cellar door could best be described as having a "rustic charm" which ultimately made it pretentious, cliché, and stereotypical. In fairness, the place did have a certain romantic charm that you'd expect from a silver screen rendition of the Napa Valley. The faux weathered hardwood door was ajar and flanked on either side by beautiful potted plants that added some colour to the predominantly wooden façade. A pitched metal roof provided a shelter and outdoor area for socialising. Wrought iron chairs and impractically small tables were evenly distributed on the paved, covered area. Even I had to admit that, despite the obvious tropes, it was quite a pleasant space to enjoy a glass or seven of overpriced wine.

The conversation coming from inside added to the ambiance and immediately drew Katie to the door. I never expected the nerves but as I stood there, admiring the view and attempting to find a distraction to keep me outside for just a fraction longer, Katie's enthusiasm overpowered me and I subconsciously followed her through proverbial looking glass.

What greeted us inside was an even more exaggerated take on "rustic charm" obviously designed to make us feel like we were in fact touring Tuscany and about to be met by luscious, rich Italian reds and, hopefully, luscious, rich Italian men.

My pragmatism, negativity, and depravity kicked in unfortunately and I saw through the façade and, instead saw subtle hints of "sex dungeon", or at least as my active imaginative envisaged one anyway. My memory took me back to that life-altering conversation with my mother and all that imagery was swept violently out the door and replaced with the soft, ambient lighting and tastefully adorned walls of a wine tasting establishment.

The tables and chairs were nicely spaced meaning that there was the potential to broodingly sit alone if you saw fit. The bar, which ran the full width of the room, was staffed by the "beautiful people" handing out tasting notes and directing people's attention to the board and cost. At a glance, I would say there were about twenty people in the bar broken up into what I guessed was two different, and very separate, groups. There were a number of young-ish ladies who, at a guess, were here for a birthday gig or bachelorette weekend. However, if it was a bachelorette party, it appeared to be not overly eventful or as debaucherous as they ones I'd previously attended. The other group looked like extended family with a good mix of old, middle and young people with even a baby in a pram thrown in. I guessed that the child, who was surprisingly well behaved, wasn't going to partake in the tasting in the traditional sense.

My instinct for booze kicked in, pushing my trepidation and mild levels of social anxiety to the side. I took Katie's arm in a delicate, yet forceful, hold and motioned her towards a vacant space at the bar. I couldn't help but notice that we were approaching over-dressed status but, to be honest, I couldn't really give a shit. One of the few positives about my brain was that anxiety could disappear just as quickly as it made its disruptive presence known. We turned a few heads, mostly from the group of girls who were obviously making some very sly judgemental statements among themselves ,which did make me feel somewhat self-conscious. Had I tucked my dress into my underwear and somehow not registered it? That was immediately where my mind went of course but a quick, subtle check reinforced what I already knew ... I was good and they were just being bitchy. There was of course another alternative that involved me being less judgemental, but I chose to ignore that.

The guy behind the bar looked to be pushing fifty and sported the most amazingly lush head of salt and pepper hair. His smile and cadence highlighted his confidence and the knowledge that he clearly had a deep understanding of the poison that he was purveying.

'Ladies, my name is Jack, and I have the distinct pleasure of guiding you through our extensive wine tasting menu this evening.' He was confident and suave, and judging from the ring he was sporting, married. 'Can I suggest the tasting menu 'social' option? It comprises three house reds and three house whites, all paired with local cheese and preserves.'

That did sound amazing but the price, which he'd strategically neglected to mention, could certainly be a roadblock to that particular option but he was confident he could make the sale.

'It is our most popular option for newcomers and it would go swimmingly on that table over there on the corner with you two lovely ladies in front of it.'

Wow, this guy was good … very good. I tried to find an excuse to check out the menu that was standing upright to my left, without making it too obvious I was looking at the price.

'So, what wines do have available for that option?' I threw a level of snobbery into my voice that my mother would have been proud of.

'Ah, great question from an obviously seasoned wine connoisseur.' With a smile and wink he handed me a menu and told me the six wines and their accompanying cheeses could be found inside. Opening the textured single fold menu I slowly tracked through the list of wines, cheese and preserves, most of which made very little sense, until I found the price. I was a little taken aback, but it was nothing out of the range of what I expected and, to be honest, may have even been a little cheaper. Fifty dollars a head sounded quite reasonable, until I remembered that the wine in this menu was 'a tasting' meaning it was really fifty dollars for a few shots and some cheese. Oh well, you only live once I guess … which is probably for the best considering my somewhat self-destructive tendencies.

'That sounds very pleasant.' There it was again, the snobbery made its way into my forced intonations. 'We'll have one each, please. And we will take your suggestion and take it at the table you pointed out.'

Katie looked at me sideways, trying to hide the smile forming on her lips. Considering I had just ordered without even asking or seeking any kind of consultation, I thought it best that I pay. I tapped away one hundred dollars and was led away by a now openly giggling Katie to the table in the corner ... I could already feel my buyer's remorse building.

When the wine and cheese arrived, I was pretty sure the waiter noticed my obvious disappointment. While it all looked incredibly classy and elegant, the portions were far from "satisfying" with the wine measured out to what would have been barely more than a standard shot. Each accompanying cheese could best be described as a morsel and one seemed to emit quite an acrid aroma. I knew I should have asked if there was any blue cheese on the board but, realistically, I should have prepared myself for this and, ultimately, the small portions.

Katie also showed signs of disappointment but deep down, I think we both knew this was going to be the deal. You didn't come to a cellar door to do tastings and leave drunk and satisfied. With all that in mind, my less than refined palate recognised that the wine was actually pretty good and the cheese ... well, it was definitely cheese of some description. One of the six types was actually pretty good.

I would love to say the conversation was deep and profound, but it pretty much just involved Katie and I sharing funny stories from our past lives. She had me in hysterics at one point with several tales of her somewhat more adventurous time at high school. As it turned out, and I should have called it knowing her current profession, she was a massive science fan-girl and managed to score a ridiculously attractive biology teacher in year 12. She even showed me a picture of him from one of his social media pages, which she assured me she 'doesn't stalk', and even now he was quite fit.

We shared embarrassing stories; in one of her biology lab lessons he'd directed Katie's group to the storage shelf to collect the tripods for a class experiment. Now, it was pretty obvious where this was going if you had a filthy mind but apparently, much louder than intended, Katie unloaded a smart-arse comment along the lines of 'I bet he is quite familiar with tripods judging by—.' Thankfully, her friend had stopped her there before she got too descriptive of what area of her teacher's body she'd been looking at but, alas, it was too late and her volume amplified by the acoustics of a lab led to everyone in the class hearing. The teacher went bright red, the rest of the class were in hysterics, and Katie never lived it down. Absolutely brilliant story that made my tales of high school seem tamer than they already were.

'So, when we work our way through this huge sampling of food and wine, what's the plan?' Katie's question seemed somewhat loaded as I got the strong impression a move to the main bar at the restaurant was high on her list of priorities.

'I'm wondering if we should at least have one glass here. It would be rude not too and, besides, Jack behind the bar, was quite the personality.' Yes, he was a married man and I was a lot of things but I wasn't a homewrecker. I always figured that just because I don't have a stable relationship, kids, a car, a house with a picket fence, actual prospects and all that other bullshit, that still doesn't give me licence to play around with a married man.

As we sat there, debating our next step, the door opened and, what came through, immediately solved our problem. All my hopes and dreams for the weekend had come true giving me a renewed vigour and the feeling of a mid-tier fairytale princess.

There, walking through the door was a group of four men. All

Films Have Given Me Trust Issues

well dressed and manicured and as an added bonus, upon first glance, two of them looked to be in my league and appeared to have no rings. My ability to spot a wedding band from great distances was actually a superpower of mine, to the point where I almost considered myself worthy of a comic book or television program.

The men walked with confidence and swagger, sporting natural, comforting smiles. Well, all except the leader, or so I assumed, who resembled a suave European playboy and carried an aura of arrogance. They made their way to the bar and, along the way, we managed to draw the attention of at least two of them.

I glanced at Katie and we locked eyes, our thoughts now in complete sync. 'Hannah, drink?'

CHAPTER 43

The speed at which Katie had sorted out two glasses of some kind of local red wine (I didn't ask questions as to what specifically it was) and somehow initiated first contact with the new arrivals was astounding. Apparently, when you looked like Katie all you needed to do was a) deliberately plan your path from the bar back to the table to force interaction with the men, b) find a remotely justifiable reason to move close enough to them to have to excuse yourself and c) smile in a polite yet 'look how hot I look in this outfit, please talk to me and my friend' kind of way.

I wasn't sure if they were as desperate as me, soliciting for a charity, or whether they were just really looking for conversation, but I really couldn't give a shit because within minutes of irrelevant conversation we had been invited to join them at the bar. While I sat there positively star struck by the level of confidence Katie exuded in her ability to 'work the audience' I struggled to comprehend how she was single and not fighting off men with some kind of large stick or surgical equipment stolen from work.

'Maybe later, boys. My friend Hannah and I' – she motioned in my direction and gave me a sly wink – 'are still trying to figure out how to spend our night.'

I had to react to having my name dropped and Katie drawing their attention to me, Hannah ... Miss Ordinary. I tried to muster all the confidence and sensuality I had and delivered what I hoped was a sultry smile and a 'I have men hanging off me but thanks for the attention and I'll consider my options' wave. However, I'm pretty sure I must have just looked ill or startled, like a small furry critter finally noticing the hunter stalking it from far, considering whether it was worth taking the shot.

Katie turned and made her way back to the table with a, 'See you later boys,' all the while knowing that one, if not all, were checking her out from behind as she lent down to put the glass of wine in front of me.

'Hannah, act cool and bored until they stop looking.'

I was sure I could pull off the bored look but cool, I wasn't so sure.

The men ended up standing at the bar doing a tasting, our good friend Jack helping them spend their money on overpriced local wine. This allowed us to surreptitiously discuss whether we should track them down later. I didn't have a chance to speak before Katie hit me with a wall of what turned out to be a surprisingly large amount of information about them.

'Okay, so, if you're interested, Mr Supermodel is in a long-term relationship with a girl living in Paris, not that I even cared or asked, the shorter one just came off a nasty divorce and the other two are ready to mingle.'

That was a lot of information thrown at me and it very much seemed designed to lead my attention towards the two single guys. Nothing against the divorcee but I had enough emotional baggage in my life without taking on anyone else's, even if only for a night. 'Divorcee is James, the other guy is Christopher and the two available specimens are, Mark and Sam. From memory, Mark has the stubble and the darker hair and Sam has really REALLY blue eyes.'

I got the impression this information was supposed to lead to a "I choose you" revelation but even someone as keen to hook-up this weekend as me wanted a conversation and a free drink or two first. Like me, Katie thought the divorcee was cute but acknowledged that anything remotely sexual in that area could have unpleasant results ... especially without details. I could see she wanted some kind of feedback from her attempt at a being a PI for her desperate friend.

'Okay, on first glance – and I do only mean on first glance – taking into consideration many factors including the sound of their names, your brief description ... ' I paused both from dramatic effect and to actually consider who I actually found more attractive. ' ... I would take either of them in a heartbeat.'

Stay classy Hannah ... I could almost hear the sarcastic slow clap coming from the rational side of my brain. Having acknowledged, and regretted, my achievement in reaching 'next level desperation' I took a massive gulp of wine, in what would have been a manner completely lacking in class, and looked at Katie who just laughed.

She put her hand on my shoulder and simply said, 'I figured as much ... I'm not judging, seriously. I was actually thinking the same thing myself, to be honest.' She gave me a wink and a smile which still managed to trigger this deranged image of Katie and I fighting over which of us was going to sleep with the one "good one" after the other turned out to be a eunuch or something along those lines.

My brain really did work in bizarre ways and it never ceased to throw up some new and strange way of dealing with my insecurities and foibles because I know that, if I had a penis and the mentality of the average male, I'd take Katie home over me any day of the week.

Katie could see my mind working a million miles an hour on meaningless, unhelpful or downright stupid thoughts and she expertly steered the conversation away from Mark, Sam and the others.

'So, on a completely different topic, how did the last day at work go with Ryan?'

I actually couldn't believe we hadn't spoken about this in depth yet after that lengthy car trip. 'Well, at one point, I actually considered committing first-degree murder, but my heels thankfully stopped me catching him before he cowered in his office like a spineless teenager.'

I maintained the perfect, emotionless façade in my somewhat psychotic mental and emotional state in that particular moment. 'Thankfully, he explained himself before I could get my hands around his neck. In retrospect, he actually did quite well in bringing me back from the brink of violence to, once again, feel that there may be some semblance of decency in his handsome body.' Wow. Once again, I'd publicly acknowledged that Ryan wasn't bad to look at. Something that I still cursed Katie for pointing out at all in the first place.

'Seriously, why don't you ask him out? There is obviously a love\hate kind of thing going on there and he very much seems to be doing the primary school thing of 'pulling your hair' to make you notice him.'

The thought had genuinely crossed my mind after a few drinks and a bout of loneliness mixed with horniness, but I just couldn't bring myself to do it. That kind of relationship, or even one-night fling, could never work.

'Honestly, not going to happen. This is not going to be one of those Hollywood moments of "girl falls for boss who previously made her life miserable" or one of those seedy office porn parodies featuring boss on employee "romance".'

I realised at that point that Katie hadn't even seen the guy so, like all self-respecting members of the twenty-first century, I stalked him on social media and discovered that, based on the photos he displayed, he really did love himself. His shirtless while fishing photo, while stereotypical and reminiscent of a profile picture on a dating app, did make me look twice at his rather well-defined body.

'Here, this is him. Have a bit of a troll through his photos and profile. I haven't done it before ... I promise.' Unsurprisingly, I actually had. Once. While mildly drunk, lonely and curious.

'Wow!' Katie did a generic, exaggerated fanning the heat away from herself gesture that told me she was genuinely impressed. 'How do you work with someone like that in the office? He is all kinds of yum.' Her statement lacked the class and elegance of the venue but clearly showed she was definitely on board with Ryan's appearance. 'Seriously, he is attractive. Like, really REALLY attractive. I have no idea how you didn't see that.'

The answer to that question was quite simple and self-explanatory. 'When someone essentially makes your life miserable for seven hours a day, five days a week you tend to see through the exterior to the interior arsehole.'

Taking another, rather large, gulp of wine I took my phone back, and in an effort to take the conversation away from Ryan, asked the lady across from us to take a photo of us. I must have been desperate because I hate photos. When people say a photo puts on ten kilos, with me it's more like fifteen at least and an extra two chins.

The lady from the family group was happy snap a picture so I got up and moved over beside Katie, kneeling down and putting my arm around her nervously.

'Smile girls.' The woman was extremely enthusiastic and ended up take four of five photos from different angles just to make sure she got it right. I'm guessing perfectionist mother but single and lonely was also an option.

'Thanks a lot, its much appreciated.'

Katie gave me a strange look as the phone got handed back to me; one that essentially said 'what the fuck just happened?' It was not my best way of changing topics but it had done the job.

'You two make such a lovely couple,' the woman said with a smile as she turned to go back to her group.

'We're not together. Just friends and totally heterosexual. Not that we have anything wrong with ... ' I trailed off as she obviously wasn't listening anymore. I looked at my phone and flicked through the photos she took. Wow, I was actually impressed with her work. Katie looked absolutely amazing and I looked acceptable, for lack of a better word. I didn't seem to have developed any more chins, and I didn't look like I'd been living off carbs and cheese for a week.

In fact, it was probably one of the few photographs I'd been in that I actually liked. I couldn't put my finger on why. Was it because of the confidence and positivity of Katie which, somehow managed to rub off to me in small amounts or was it simply that the wine had kicked in? Probably the former, because I was nowhere near drunk enough. I handed Katie the phone to check out the photos and opted to make a bar run, unceremoniously finishing my glass on the way. Lining up at the bar, I realised I probably should have actually asked her if she was ready for another one ... oh well, too late now.

Of course, when I was involved, one more wine turned into three, and in a remarkably short and expensive space of time. The conversation was not so subtly redirected by Katie back towards Ryan and my every growing level of confidence and wine induced 'buzz' brought up a whole range of conspiracy theories.

'He can't be that big of an arsehole, surely. He does look like he'd be a great—'

I cut her off there before she put ideas and visions in my head that I neither needed or wanted. 'Look, do you want me to try and set you up with him?'

As it turned out, that came out rather louder than expected but not quite enough to bring all conversation in the bar to a halt and, most importantly, the guys we were contemplating to meet up with, didn't hear.

Katie just kind of stared at me with these faraway eyes that I hadn't seen from her before.

'Really? Wouldn't that be, you know, weird?'

Finishing off what was left in my glass, I answered her without really thinking of the consequences of my response but, in typical Hannah style, there was no filter when booze was involved. 'I don't want him, I have no interest in dating him or sleeping with him, so if you're interested, I can at least see if he would be up for it.'

In a venue like this, I couldn't stand having an empty glass for too long but the dark, almost medieval feel of the tasting room was getting the better of me and, on a completely unrelated note, I saw the boys had left.

'I guess that would okay … if you were okay with it. I've never met the guy, but I'd be willing to have a drink with him if he was keen. Only if you're good with it. He's your boss after all.' I could tell she was cautious, but I fobbed it off and made a promise to 'see what I could do'.

Katie seemed content with that and, now more than willing to follow my suggestion in moving to the main bar\restaurant area. It was nearing 7pm and I figured that a) we could actually eat a proper meal, b) those men would be there, thus allowing us to continue to play Katie's game of 'hard to get' and, most importantly, c) the drinks (fingers crossed) might be cheaper and more varied than the local wine.

I grabbed her hand and went to lead her away but suddenly became aware of that same lady from before looking at us with gooey eyes and an expression that reeked of 'such a happy couple'. Fuck it, I held Katie's hand tighter, and we made our way through the bar and out the side, waving to Jack on the way.

CHAPTER 44

The restaurant and bar area were in complete polar opposition to the almost gothic tasting room. It was spacious, well-lit and, considering the location out of town, buzzing. That being said, it was a Friday night and places like this would have attracted weekend visitors and the odd party bus. Another completely random thought ... a party bus could really liven up the evening, until reality kicked in and I came to the realisation that most party buses usually involved young, out-of-control university students or twenty-somethings looking to simply write themselves off and have a good time along the way. So, high-end boutique winery was probably not high on the list of places to visit.

As we moved through the bar, trying to maintain the poise and grace of two mature, classy ladies, I noticed about half-a-dozen tables of couples or groups of four of eating and engaging in conversation. There was more than one example of fake, contrived laughter but all in all, everyone seemed settled and enjoying themselves. The main bar had much more subdued lighting and contained a dozen or high tables and adequate space at the bar. It was relatively empty except for a group of four, obviously on a double date, an elderly gentleman sitting at the bar and the group of boys we were, to an extent, pursuing ... for lack of a better word.

I could continue with the façade of 'playing hard to get' but the wine had really removed any sense of self respect in that regard and, while I wasn't going to start flirting with all the subtlety of a panda bear in heat, I sure as hell wasn't going to turn away any advances.

'Alright, cocktails! Do you trust me?' Trust wasn't really an option in this case because It was Katie, and I was honestly at the point of 'I don't care, just put a drink in front of me that isn't beer.'

'Of course, as long as it doesn't have one of those cringey sexually suggestive names, I'll have any cocktail you throw at me … metaphorically of course.' I added a little wink at the end in some poor attempt at humour but it elicited a kind of pity laugh from Katie as she made her way to the bar.

It was strange, as soon as she left I begun to feel incredibly vulnerable and alone. A sense of subdued social anxiety started to build up; being in a bar, at a winery, dressed up and away from home felt so surreal and without Katie right there, even though she was only a matter of metres away, felt scary.

'Hannah, wasn't it?' The voice from apparently nowhere startled me and, upon coming back to a sense of reality, I was greeted by one of the guys Katie had been talking to.

Okay, deep breaths Hannah, you can do this. Calm, serenity, peace and all that other bullshit you hear from the yoga and meditation classes you never attended.

I just stood there, taking in the guy's features. This was either Mark or Sam, because he wasn't the European Playboy and he was too tall to be the divorced guy. He exuded strength and confidence, was clean-shaven with a nose that clearly reflected past involvement in a contact sport, probably rugby league. Hopefully he was more intelligent than the other footy-heads I'd slept with, the last of which couldn't figure out how to unlock the front door while trying to do an early morning runner. If I were him, I would have been doing a runner as well because, for someone who promised a marathon, he managed to instead run one hundred metres in world record time. He definitely won, but I didn't even get out of the starting blocks. After possibly the most mediocre two minutes of my sexual life, he'd even had the nerve to ask if I finished. Moron.

This guy, Sam or Mark, his nose wasn't that messed up and,

besides, he had the most amazing blue eyes that distracted me from every other aspect of his self. Blue eyes ... so, based on Katie's notes, this must have been Sam. Alright, here we go; roll that dice and pray you put the evidence together correctly.

'Sam, isn't it?'

Nice. No look of revulsion appeared and instead, he nodded and seemed impressed by my basic ability to recall a simple name. 'I'm guessing Katie mentioned our names. She seemed quite aloof that one or was the "mystery" all just a bit of a performance?'

Katie showed up at just the right time, two iridescent green cocktails in hand, which I assumed from my vast experience with expensive cocktails in movies, were Grasshoppers. Slapping the drinking in front of me with the playful elegance of a trained seal she answered his question, removing any semblance of mystery or class that we had previously held.

'Definitely just a performance, and a pretty dismal one at that. Playing the "we're untouchable" role isn't easy after a few drinks.'

We all shared a laugh, and Katie and I exchanged a look of muted success and Sam now brimming with confidence and the look of someone up for a challenge, turned and ushered for his friends to join us. Before Mark and the other two even arrived, I had made up my mind ... Sam was my target. Now, I probably should try and let Katie know so we both aren't shooting for the same proverbial moon. In a way that seemed incredibly subtle in the planning phase, I picked up my phone to 'reply to an earlier message' I sent Katie a text with one simple word: 'Sam' ... and an emoji best left to the imagination. The fact Katie's phone dinged immediately after I clicked send, probably gave me away, but the damage was already done.

'You two need a moment?' Said Sam with a cheeky smile.

'Nope, not at all. Hannah was just letting me know she thinks you're cute.'

Fuck. Thanks Katie. While I know I can be quite forward at

times, some would call it sexually aggressive almost, but that was a first. I blushed, she laughed, Sam blushed, the rest laughed. It was basically a laugh\blush festival of embarrassment. 'Sorry Han, just figured that would save a whole lot of small talk and clear up any possible confusion.'

She'd meant well and, in all honesty, she was probably right, but a little fucking warning would have been nice … maybe a not-so-subtle text message back to tell me 'Hey Hannah, I'm going to basically tell this guy you want to sleep with him.'

I'm not really sure whether that was a positive start to the interaction or not considering it realistically, conveyed the impression of 'I'm easy prey … come get me!'.

CHAPTER 45

The conversation with the group of men was surprisingly normal, for lack of a better word, and contained no sexual innuendo, vivacious flirting or drunken slurring. Was it sad that I was kind of disappointed? I was generally a lot more confident talking to men after a few drinks and tonight was no different. In fact, the very real possibility of a hook-up that was a) pre-planned and b) lacking in the anticipation of regret and self-loathing made me sound less like a drunken crazy person than normal, which I took as a big win.

Christopher really showed little interest in the conversation but, in the interest of being a good wingman, he was respectful and genuinely charming when he chose to involve himself. It turns all four of them worked as teachers on the coast and had decided to bring the divorcee, James, away for the weekend to try and distract him from, as they described her, his "bitch of a harlot of an ex-wife". Very descriptive and in no uncertain terms made us well aware that the divorce was far from amicable.

He and Katie seemed to bond, with her caring, empathetic nature that I witnessed on that fateful first encounter in ER seeming to kick in. There was enough physical contact, hand on knee\ shoulder, and eye contact to form a connection and gain a level of trust for him to want to share, but there genuinely seemed to be no interest sexually from Katie. That being said, I'd have never witnessed her in this situation and, if she in fact was after something more from James, she was doing an incredible job at forming the initial connection that would be crucial to someone with James' current trust issues.

I was trying to both talk to Mark and Sam and, in a morbid kind of way, listen into the story of someone else's misery and pain. I shouldn't get off on that kind of thing with it being so personal and emotionally crippling but someone with my level of fucked-up-edness (yes, that's a technical term) kind of felt mildly better knowing other people's lives weren't perfect.

'James, Hannah here obviously wants to know the story as well, because we asked her about what she does for a living five minutes ago and all we are getting is blank stares and the occasional "ah hah".'

I went bright red and hoped beyond hope that Mark had been exaggerating. As it turns out, he had been, but only slightly.

"Sorry." Was all I could come up with, but they seemed to take it in a light-hearted, "she's just a stickybeak" kind of way.

On a positive, Sam seemed to understand my curiosity but was also very clear regarding what he thought would be an okay level of "bringing down the mood".

'Just once, share the story and let's move on. I don't want to be the arsehole, that's normally Chris' job after all, but we came here to escape this ... just for a few days.' He was forceful, but there was a clear sense of understanding in the tone of his voice. This actually drew Christopher, who I'm assuming prefers "Chris", into the conversation and his expression even changed from "arrogant twat" to "love ya, mate".

James downed the rest of his beer and proceeded to give us the short version of his misery. His wife had basically been cheating on him with one of the executive from his school for an extended period of time. To make matters worse, it seemed that it was quite widely known in the local community. So, he'd come back early from some training that, in a crazy and totally believable coincidence, had been organised by said executive and was to take place over two days in the city. James got sick and drove home at the end of day one and in an effort to surprise his wife, didn't call ahead to warn her of his impending arrival.

I could tell that part of him wished he had and that he'd continued to live in a state of ignorance to the sordid affair because, according to her, she still loved James immensely and that this was purely physical.

In my experience "purely physical" roughly translated to "fit and toned" or "well endowed". In a way, it seemed he was like me in that living in a state of denial would have been a solid preference to the emotionally destroying pain of what he'd walked in on.

He was met with, and to avoid any more vulgarity being attributed to me I quote James directly, '.. my wife, spread eagle on the couch, a brand-new one at that. That prick was balls deep in the love of my life.'

Faced with this level of heartbreak and anger was one of the reasons I wasn't sure I could do the relationship thing. Poor guy had turned around and walked out without saying a word. His wife hadn't even gone after him. I'd hoped she just wanted to get dressed and say a cordial goodbye to the gentleman caller first, but the cynic in me assumed the reaction was 'oh well, we're pretty much fucked, so we might as well finish'.

Poor guy, I could understand Katie's response and the innate need to physically comfort him with that delicate, caring touch of hers. Hopefully, that story was the last downer of the night.

'Right, more drinks it is. My shout.' Chris broke the awkward, post miserable story silence and did one of the things any man can do to make me happy … buy me booze. My opinion of Chris changed dramatically as, after a fairly short wait, he made his way back with a tray of drinks. Beers for the boys, bubbly for the girls and, the most horror inducing sight one could face in this situation: tequila chasers.

Deep breaths, Hannah … they will not defeat you and you will hold the contents of your stomach.

The conversation from there pretty much revolved around work and how all of us, except for Katie and James, pretty much hated our jobs. The idea of a teacher hating their job was certainly not an out of the ordinary revelation but Chris, who had finally opened up and lost the cold exterior, was close to quitting and moving overseas to live with his girlfriend.

Apparently, despite appearances, cash was an issue. As was getting the documentation and finding a way to end a long-term lease on a cute little place on the beach early (he had pictures). He became a lot more human after he let out his first expletive: 'Fuck real estate agents!'.

Thankfully, the gap between the rounds increased and everyone started to sit on their drinks a little more, which was probably going to help me save some dignity later on. Realistically compared to a normal night out at home, I hadn't drunken excessively, but the tequila and lack of food that wasn't stinky, overpriced cheese was a big x factor.

Mark disappeared for a few minutes while in the middle of a conversation about our families, which I avoided like I normally avoid shots and public transport, to order some food for the table. Winning!

I had never been so happy to eat in front of a group of attractive men which, under normal circumstances, would have ended in gut wrenching anxiety and a fear of spilling something all over myself. Another, much more welcomed, benefit of Mark's disappearance was what seemed like a pre-organised reshuffle of the seating arrangements with Sam now sitting next to me. So close, in fact, that he was able to discreetly place his hand on my thigh in a somewhat sensual fashion which resulted in goosebumps and a little spark that shot through my body, bringing me into a heightened state of anticipation.

His amazing blue eyes met mine and he gave a subtle smile and a wink. I really do have an obsession with eyes ... and showers

… but his were just amazing, certainly worthy of waking up next to tomorrow morning.

I'm pretty sure Katie knew exactly what was happening under the shroud of the crowded table because she also gave me a cheeky smile and a look of "someone's getting sex tonight". She'd planned this … devil woman!

I was shocked and disgusted and totally embarrassed at the … fuck, who was I kidding? I loved this girl!

CHAPTER 46

Chris, who it turned out was a really nice, genuine guy … totally not my type … left early, pretty much straight after we greedily devoured the food Mark had ordered for the table. It was kind of sweet really, turns out he'd agreed to FaceTime his partner as scheduled, even though he was away for a lads weekend.

Mark had been drawn to a woman at the bar who was obviously single and putting herself out there. James, after developing a little more confidence thanks to Katie, made some smart-arse comment about making Mark needing to make sure he had cash with him. It was a pretty class-less comment but, as James pointed out after seeing Katie's sudden change in demeanour, it was an ongoing "in joke" the guys had thanks to an unseemly, yet retrospectively amusing event, at James' bachelor party.

Sam had been politely prying into my background, family, relationships, job etc. but I didn't really want to go into anything. Feeling like either a failure or a fuck up in any or all of those topics would merely have accentuated my mental and emotional "complexities". Those "complexities" also happened to be the greatest birth control known to man because no one wanted to sleep with you, let alone form a relationship with someone who was a self-confessed red-hot mess. I opted for the safest option and settled on work, explaining the monotony of a government desk job and the mundane nature of the workplace itself. I was pretty sure he also picked up on my total disdain of public transport, something I almost unnaturally fixate on, because I mentioned on several occasions my bus\train experiences ranging from funny, to dirty, to outright disgraceful.

All the while, Sam's soft hand continued to rather delicately make its way further up my thigh until it settled uncomfortably close to my underwear. This quite naturally increased my breathing, blood flow and nerves which was unusual as, while it had been a while, I was quite familiar with the lead-up to meaningless sex.

Was this going to be different? Was he the one? Was Sam finally going to be the kindred spirit that guided me through the darkness of uncertainty into the bright sunlit field of relationship bliss?

Fuck no!

I wanted one thing from this guy and he met all the criteria. One thing and then he's off packing. No one in any winery, no matter how classy or how much I've drunk, could break through the uncertainty of me and my relationship with relationships. Katie could tell where my mind was going, of what thoughts were racing through my head trying to avoid the anxiety and fear and finally made the move.

'Okay gentlemen, it's been lovely but I'm taking Hannah back to our cabin via a treacherous walk through a vineyard.' What, don't kill this on me Katie ... please! 'You are both however, welcome to join us. There is wine and a hot tub, but neither of you are going in naked so don't get any ideas!' She gave them this look that had the amazing double meaning of "I'm deadly fucking serious" but in a playful kind of way.

Considering Mark was occupied and Chris was probably on a video call that was either incredibly romantic or filthy and involved pixelated body parts and over the top descriptive language, both James and Sam agreed to join us. James made a quick b-line to Mark to let him know what was going on, but he was too busy trying to sweet talk the girl at the bar. He even introduced her to James as "his divorced friend" which prompted a short and obviously miserable exchange of words. To call it a conversation would be very much overstating it.

While James was occupied trying to give a simple message to Mark, and Katie and I were gathering up our things, Sam leaned into me and gave me a rather suggestive kiss which, despite being a mere peck (no tongue or anything) certainly indicted he had other intentions.

As we left the bar through the main door as a group, I was surprised, and slightly disappointed Sam didn't at least try and hold my hand. From an emotional perspective, I really didn't want it, but knowing the path we had to cross and the booze I had drank, I might have needed it. As we made our way through the car park and down to the gate, Katie gave us all a motivational talk, preparing our guests in a very exaggerated way, for the short journey through the vineyard we, unfortunately, had to take.

'Okay, stay close people ... its rough in there. Seriously though, flashlight on your phone might be a good idea.' She did make the walk seem more daunting than it probably would be, but still, the talk needed to be had because the last thing we needed was a rolled ankle or, even worse, any injury that would prevent sex. 'Hannah, since these boys won't hold our hands to keep our delicate selves safe and stable, we'll have to hold hands.' She paused, waiting for a reaction but all she got was stunned silence and, disappointingly, not even an objection. 'Hannah, you have the key right?' Fuck ... where was the key? What could I have ... I looked over at Katie who had a cheeky smile on her face as she openly twirled the key on her finger. *insert internal sigh here*

CHAPTER 47

After making a big deal about the path that was, according to the tales of yore, more treacherous than a hike up the slopes of Everest, everyone made it quickly and unscathed. As it happened, doing that walk while drinking actually made things easier ... just like most other aspects of my life. If only they would let me go to work tipsy, things might be significantly better.

The cabin was well-lit and looked as amazing as I remember. Considering how mild the night was, Katie and I left James and Sam outside in the entertainment area and went in to grab some drinks. 'So,' I asked Katie as I rummaged through the cupboard for some wine glasses, 'you aren't actually going to sleep with James, are you? Not that it's any of my business but that just seems like a really messy situation.'

She took the lid off a bottle of what, unfortunately, seemed to be a red from the local winery. Katie gave me a look of, what the fuck are you talking about?

'What? No, not my cup of tea by any means. He's a great guy, but he doesn't need what I can offer him right now and he made it clear he wasn't after a fling.' Wow, that was different, a man making it known that he wasn't after a no strings attached night of passion with a drop-dead gorgeous specimen like Katie. 'I asked him over because it would have been damn rude to leave him there on his own and the only other alternative was to let you come home with Sam on your own. I'm not that trusting of anyone these days.'

I hadn't even thought of that. While I was pretty confident

Sam wasn't some psychotic serial killer, the scene was perfectly set for a generic slasher film and I wanted no part in that at all.

'Thanks. That "safety" kind of thing actually slipped my mind.'

Katie took the drinks outside into the entertainment area, which was subtly awash in ambient illumination of the pool lights and one strategically placed above the hot tub. This created an iridescent glow on the undisturbed water which was already emanating visible waves of heat. I wasn't going outside without two things: music and, more importantly, a visit to the loo all the while thinking about what to actually play. Through my experience, the right music could make or break any situation, acting as a force capable of destroying the best laid plans ... especially if you played One Direction.

I made my way outside, adjusting my dress to ensure everything was where it needed to be and played my The 1975 playlist; crossing my fingers that it was not a choice I'd regret. As the smooth, and somewhat ironic, sounds of 'Frail State of Mind' came through the speakers at an acceptable volume, I was met at the door by the sight of two grown men stripping down to their underwear, while Katie sat, drank, watched and laughed. Two things came to mind: *What the fuck did I just walk into?* and *I bet they're thankful it isn't cold outside.*

Here I was, standing there in a state of stunned surprise as two men we barely knew undressed. This was certainly not what I signed on for. There was certainly no desire for more than one passenger on this train but, fortunately, the simplest explanation is often the right one.

'I told you boys, you're not hopping in naked and I sure as hell hope your underwear is clean and you have no skin conditions.' Oh, that makes so much more sense ... they were getting in the hot tub and Katie was just having a good old, shameless perve as they stripped down. As they slid into the water she said, 'Don't spill any fucking wine in the tub!'

I couldn't help but notice how average a body Sam had. That sounded horrible, but average was not a bad thing, it gave me a little more confidence knowing I wasn't chasing some muscular guy sporting rock hard abs and the well-defined body structure of a profession trainer. Average was good and, in Sam's case, it seemed that average was a good summary of all of his important body parts ... not that I'd looked, of course.

The whole situation was relaxed and very laid back with Sam and James in the spa, obviously trying their very best to not spill their drinks through fear of Katies wrath. Katie sat on the edge, dangling her legs in the water and then there was me, awkwardly sitting off to the side in a deck chair drinking at a pace far exceeding that of the others.

'So, Sam or Samuel?' Wow ... what an absolutely amazing contribution to the discussion, Hannah. At least it hadn't been an emotional outburst or a verbal opening of the flood gates, I guess.

'It's Sam, but you can call me whatever you want.'

I'm not really used to seductive looks, as I normally just get the 'skip the small talk and let's get it on looks' from men so it was very different and a little bit nice. I'd love to have been able to come up with another more descriptive, intelligent word but nice summed it up perfectly.

'I'm just putting it out there ... ' Okay James, where was this going? Please involve drink top ups and a situation that could speed up a progression to the bedroom. All this lead-up and subtle flirting was driving me nuts! The anticipation was literally welling up and I could feel the need to just get on with it. As I said before, I've never been one for the journey, just the destination, and in this case I'd been waiting to get to the destination for far too long. ' ... how about you girls join us? There is plenty of room and, considering where you are staying, I'm assuming you brought a swimsuit of some description.'

Shit ... I really should have seen that coming and prepared

myself for this very situation. As soon as Katie mentioned "hot tub", I really should have been able to join the dots and see the bigger picture here ... her end game. Get us in the water with some guys and things will happen.

'Hannah? You with us?' Apparently, I must have gone off into my own little world for a period of time because when I once again became aware of the actual conversation, Katie was at the door to the house with a glass, ushering me inside.

Always the follower, always the girl that resonates to the one strong personality, I followed her without asking any questions. 'I don't know whether I can ... ' *insert unsexy hiccup here* ' ... do this. I kind of just need this ... whatever that is that's going on outside ... ' I haphazardly pointed at the rising steam visible through the window from the unseen hot tub, which was partially obscured by the wall. ' ... I'm not used to all the lead-up.'

I could feel my breathing increase knowing that I had working myself up so much over the pursuit of what would be a night of meaningless, and probably disappointing sex. It was kind of sad that my inherent negativity and lack of any self-belief or esteem had wormed its way into even this type of situation.

'I just want him to fuck me, or not. Either way, this is ... ' Katie stopped me and led me into my room which was, just as I remembered, littered with clothes both clean and dirty. She riffled through my bag and found the more conservative one-piece that I also brought along and handed to me. What the hell was I thinking, canary yellow?

'Put it on, go and join him, be your ... normal? Ok, probably not *normal*,' She said with an empathetic, understanding smile, 'charming, or flirty self. I promise I'll have James out of your way within twenty minutes.' She gave a cheeky yet sincere wink and left me standing there, swimsuit in hand and unsure of my next step.

Fuck it! I stripped off and got into that swimsuit in record time, making sure to avoid looking at myself in the mirror knowing full well that there would be clear signs of alcohol induced bloating.

It was done, and I was relieved. Katie had my back and life was good. She'd made the decision for me and it made me breathe a little easier. I still genuinely had no idea why I had worked myself up so much over this. 'Shit! I forgot to ... ' I didn't even finish my sentence. Now, a little unsteady on my feet I race into the kitchen before Katie and grabbed my phone. I'm hoping I won't regret this in the morning ... famous last words if I'd ever heard them. Surely, right up there with that guy from *Goldeneye* who'd screamed 'I am Invincible!' before dying in an ironic, brutal fashion. Anyway, I picked up my phone and opened up my messages. Who would have thought that I'd be messaging Ryan, drunk, at some ungodly hour?

H: Strange time I know but hear me out.
This is my friend Katie and she thinks you're cute
Can I give her your number?
By the way, you're still an arsehole.

I add the picture we took earlier in the night, click send and immediately contemplate what was going through my mind when I decided send that without asking Katie ... and to write that last line that may or may not get me fired. Oh well, it's done now and I'm sure the inevitable hangover in the morning will distract me from potentially poor life choices.

Okay, here it goes ... I topped up my glass to a level that suggested 'I really like this fine, fruity pinot' and not 'I'm drunk and want to get drunker'. If I hadn't near slipped on my way out the door, I could have possibly pulled it off.

Upon finally making it safely outside again, I look around and noticed two very important, and not-so-subtle, details. James wasn't there and Katie was in the pool already. She either got changed in record time and somehow surreptitiously snuck past me or, in the less likely scenario, she was as naked as the day she evacuated the womb.

Sam had activated the jets which, unfortunately, drowned out the music and any semblance of a chance of a quiet conversation.

'WHERE'S JAMES?' Wow, that was louder than I expected.

'WHAT?' Strangely, I heard his response quite clearly.

'WHERE IS JAMES?' I repeated with vigour.

'HE'S IN THE BATHROOM I THINK. By the way, I can hear you fine without yelling, luckily. But I'm pretty sure the winery guests will have heard you as well and are probably looking for James as we speak.'

I could feel the embarrassment build at another amazing 'what the fuck, Hannah' moment.

'He's in the bathroom, Hannah. Relax, no need to yell.' Katie had to chime in with her sarcastic, yet gorgeously playful, contribution just to reinforce the extent of my combination of drunkenness and nervousness because, by this point, the wine had certainly taken hold.

I slid into the hot tub fighting the chaos and disruption caused by the active jets, the heat of the water welcoming every part of me into a wet (obviously), comforting environment. I placed my wine on the edge in a hopefully secure position, and laid back and took in the warmth, the subtle chemical smell and the knowledge there was a near naked man sitting mere feet from me, mesmerising me. *Deep breaths, Hannah.*

I was immediately taken aback by the sudden, yet controlled motion of Sam's hands and mouth. I've seen *Deep Blue Sea* so I hate to compare his movement to that of a marine predator because I'm pretty sure he had no intention of eating … wait, I'll stop right there because I'm not sure how I feel about finishing that sentence. His hand made its way immediately to my waist which he used to pull himself in, nuzzling into and kissing my neck rather delicately.

It felt amazing and I just ran with it, welcoming the physical contact and connection that wasn't just a tongue down my throat.

He pulled back suddenly while keeping his hand stealthily planted to my thigh as James returned. I liked that he wasn't what I call a "trophy hunter", he didn't feel the need to show off to his mates.

I was still yet to see how Katie was going to get rid of James though but, through sheer luck, or you can call it serendipity, she didn't have to.

'Hey man, we need to go. Mark just rang and, as usual, he's in some strife.'

I felt somewhat deflated, it looked like the bubble had burst and it was going to be Hannah and an empty bed. Oh well, I might just sleep right here in the hot tub. It was so warm and welcoming and, if it wasn't for the high probability of drowning, I may have considered it.

Sam just looked at me, his hand still firmly in place and I turned to faintly make out calculations running through Katie's mind, trying to think of a solution to keep Sam here.

James proceeded to dry off and get dressed right there in front of us as he retold the story of woe that had befallen good old Mark.

'He ended up going back into town with that girl but they got a flat near "something tree lane intersection". He needs a hand because, as it turns out, she had no jack with her. He also said he wants fifteen minutes or so which means he is probably doing the dirty in the backseat or the bushes as we speak.'

Katie chimed in loud and enthusiastically, she'd had a light bulb moment and I could nearly see the metaphorical glow appear above her head ... or was I just seeing things now? 'I know exactly where that is, it's about a ten minute walk that way.' She pointed roughly towards town and, if she was faking the local knowledge, she was doing a pretty good job of hiding it. 'I'll walk James there with the jack from our car, because I'm assuming your pretty handy with things like that.' She said pointing at James. Now I know Katie can change a tyre and do just about anything else she put her mind to, but I could kind of start to see her deviously sexual scheme come together in her head. She continued as she too got out of the pool, immediately drawing James' eyes and, more discreetly, Sam's. 'Sam, can you do me a favour and stay here with Hannah until we get back? Sounds silly, but being so close to any kind of bar and having the big scary outdoors right there I'd feel better if she wasn't left alone.' Great play acting, she did the innocent, naïve city girl act so well. 'Besides, there is no point us all going.'

Sam took a socially acceptable amount of time to agree without sounding too enthusiastic, giving me a very cheeky wink in the process. Everything happened so quickly but within five minutes it was just Sam and I, *The 1975*, the hot tub and some empty glasses.

CHAPTER 48

As if on cue, the timer clicked and jets stopped abruptly, leaving us in the peace and serenity of a pitch-black night sky and 'Somebody Else' now playing through the speakers. Certainly not a song I'd associate with this situation with lyrics such as …

I don't want your body
But I hate to think about you with somebody else
Our love has gone cold
You're intertwining your soul with somebody else

… the music though, the rhythm, was smooth, peaceful and a subdued sense of sensuality. Sam's firm grip pulled me in close to him and our lips met in a torrent of, what I'd normally describe as, "yuk". I'd never been a fan of tongue down the throat, but I ran with it on this occasion.

His hands started to go to places that left no doubt as to his intentions and we seemed to be on the same page: let's get this done. He only stopped to stand, take me by the hand and help me out of the hot tub. His "anticipation" was quite visible considering all he had on was underwear which had obviously become skintight. I had that giddy, schoolgirl "butterflies in my tummy" kind of feel, but that could have been the booze as well. His ever so obvious penis was now, to me, somewhat comparable to a celebrity meltdown in that you can't look away despite knowing you probably shouldn't be so enamoured with it.

I'd had enough of the trailer, it was time for the feature, so I took his hand and guided him to my bedroom. This was it. Game on. I'd been fixating on for this weeks. He was careful to close the door, knowing that Katie would, at some point be back home. I did something then that I have always dreamed of; in one sweep of my arm, I pushed everything off the bed in a fit of, what I guess you'd describe as passion but I'm going with speed and ease.

He shimmied out of his wet underwear and crawled under the covers, turning my sheets immediately into a tent in the process.

'Your turn.' I removed my swimsuit in an efficient manner lacking any pomp, sensuality or ceremony. I could feel his eyes work up my body from feet to face, along the way pausing to pay particularly close attention to my various lady parts. There was no sounds of revulsion which was a big win and he seemed particularly impressed with my "groundskeeping".

'Move over, that's my side.' Fuck, what a time for the OCD\ love of routine to kick in.

Mind you, he didn't say anything, but I got a quirky look and he complied without question. I crawled into bed and was immediately unsettled by the unpleasant caress of a wet fitted sheet, another bug bear of mine. I really should have made him dry off better, but that ship had well and truly sailed. I didn't have time to worry because his hands and lips were all over me, as was the occasional unwanted stab from his lower appendage.

'Shit, condoms. I'll be back, I've got one in my wallet.' Nice, proactive in the birth control department was always a win. He was out of the bed and shooting across the floor like his life depended on it. It would have been brilliant to see him dash naked across the kitchen, out the door, into the entertaining area to collect his clothes and his wallet, all the while sporting a decent sized erection. I really should have told the poor guy I had brought a few and that they were in the suitcase that he could have reached from the bed. I giggled to myself at the comedic value of that scene.

It seemed like an eternity of me laying there, naked, feeling somewhat "ick" from the wet sheets, waiting for Sam. When he made it make back and closed the door, things happened fast. Might

I say, I was really impressed at the speed in which he managed to get the condom unwrapped and on. Hopefully that would be the only thing tonight in which he would show unnatural speed. As soon as that thing went on, things happened really quickly and surprisingly really well.

He seemed to actually care and pay attention to what my body was telling him I wanted. There was a motion, a fluidity to his movement and every action and, for once in a long time, I felt like it wasn't just running through the motions. There was a strong sensation and a sense that every movement, every touch and every moan felt good and that I didn't want it to be done and dusted in fifteen minutes. He knew where everything went, where everything was and didn't start and end at just penetration.

There was no kissing or any real intimacy, once that metaphorical bell rang which, while somewhat strangely, added to my enjoyment in that it made the temporary nature of this connection more real. It was everything a one-night stand should be and that made emotionally messed up me happy. It was like the best of both worlds, really: a guy who actually wanted you to have a good time, but who you would also push out the door in the morning after an awkward breakfast.

Sam worked hard and I didn't even have to fake it in the end. For the first time in a while, I felt satisfied. Possibly only for a few hours, or days or, if I'm lucky, weeks, but I was in a state of bliss. He looked at me with a sense of pride, of accomplishment, because guys generally based the success of their performance on vocal reactions ... and I was fairly vocal. But what was I missing ... Fuck, poor guy hadn't finished.

That was unusual for the men I brought home, they usually won the gold medal while I brought in silver, bronze or am disqualified. With a little work, and not much effort really, he was done and he looked exhausted, "drained" so to speak.

The post sex clean up was quick and actually involved some

level of conversation as, apparently, the act had sobered me up enough to talk about the weather. Great move, Hannah. *The weather*? Couldn't have come up with a better topic?

He crawled back into bed with me after a dash to the garbage bin, kissed me on the forehead, thanked me and rolled over. Within a matter of minutes, he was snoring and I was laying there contemplating and basking in the fact that he hadn't tried to continue said conversation with me … plus, I'd just had sex and it was actually good.

I registered Katie come home about half an hour after I turned the light off as the light peaking in from under the door disappeared and I heard her door close. I didn't hear any conversation and didn't want to bother her so I rolled over and started to drift off … Fuck! I forgot my pills … always, just as I am about to sleep. Five minutes later, dosed up and having held off the urge to pop a pain killer, I drifted off … again.

CHAPTER 49

The sharp ray of morning sun awoke me early and reminded me quickly of the excessive amounts of red wine and cocktails I'd drunk during the night. I was dehydrated, my hair was a dishevelled mess, and I felt gross. Shards of memories of last night helped me to gingerly put together a picture of what happened. I wasn't blackout drunk and remembered everything, but as always, sequencing and clarity was an issue in those first few minutes of being awake.

I looked to the other side of the bed to find it empty. The lack of male clothes on the floor too, suggested that Sam had done an early morning runner. The anxiety of having to interact with him in the morning evaporated and I let out a sigh of relief.

This time, however, I did feel bad because he was a nice guy and an above average lover. But, ultimately he was just a tool I'd needed. That sounded horrible and came across as me being a heartless, uncaring bitch, but I couldn't pretend it was anything more. I'd never given him the impression that it was "going anywhere".

This was one of the positives of my state of mind and my issues and confusions surrounding relationships. My psychologist seemed to think that my way of thinking could also be contributing to it, but I choose to ignore that and live in, what she called, repressed denial.

I got dressed in a simple white dress and did my hair in a ponytail to "take the edge off" the delightful combination of sex hair and morning after a night out hair.

I tried to avoid eye contact with myself in the mirror but that iridescent glow in the aftermath of yesterday's sunburn was too hard to ignore. At least the booze had the added effect of distracting me from the discomfort. No one had mentioned anything, which meant that maybe, just maybe, it wasn't too obvious. I found it bizarre that the knee I'd had surgery on, the one that caused me continual grief, was emanating a dull ache. The kind that I normally get in the evening thus giving me an excuse to ride the prescription opioid train, one that I was desperately aware that I needed to get off. The only problem with that was that I generally didn't do the "self-improvement" kind of thing very well and they do go so very well with a whiskey or a few wines before bed. Surely I get credit for knowing that it wasn't particularly healthy ... surely.

I exited the room and was met by Katie who was thankfully in the kitchen, already in her swimsuit and a floral sarong, making coffee and what smelled disturbingly like burnt toast. Our eyes met and she gave me the most vibrant, toothy smile I've seen, one that oozed self-satisfaction in the knowledge that she'd helped me to hook-up.

'Well, well, well. Look at you, all chirpy and glowing. If I didn't know any better I would think that was the look of someone that just had some pretty amazing sex.'

I didn't look "chirpy", I never did in the mornings and the glow she was talking about was more than likely my back.

'I don't kiss and tell but, yes, we had sex. Yes it was amazing, and no he's not still in the room. He did a runner, must have been early this morning.'

Katie seemed a little taken aback. 'Okay, two things ... how do you feel about that? It doesn't bother you?'

I think she knew the answer but still wanted to do the check in to see that I wasn't suddenly smitten with Sam and was about to go all "Juliet" on her. 'Doesn't faze me at all. In fact, I'm happier that he is gone. One night, that was all I wanted. I don't really want to see him again to be honest.' My headache started to kick in and I realised that last comment sounded incredibly nasty, but it certainly wasn't meant that way.

'Well, you may have to see him again because he left his phone here and it's been going off all morning. Guy must be pretty popular, or he just had his cronies ringing it to try and find it.' She held up a sleek new iPhone and waved it around just as it vibrated and lit up briefly signalling another message.

Fuck.

I decided at that point the cure to all my aches, pains and perceived problems was a coffee and a swim because hard liquor at this time of the morning was frowned upon. The sun was already bathing the entertainment area in a welcoming warmth and it seemed liked the best place to get my caffeine on.

The coffee Katie brought me was – and I say this with love – tepid and near undrinkable, but in the interest of friendship and needing a liquid to wash down the cocktail of paracetamol and bipolar medication, I tolerated it. We sat quietly around a small table directly exposed to the morning sun which created a sadistically pleasing burn on my shoulders reminding me I was in fact alive.

'So, how was it?' A simple question and a perverted smile was what I got from Katie and, to be honest, it was nothing less than I expected.

'I'll save you the gory details but it was exactly what I needed. He and his bits did everything they needed to and … that's all she wrote.' I tipped the last half of my coffee in the pot, plant hoping that it wouldn't kill it, got up to go and get changed for a swim, it might wake me up a little. 'I'm going to get my swimmers on and do my teeth before they rot in my mouth from that coffee. Thanks for that by the way.' I gave Katie a wink and headed off inside, noticing a figure walking across through the vineyard as I closed the door. All I could think was *please, don't be Sam!*

I slipped into the one-piece again because it was right there in my room, still somewhat damp, but easily accessible and it would hide any post night out bloating. I took an excessive amount of time to apply the sunscreen, even though the damage was done, and to tidy myself up. If I had laid down I could have slid into the pool with the amount of sunscreen I applied, but the aroma of coconut was pleasantly pungent and reminded me of the beach. Taking in that scent, one of my few non-guilty pleasures, I was feeling a sense of peace and zen and all it had taken was a night of better than average sex and some time off work. I was however, missing something and I couldn't quite put my finger on it until I realised I probably needed to put my phone on charge. I find it nestled away on the floor after being flung off the bed at some point last night and there were two messages … both from Ryan.

Fuck!

Between the nervous flirting and the eventually passionate result I forgot that I'd messaged him. To make matters worse, I hadn't mentioned to Katie that I had any intention of sending him photos of us last night while drunk.

Okay, deep breaths Hannah, it's all done, put your big girl pants on, move on and start to think about possible future career choices. Maybe I could work in that Bubble Tea place? I unlocked the phone, held my breath, despite my internal pleas, and opened the message.

R: Nice photo, you both look gorgeous.
There is nothing going on with my love life at the moment
Thanks for thinking of me … I think.

That wasn't so bad. He seemed calm and okay with the drunken, random message and, also, he didn't mention code of conduct … in the first message anyway. Okay, next message … let's do this.

R: Surely, I'm not that big of an arsehole?
I did just give you two weeks off.
☺

That's right, I'd called him an arsehole. I actually forgot that really important component of the message. At least he'd seemed to take it with a little jest or, was he just waiting for me to return to give me the old "clean up your desk and get out!" speech. Jokes on him, it was not all that easy when working for the government because there would be "mediation" and "development plans" and all that touchy feely nonsense.

From what I could make out, you pretty much have to steal money or burn the place down to get let go from a government job ... or sleep with an intern, but that was out of the question considering my lowly status.

I was clever enough not to respond until I had the chance to speak to Katie. Afterall, I didn't want to be too presumptuous and take the drunken affirmative from last night as gospel.

'Katie, can I see you for a minute?' I yell through the door hope that her hearing was near superhuman.

'What's up? She slid through the door like Kramer from Seinfeld and near knocked me off me feet. I was taken back to say the least but it got the heart rate up, reminding I was in fact still human.

'So, remember last night when we were talking about Ryan and I asked if you'd like me to—' I didn't need to finish my sentence, she must know me well enough to register the lack of thought in my drunken decision-making.

'So, I'm assuming you messaged him last night?' She was an astute girl.

'And ... I also sent that photo we took at the winery.' Without any distinct pause I threw in a panicked and forceful, 'Please don't be mad!'

She let out a nervous smile and for the first time she showed a little hint of self-doubt, I think there was a hint of concern that Ryan wouldn't have found her attractive or that he wouldn't be interested. 'So, what's the verdict? Did I make the cut? Worthy of a coffee or dinner with the biggest arsehole in your office?' She hid that now obvious self-doubt under a thin veil of sarcastic humour.

'He wants your number and he said you were gorgeous.' There was a stunned silence while she took in this information. She genuinely seemed surprised but, at the same time, a little nervous.

'You can give him my number and tell him to give me a call whenever he wants … as long as you are okay with that.'

I was okay with it … I think. Until she'd mentioned it, I hadn't even considered how it would make me feel or why that should even make a difference. Now, with those few simple words my brain had switched to "how can I cope with this change in the situation" mode. My head immediately started to hurt while in that fraction of a second, I went about contemplating every worst-case scenario possible.

'Of course I'm okay with it.' For some reason a seemingly forced, uncomfortable noise that I thought was a laugh squeezed its why out creating a somewhat awkward, but brief, silence. 'Why would I have a problem?' *Deep breaths Hannah.*

'Is anyone there?' A somewhat familiar masculine voice penetrated the somewhat uncomfortable gap in conversation which, was very much welcome. At the same time, a disembodied male voice opening the door to your cabin in the middle of nowhere without any 'hey, can I come in?' is somewhat disturbing. 'It's only me, James. I came looking for Sam's phone. He said he might have left it here last night.'

Katie moved towards the breakfast bar and held the phone up, waving it enthusiastically. 'Is this it? It's been going off nonstop since early this morning.' She handed it over to him and he tapped the screen, noticing the sheer volume of messages that must have been displayed and a battery level that was probably pretty low. 'Couldn't he have come and got it himself? Too hungover I'm guessing.'

I stood there quietly all greased up with sunscreen wearing nothing but that yellow, partially damp, swimsuit, trying to look somewhat nonchalant.

'No, he had to go. His wife's sister had gone into labour early and he had to run back home to sort out the kids.'

I went numb.

To call what followed "stunned silence" would have been an understatement. Katie looked at me and I could just imagine how I looked as I could feel the colour drain out of me completely and my brain just shut off, entering caretaker mode. I was numb, not with anger but with the sensation of 'I knew this was too good to be true'.

'No one told us he was married, what the fuck was the go with that? Do you really think it's ethical to come back to a cabin with two single girls, as a married man?'

Katie lost it, but I hoped beyond hope that she wouldn't mention that Sam and I had played the proverbial beast with two backs. Regardless of how I felt at this moment, and I couldn't accurately describe what that actually was, I didn't need or want to break up this fuckwit's marriage.

'What the actual fuck were you guys thinking?'

James was silent, dead silent, obviously trying to find a way to face the mighty onslaught of Katie's wrath. He did however, make a rookie mistake, he spoke when he really should have just kept his mouth shut.

'Ummm ... it's not as if you guys slept together, what's the problem?'

All I wanted to say to him at this point was, *With verbal self-control like that, it's no wonder you're a divorcee,* but my common sense kicked in and, I don't think I could have said anything even if I wanted.

'He was all over Hannah all night, you saw that surely. You can't stand there and justify to us with any seriousness or credibility that what he did was remotely right.' Katie was furious, I could feel the intense seething build up inside her to the point where I feared for James' safety. She did, after all, probably know all the pressure points and delicate parts of the human anatomy. Oh, he's going to speak again, I could see it coming. I just wanted him to shut up and leave so I could start to put this behind me and move on. It's not that I actually wanted to date the guy.

'Look, he's a decent guy. He might not have mentioned anything but he did leave straight away when Hannah came onto him pretty hard after you and I left.'

Oh shit, this was not going to be pretty.

'GET OUT! Take his fucking phone and fuck off right now. You have the time it takes me to get that cork screw off the bench to be out the gate.' He obviously didn't know Katie, and wasn't sure how to react so he stood there, in a way that reflected the utter disbelief of the situation he was in.

Katie started to move towards the bench, finding the corkscrew with deadly efficiency. 'Do you think I'm joking? Because you don't have long to get off this private property, of which you entered unannounced, before you test if I am actually bluffing.' She took one step towards him and he turned and started to walk with purpose out the door and towards the gate. 'Don't walk ... I never said anything about walking. Run you prick and I better not see you or any of your cronies again.'

James moved pretty quickly after that and the last words we heard from him as he sped off through the gate were, 'I'm sorry.'

Katie turned and gave me a remorseful look. She knew I didn't want anything from this but she also knew where I stood on married men. 'Do you think I scared him enough?' That was much better than the "are you good?" question that I'd expected. I didn't stop me from answering what expected and, to be honest, what I needed.

'I'm good ... I think. Him lying to me doesn't bother me in the slightest, it's him lying to his wife that makes me feel like shit.' This was one of the many reasons why I just feel relationships aren't for me. I'm not resilient enough or confident enough to know that I am good enough for someone to want to spend the rest of their life with me. The fear of living with this constant doubt that your perceived "better half" is in fact just that. The thought that they would either inevitably toss me aside for someone better, someone prettier and less crazy or that they'll get some kicks on the side. Either situation ended in me a broken mess or left in the dark just like Sam's wife.

I didn't want to be like Sam's wife and I didn't want to be like James, tossed aside for someone else. That fear all stemmed from a complete lack of self-belief and self-love, I know that, but after being single for so long I just didn't know whether I could trust myself not to put myself in a situation where I would either get hurt, or worse, talk myself into getting hurt through a sense of paranoia, fear and loathing.

Katie made her way over to my miserable self and gave me a hug, one that made me slightly uncomfortable considering the small amount of clothing we were both wearing. In typical Hannah style, I did my best to push all that aside in a manner that was far from healthy.

'Oh ... I'm going to send Ryan your number before I forget. On a side note, I know for sure he is single ... or, at least not married. Probably should double check first, considering he is an arsehole.'

I smiled and did my best to push away what I felt for Sam's wife and try to convince myself that I was okay with Ryan and Katie going on a date. I tried to bury all my hypothetical worst-case scenarios and focus on something positive. All I could come up with was: *I want to go home.*

INTERLUDE: THE PURSUIT OF HAPPINESS

After yet another fight with Will, I sat at that sad little table in my sad little study and instinctively picked up a pencil. Another round of pointing fingers and excuses as to where he was last night. Another broken glass, slamming of the door, and the numbness that followed. Will was so very flawed but he meant well. I realised that could only go so far when I had no idea who he was with, who he was messaging, or how to respond to his ever increasingly emotionless façade. The worst thing was, I stopped actually caring if he was sleeping around or not because if I cared, it would hurt, so I made myself numb with booze and music ... depressing bloody music.

So, pencil in hand and with some time, I wrote. Well, at least I tried to, but nothing seemed to work and it was all just disjointed. It wasn't even a novel, or a continuation of what I had written before or even a fucking story. I had to admit to myself that my dream was dead in the water and that my relationship with Will was going the same way.

Were either of those things really a big deal though? Maybe I was better off riding solo; no commitments, no pressure and no one to let down or be let down by. As a way of finally burying my hopes of writing once and for all, I had a glorious send off. At eleven in the morning, on a Sunday sometime in winter, I poured a sizeable glass of whiskey and I sat down, I wrote words and I cried. I cried because things needed to change and the safety of my shitty routine needed a paradigm shift for me to grow up and survive.

I had to leave Will, I had to stop pretending I'd write the great Australian novel, and I had to start to grow up. Everything that permeated my every thought in that brief, single moment, would've made my mum incredibly happy. Those words, they originally made no sense, they were random thoughts, but the more I sipped on that cheap bullshit whiskey Will had left behind, the more they formed patterns and started to take shape. I think I'd written a poem.

Films Have Given Me Trust Issues

*Shards, man-made reflective windows into
ourselves,
All that remains of a mirror hiding in an empty
room.
The pieces consume the cold floor
Like jigs of a forgotten puzzle
They rest there, alone, forgotten, broken.*

*Signs of its beauty remain.
The teak stand, the inscription of ownership:
'Happy Anniversary, Hannah'
What inspires the most pride is that it is still itself
Despite being shattered, it still shines. It's still a
mirror.*

*The question permeates through the dank,
What destroyed it? Why?
The dust, the webs tell it all,
It has slipped from memory,
Humankind has chosen to forget or ignore its
uncommon beauty*

*Some light penetrates the darkness, unwillingly.
It reflects outwards allowing the beauty of grey
To permeate the abyss,
The darkness of all that is forgotten.
For a brief moment, the mirror remembers itself,
it shines.*

*The light fades, the room goes dark again.
Normality is returned, the chaos of light has
faded.
The broken mirror is still there,*

*The room is still empty and forgotten.
But for a brief time the mirror once again lived.*

I read the poem once, twice, downed what was left of my whiskey, and I threw it in the bin along with the pencils and my notebook. Time to move on, time to grow up and acknowledge that a guy justifying cancelling plans on my birthday to help his mate "move house" was not worth my sanity. Happy Birthday, Hannah.

As far as things went with Will, he hadn't technically moved in, so nothing about his personal details were affiliated with my living situation at all. I rang him, slightly tipsy, and explained the situation and, to my credit, I didn't give him a chance to rebut or sweet talk me. It was the most honest break up in the history of Hannah.

'Will, we're done. I think we both know this is not going anywhere … no, just listen .. and frankly, I don't think I want it to go anywhere. I think you'll be better off with someone else and I'll be better off on my own. I'm packing up all your things this afternoon … no, shut up and listen … and I'll drop them off at your mum's. By the way, I'm keeping that bottle of whiskey you left.'

With that, I'd hung up and spent a surprisingly brief period packing up Will's things. It was kind of depressing, the lack of connection or presence he had left. A few pairs of underwear, a shirt, a toothbrush, a box of condoms, and an Xbox was all that he had bothered to leave at my house. A miserable haul for a mediocre relationship, but boy did he make-up for it with length, girth and technique. To give him some credit, he had an uncanny ability to say the right thing, to comfort me when I was at my low.

I spent the rest of the day cleaning compulsively, metaphorically tidying up my life in the hopes that it would change things. Despite all that, as I had previously learned, change scared me and, ultimately, I was mopping up tears as much as I did old pasta sauce from floors.

At the end of the day, I sat down with yet another glass of whiskey and fell asleep on the couch watching re-runs of *Melrose Place*. I knew then that I had hit a low because that show really was utter shit.

PART VI:
Inside Out

CHAPTER 50

I woke up with a dry mouth and an intense pain in my bad knee. I'd fallen asleep in a really uncomfortable position and my middle-aged body was making all kinds of complaints in protest at the discomfort. With the changing of scenery from green to the grey of suburbia, I figured we must have been getting close to home and the safety of my little "fortress of solitude" ... and sadness, but I generally didn't add that last part.

Katie had packed us up after a morning swim and an early lunch of a dodgy salad roll from a store in town. She could tell I wasn't feeling it and that what I might have needed was the security and safety of home. To be honest, she was right. While I wasn't one hundred per cent sure she really wanted to cut the trip short, I could also tell she wasn't overly fazed at the prospect of not seeing any of those guys again.

'So, I feel like an idiot for getting even remotely worked up over the Sam thing,' I said.

Katie jumped a little, not realising I'd woken up. 'Ummm, Hannah ... ' She was smiling, but I had no idea what at. She pointed at the side of her mouth. Maybe she was crazier than I— And there it was, the sudden realisation that she was in fact warning me of a stunning globule of drool that had managed to establish itself just under the corner of my mouth. I wiped it away, ignoring the embarrassment I would have felt if it was anyone else.

'It's not as if I even wanted to see him again, and I don't hate myself. I hate him for being for doing that to his wife and for reminding me why I question the value of a lasting, monogamous relationship. Because If I was her, I couldn't cope.' I could feel myself getting worked up again.

'Maybe they were polyamorous?' I tried to compute what that even meant, was I really that out of touch with life? 'You know, basically a relationship that is non-monogamous where everyone knows and is cool about it.'

I had a light bulb moment, one that was so devious and amazing that it just might make me feel a bit better. 'Okay, I am out of touch but that kind of sounds credible, more than credible in fact. I'm just going to tell myself that he was in a poly ... whatever relationship and that it's all good.' There, all the loose ends tied up and internal, exaggerated crisis avoided.

'But, on the other hand what if—' With all the power and might of Zeus, I interrupted her and blocked my ears like a four-year-old, or a twenty-year-old male, both are as mature as each other after all.

'Shut up, shut up ... I'm not listening ... lalalalala!'

She obviously did it for, what she called "shits and gigs" but knew exactly when to end it. There was a happy, contented silence broken only by the vibrations of the engine and the music which played the significant role of soundtrack to a premature ending to a time that promised so much. Unfortunately, this reminiscent of that college guy I'd accidentally took home one Friday night. The first and only time I slept with a guy more than ten years younger than me. Expecting a vigorous, powerful twenty-one-year-old stud, for lack of a better word, I was in fact "rewarded" with a mess on my hands after about thirty seconds ... yes, thirty seconds ... of physical contact. Not only did he finish quickly but left even quicker ... the very definition of premature. Ahhhh, good times, I say with a massive internal face palm.

We continued to hum along in relative silence, the scenery moving at a speed that became somewhat incomprehensible. The music was the metaphorical third in our road trip return and it was soothing and caring in its interactions with us. I knew I had to say something, to express in no uncertain terms my gratitude in pulling the proverbial pin on the trip.

'In all seriousness though, thanks for taking us home early. I know this was supposed to be a big, happy weekend but I fucked it and you helped me with damage control. Thank you, genuinely.' That was probably about as emotional a 'thank you' I'd given recently. I really did appreciate what she'd done for me in getting me through the somewhat unjustified emotional response to what I would from now on be calling "The Sam Situation".

Her eye contact was immediate, heartfelt and genuine. As she refocused on the road and, you know, avoided any motor vehicle mishaps, I felt the need to take control of the music, one aspect of my life in which I actually felt confident in making big girl decisions. Scrolling through my phone, knowing the Bluetooth adaptor we had for the car was only borderline reliable, I went with something that, if you can believe it, was apt, upbeat, depressing and comforting all-in-one four minutes of amazingness: 'Rescue Me' by Marshmello and A Day to Remember ... a somewhat ironic choice.

The opening guitar hook and the lead into the beat focused me and I sat there, considering just how fucking stupid this whole situation would seem to people on the outside looking in. I wished I could accurately convey the sheer unpleasantness and unease that flowed through my very being at the very thought of knowing I had fucked a married man who had outright lied to me, albeit by omission. Even though I had no interest in him, that kind of shit was just bad juju.

We'd just turned off the motorway and were making our way through seedy back streets, dodging young people under the influence of any number of legal and illegal substances and Katies phone rang. With sheer disdain for the law she hit answer and put the phone on speaker ... wait, did she really want me to hear a private conversation? As long as it wasn't some gory description of a ruptured testicle or something that would result in her being called into work, I'd be happy ... I think.

'Hello, Katie here.' It was a nice, completely impersonal yet welcoming greeting that was far from the 'Hey you' that I was often met with.

The voice on the other end reeked of arrogance and seemed quite familiar ... fuck!

'Well that's a good start, Hannah gave me the right number.' Ryan really did work quickly. That was a shamefully brief turnaround between getting a number and calling. Definitely no playing hard to get here. 'I'm Ryan, Hannah's boss who is apparently an arsehole.'

His 'look how funny I am' laugh, while somewhat suave, kind of reinforced my original arsehole statement.

'Okay, hi ... I guess. Didn't take you long to call me. I figured someone like you, a "not arsehole", wouldn't be that desperate.' Well played my friend, well played. I give Katie a little clap and wink and relaxed, seeing that Katie was seeing through this faux "cool" phone façade he was putting on.

'Um ... not, *desperate* but very impressed by how gorgeous you are and, while Hannah scrubbed up alright, you were ace.'

Wow, what a feel-good statement that was but, to look on the bright side, at least he didn't refer to me as hog-like in appearance. Katie seemed both impressed and disgusted by the statement and I had the feeling Ryan's chance of a date rested precariously on a knife's edge.

'Get to the point, James Bond.' I thought that Ryan wouldn't take the empowered, forceful response but he seemed to eat it up ... maybe he was a bit of a sub under all that bluster. His tone changed a little and it brought a smile to my face.

'I was hoping we could meet up for lunch, maybe tomorrow? You know ... casual, conversation and good food.' There it was, right at the very end, that regained confidence. Katie looked at me and gave me a 'what do you think?' look.

I blanked. How did I feel about this?

'Okay, lunch is fine. There's a café in town, just next to that shitty, overpriced pub near Central Station. I'll meet you there at one, for lunch. *Just* lunch.' My brain went into caretaker mode, calculating the pros and cons of Katie deciding on this date but, ultimately, I had given her the thumbs up and I had to live with that.

'Okay, see you then. I look forward to it.' He hung up and I had no doubt his confidence had been restored.

Katie looked at me with a look of almost fear. 'Are you sure you are good with this?'

I had to be, she had said, 'yes' and I was the reason they'd even spoken. With a smile that I was sure was readable as uncertain, I responded with a simple, 'Sure'.

CHAPTER 51

After twenty-four hours or so away with Katie, home felt particularly empty and even less glamorous than before. She had dropped me off no more than an hour ago and I had already unpacked, by which I mean filed clothes into dirty and clean piles and parked myself on the couch with a cup of tea. Yes, tea was rather unusual for me after the regular drama that was Hannah but I figured drinking this early might not be the best idea in this particular mindset.

I didn't even put on music or the television, I sat there with a book haphazardly thrown open on my lap to make it look like I was planning on reading, and contemplated what I had just done. I had set-up my best friend with my boss, who I was still convinced was unworthy of her attention. In my little old mind, there was so much that could possibly go wrong with this but, in typical me fashion, even considering these, I continued to formulate worst-case scenarios. They stewed away in my head, eating away at every logical thought I had like a cancer.

What was there to worry about, you may ask? After extensive thinking and a bout of unfathomable paranoia, I came up with a number of scenarios that physically hurt me to think about: she could fall head over heels in love with him and run away, get married and have little arsehole children with him, thus taking her away from me. Alternatively, he could convince her that I was in fact the arsehole, leading to her becoming more aware of my many flaws and faults, also resulting in a friendship divorce.

Embarrassingly, what ate away at me the most was that she'd have someone and I wouldn't. Someone that I had had a role in setting her up with and someone who could replace me. I felt really selfish because, in this case, even I could see that it was very much a case of 'I don't want him and I don't want a relationship, so why should you?' Sometimes, when I entered one of these cycles or, as I like to call them "whirlpools of misery", I overthink things so much that I physically hurt. My brain burns and my breathing became erratic and, worst of all, my heart hurt in the soppy, woe is me, emotional way. This was, ultimately, my fault. I had no one to blame but myself. I put myself in this situation by putting Katie in contact with Ryan.

I guess, deep down, I'd kind of hoped she wouldn't be into him and that nothing would change. Fuck it ... I needed a drink!

The dusty old bottle of red wine I found at the back of the cupboard went down a little too well and, unfortunately for all involved, on this occasion I became one of those hopelessly depressed drunks, who sat there and alternated between fits of near hyperventilating, uncontrollable sobbing, and self-imposed anger.

I contemplated calling Katie to try and talk things through with her, under the guise of a far-fetched tale of "this happened to a friend" to try and see what advice she could provide but I was sober enough to work out that it wasn't the best course of action going forward. At that point, I did the only thing I knew would possibly help get me out of this funk; I put on some music and had a shower.

I was conscious of not making the temperature too hot because of the sunburn on my shoulders, another product of a complete lack of planning and jumping into things without thinking. I stood in the bathroom, surrounded by steam, stark naked, feeling vulnerable and weak at just how little it took to break me down after being on such a high. The joys of bipolar I guess, but in this case, it approached the pinnacle of a semblance of control. I looked down at my imperfect figure which I thought, at this very point, was a good reflection of my imperfect mind. Strangely, couldn't help but consider what Sam's wife was doing now and how she would react if she knew what he had done.

Practical Hannah exerted herself for the moment and a consideration of hot water use kicked in, pushing me into the steamy cubicle. As the comforting heat of the water washed over my body, running down my face and kissing my eyes with a subtle sting, my brain did a famous double take. It was like that a simple step into the water had shifted my focus once again to Katie and Ryan.

Fuck ... they hadn't even gone on a date yet and I was already building a life for them together without me. *Deep breaths, Hannah ... Listen to the logical part of your brain, just once and trust that it is just a date. Nothing more, nothing less, and it is not the end of the world.*

I craned my neck back and took a face full of the shower, running my hands through my hair, considering that it really needed a wash.

Everything will be okay. I'm overthinking things ... I'm paranoid ... trust her and trust in what we have.

A sigh of relief and a feeling of inner peace washed over me and everything was suddenly good. Until I stepped out of the shower and was once again faced with an empty place and a shitty song that had somehow found its way into my playlist. Who the fuck was Luke Combs anyway?

CHAPTER 52

I slept fitfully, tossing and turning, and countlessly kicking off of every bed cover possible. It certainly provided me with the knowledge that I really needed to wash my sheets again and possibly ... no, *definitely*, my doona too. Even the Oxy and red wine didn't put me down, it merely provided me with that funky buzz and relief from physical pain that made it ever so appealing.

I found a copy of *The Great Gatsby* on my far bedside table and I had no fucking idea how it got there but, figuring it was a gift from some guardian deity, I opened it hoping that it would bore me to tears. East Egg, West Egg, green lights and all that symbolic bullshit was just too much for me, but it did focus my brain to the point where I did drift off. Unfortunately, though, I dreamed, and Freud would have had an absolute field day with the mess that my subconscious generated that night.

As fair as nightmares go, this was up there and it genuinely shook me up. I woke in a cold sweat that only added to the need to wash the sheets. I was in a happy relationship with three little mini-Hannahs, living the great Australian dream. I must have been pretty career motivated or just straight up rich because in this dream I could actually afford a house ... in the city! That in itself made this as far from realism as possible, let alone the fact that I was settled and in a stable relationship.

The husband my subconscious created was, from the lingering memory, perfect in most ways: handsome, intelligent and stable. Basically, everything that I wasn't rolled into a neat little package who, conveniently, didn't seem to have a name. Nightmare, surely not ... it had to be a dream, a fantasy utopia, a fantasy world worthy of aspiration. Nope, my dream husband was fucking Miss Perfect, outright denying it until I happened to walk in on them in the shower, MY DREAM SHOWER, going at it like wet, soapy rabbits. There she was, perfect body, perfect breasts and beautiful and I was still plain old Hannah … even in my dreams

I couldn't improve myself. I didn't say anything; I just stood there as they laughed at me. I cried and they laughed and the last thing I heard before waking up was, 'This is just how it is going to be from now on … for once in your life, live with it!'

My brain managed to find a way to mess up my day even more and pick away at all my little eccentricities, fears and feelings of paranoia in one tiny, yet incredibly vivid, dream. Even from those first seconds when I managed to control my breathing, bringing myself to the reality of my empty room, I knew that my dream husband, platonically of course, was Katie and that bitch banging him in the shower was Ryan. For once, my life had felt somewhat happy and now it was all going to change and I had no idea what to do or what to say.

It was 4am and I was still lying in bed naked, clammy sheets sticking to my body now wide awake and terrified. This is one of those moments where, if I had access to a man, I would go about having regretful sex and quick 'goodbye' to try and get my mind of things. I think that I could act as a substitute but I really didn't have the energy to put that much effort in … I just needed to starfish my way to victory and that wasn't possible really when you we're riding solo.

I reached over, picked up my phone and started scrolling through social media to try and distract myself enough to not message Katie because surely it was too early to message. Was it? Was 4am really too early to message your best friend? Maybe it was okay?

Deep breaths Hannah, of course it's not okay … its fucking 4am!

I did the next best thing and I scrolled through her status

updates and posts ... in a non-creepy, stalker-ish way. Just simply out of curiosity and boredom. I registered a new post on her wall and I got that immediate dopamine hit ... she had tagged me! 3.30am, no more than thirty minutes ago: *'Great night away with my Hannah. Thanks for putting up with my driving.'* She'd even added a laughing emoji and a heart and the photo from the winery that I'd sent her. I hit the "like" and felt somewhat gratified that I was worthy of a social media mention. While not an influencer or celebrity by any means, she had over three hundred friends!

I know, it really didn't take much to impress me but for someone who was a bit of a digital hermit, I found that quite an achievement. How could I possible be upset with the prospect of this amazing girl going on a date and finding a level of happiness that I didn't have?

This could be my opportunity to "save her", this could be me keeping up my end of the deal that we made what seemed like years ago. I should be happy but instead, I'd "pulled a Hannah" and made it into something it didn't need to be. I'd turned it around and brought it back to being about me because, all I could think about was, where is my "being saved moment?" I didn't mean to be, but I was such a selfish bitch. This ... this right here, is why I really didn't like myself very much.

CHAPTER 53

wandered around my place mindlessly for a few hours, doing the shit I hated but that really needed doing. I even washed and put away clothes and washed and changed my sheets which, depressingly, gave me a strange sense of accomplishment ... it was one part of this morning that I could actively take control of. I owned that fucking washing machine and I made it my bitch! I maybe got a little too excited about that, but uncontrolled mania is one of the few joys of the old bipolar. Now, time to bask in one of the other benefits ... crazy levels of online shopping because of course I could use some new towels, a coffee maker, and a whole mess of gym gear, just in case I decided to actually use that gym membership I was scammed into.

I really need to cancel it, but the really fit attractive people at the counter always made it so hard with nothing more than a smile and their promise of a gorgeously sculpted body. I sat at the breakfast bar with my third coffee and laptop and off I went on a glorious shopping adventure in the amazing digital world of commerce. I kind of felt like one of the vapid characters from *Sex in the City* – if they were mentally fucked-up shut ins.

About 8.30am, there was a knock at the door and my heart sank. *Please don't be mum ... please!* I know, she'd thought I was away for the whole weekend but this woman had superhero level of abilities when it comes to being nosy, detecting vulnerability and knowing when I was home and in a shit mood.

'No one's home ... come back in two weeks when Hannah is back from a shopping holiday to Barbados. I'm the housekeeper ... Ellen.' Now, I never thought that would actually work, but you can't win a prize if you don't play the game. Regardless of whether it worked or not, I genuinely had no intention of opening the door and, for once, my place was actually clean. 'Okay, "Ellen" Can you tell Hannah, when she gets back from Barbados that is, that Katie stopped by with a coffee and a bacon and egg roll?' Katie's exceptionally sarcastic humour brought me back from my mythical Barbados get away, which was probably a good thing. Nothing against Barbados, but who the fuck goes on a shopping getaway to the Caribbean? 'Also, Ellen? I suggest you don't go through Hannah's bottom draw because its loaded to the brim with se—' I cut her off, afraid of the neighbours hearing a scarily accurate description of the contents of my bottom draw and made my way to the door, forgetting that all I had on was a robe … nothing else, just a robe covering my Adam and Eve levels of nakedness.

'Hold up, I'm coming.' I opened the door and was hit with a subtle breeze and the vibrant colours of a near perfect, clear morning. 'You did say coffee, right? Because that means I can turf the instant swill that I'm drinking over here.'

I could smell the salty, greasy goodness of the perfect bacon and egg roll and the fresh, roasted aroma of barista coffee. A panacea for the woes of a restless night and the gritty aftertaste of my instant coffee and questionable milk.

'Hannah, best do up the robe, girl, because I'm seeing bits that you probably don't want me to see … unless? Why Hannah, my dear, are you trying to seduce me?' Katie smiled and winked, and I blushed and ran, ungraciously sliding into my room to find underwear and some type of clothing which happened to be a pair of white scalloped shorts and my favourite white, "Central Perk" t-shirt.

Deep breaths Hannah … she couldn't have seen anything more than … pretty much everything. Fuck!

I walked out and Katie had thankfully dumped my old, stale

homemade coffee and put an impressive looking roll oozing yolk, grease and barbeque sauce on one of my plates. Still somewhat embarrassed, I grabbed the piping hot flat white and took a cautious sip ... perfect temperature.

'Hannah, I wasn't looking, promise. And even if I was, wow! You really do look good ... that's if I saw anything of course.'

I blushed and couldn't think of anything to say because every time I looked in the mirror all I could see on this supposed nice body was flaws and imperfections.

'Thanks.' I mustered up the courage to say.

As I sat there enjoying Katies company and the bacon and egg roll a little too much, I noticed two things: Katie didn't have any food, only the coffee, and she was wearing a cute and casual little sun dress like she was going ... and reality hit. She had her date with Ryan at lunch and was probably heading straight into the city. That kind of killed the mood a little because I just, for lack of a better word, stopped.

Deep breaths, Hannah.

I had to break the imposed silence.

'Big date today ... excited?' Wow, even I registered the insecurity in my voice.

She shuffled around in her seat, obviously registering my discomfort. 'Yeah, will probably be a bust, but I'm interested to see just how much of an arsehole this guy is.' Her tone was obviously designed to bring things back to normal. I could tell in that probing, yet caring, look that she knew something was up. Something had changed, and she had no fucking idea what it was. Hopefully, I would keep it together and she'd just put it down to my fucked-up brain and move on.

For some reason, I couldn't maintain eye contact and dropped my head, studying the scribble written on the top of my coffee lid.

'Hey, you are okay with this, yeah? You did say you were cool with it.' There was a little bit of uncertainty creeping into her voice and a slight hint of agitation ... she knew. 'This was pretty much your idea, Hannah. I wouldn't have even considered ... '

I looked up, met her eyes and I tried ... I genuinely tried to control what I knew was going to come out of my mouth. I wanted to stop, but I couldn't.

'I really don't want you to go on the date.'

There was quite a lengthy, awkward pause. I hurried on, 'I know, I did this, but I've changed my mind ... I don't think I can do this.' There it was, I had opened Pandora's Box and it was usually at this point where I lost complete control over what I said and how I reacted.

'Hannah, it will be fine. It's just lunch and I probably won't like the guy anyway.' Katie walked over to me and put a comforting hand on my shoulder. 'Besides, you did tell me he was an arsehole and I'm sure you're a good judge of character,' she said with a caring, disarming smile.

'But what if he isn't an arsehole to you? What if he's charming and suave and you marry him and have kids and ... ' Here we go, my verbal tirade of disconnect from reality and all things logical had begun. 'You'll leave and won't have time for me anymore and ... I need you.'

Deep breaths, Hannah.

'Calm down, it's all good. All of that is so far-fetched, Hannah. You are talking this up and turning it into something that is just so totally removed from reality.' I could sense she was getting frustrated and, even then, I couldn't blame her. 'Han, have you taken your meds this morning?' There was genuine care in that statement but I just heard condescension.

'I have, of course I have. I do have some self-control!' I slammed my coffee down which, considering it was held in a fragile, environmentally friendly, takeaway cup, resulted in a literal "hot mess".

'Wow ... I've seen a breakdown, Hannah, but this is just a

fucking tantrum. What are you doing? Just tell me what you want from me?'

I walked towards the fridge and, for no reason at all opened it and considered the sad, emptiness and tried to take stock. 'I don't want you to go ... call up and cancel. We'll find you someone else.' It come out far louder, and far more forceful than intended. I'd lost it. Katie put her coffee down with a lot more grace than I did and walked away, she couldn't even look at me.

'Hannah, based on the way you're reacting, would it even matter who it was? I love you, Hannah, but I can't just "be yours". You might not want a relationship, but I might, and I need to figure that out for myself.'

I could feel my frustration building, it wasn't anger but I was getting there. The cold sensation on my face was starting to numb me, but I didn't care. I couldn't look at her. I was too embarrassed because I knew that I was really the arsehole.

'Please ... please don't go?' Here it came, the begging ... fucking pathetic Hannah. *This is why you can't hold onto anyone ... friends, men ... family even.*

'I'm going, that's just how it is. I know you've got problems and I know it's hard, but I can't make every decision of my life based around your needs. Hell, I'd been looking forward to this weekend for weeks ... optimum word there, weekend. I did what I thought was right for you and brought you home early because you fucked a married man and I was worried you couldn't cope. That was for you Hannah. Now, you expect me to cancel a date that YOU organised because YOU are having second thoughts?'

I closed the fridge and I sat down on the cold, kitchen floor and I stared at the wall. Everything she said, I knew was right. There was a constant war in my head between the logical and illogical parts of my brain and, once again, the illogical side was winning.

'Katie, please—'

She cut me off. 'Hannah, no ... this is going to keep going

around in circles. You're spiralling. Stick your head in that ridiculous cache of pills, take something to calm you down and have a rest. I'm going on a date and there is not one thing' – She was furious and I was now bawling my eyes out, hiding in a corner in my kitchen – 'that you can say to stop me. Cruel to be kind, Hannah, cruel to be kind. You are my best friend, but today I'm coming first.'

I heard her pick up her bag and make her way to the door. 'I'll call you at some point.'

With that, she slammed the door and I was on my own on this perfect morning. The harsh cold of the floor numbed my body, but I wished it would numb my mind. All I could think to do was beg, was to plead to the empty room hoping that Katie would somehow hear and come to my rescue.

'Please don't leave me.'

CHAPTER 54

Time passed on that cold floor, the bacon fat congealing on the plate still resting on the breakfast bar, and I had no awareness of the passing hours. It was just me, my inner self going through everything with a fine-tooth comb. Having an argument with someone I loved, and who obviously cared for me, was an unusual occurrence for me. What I'd learned in that brief exchange was that it was possibly the most humiliating experience I can imagine going through.

It was a new, and far from exciting, way to experience a strong sense of self-loathing. My experience with Katie was obviously very unique and, to use the scientific term, the fucked-up-edness of my head, created a whole new level of problems that, most would see as being "made up". In other words, many people I've encountered in the past and present would have simply told me to sort my shit out and stop being a whiny bitch. I probably am a whiny bitch, but only really within my own internal monologue and mostly towards myself … and fucking public transport!

All of this really did begin, escalate and end up with me becoming so unsure about what Katie even did, what she'd said, and how she'd responded. I completely lost track of what I said, did and, as a consequence, I drunk.

With someone as messed up as me, this made things even more challenging as I automatically took every little look, every annunciation and every movement to the nth degree. With Katie, one of the few people who I felt genuinely cared about me, I just wanted so much to become that serial apologist. I wanted to say "sorry" and to take responsibility for the whole thing. I wanted to hurt because I was the cause and hated myself more for that.

I practiced the best way to apologise. I worked through the "I'm fucking angry" phase in the short term and I continued with my somewhat unhealthy tendency that I'd developed over the years to beat myself up, to punish myself, to make amends and to avoid any conflict for any future situation.

I didn't want to feel this way again. This originally sounded fantastic on paper but, even in my spiral, I realised that this was an easy way to become the scapegoat, a way to internally beat myself up, to shoulder the blame and move on because I just didn't want to be hurt or to hurt her. I didn't genuinely feel she would take advantage of this, but I had enough flaws without adding to it. Overthinking things, as usual, I saw a potentially more serious consequence if I went down this painful path. The idea that I would radiate this attitude, that people would see this weakness and, like the proverbial Great White, take advantage ... they would see someone so down on themselves that they are willing to apologise and take the rap for everything rather than face any ensuing conflict. I was all over the place, conflicting thoughts, emotions and reactions.

Breathe.

I was spiralling. I could feel myself falling and saw no way of getting back up.

Deep breaths, Hannah ... just breath. Funnily enough, it's my mum's voice I hear in my head trying to calm me, trying to guide me out of this expanding hole.

It felt somewhat embarrassing to say, but I was so much more comfortable at acceptance and making amends than I was at fighting. To quote one of my guilty television pleasures, *The Simpsons*, I needed to become a 'cheese eating, surrender monkey.'

If I wanted to get all reflective and deep, I didn't want to fight because I didn't want to lose those few friends who actually gave a damn. Ultimately, I couldn't risk anything on the chance that the people who I cared about, Katie, might finally realise that the investment that they'd made in me as just too "high risk" and that it might be best to bail while ahead.

This was why constantly gravitating towards one person and not having a partner was beneficial ... it was damage control, it was all about not putting yourself in a situation where you can hurt people that you forge relationships with, or about the inevitable hurt I would feel, that the impact that I was scared of would ultimately break the thin veneer that remained.

Breathe, Hannah.

I didn't know what time it was and I didn't care. The place was empty and I was alone and scared. At that point, I needed peace and I needed it all to go away. I wanted to stop feeling like I did now and I never wanted to feel like this again. I couldn't hurt her again because it was hurting me as well.

This was not a suicide note, it wasn't a plea for attention. I didn't want to die and I didn't want to "call for help", I wasn't going down the cliché "emo" storyline.

I just wanted to stop feeling things for a while because I couldn't be normal like everyone else. I forced myself to get up and I brushed myself off and thought about how pathetic I must have looked. In that a moment of logical stupidity, I did what I did best, I put on some music. I took a few too many pain killers and far too much whiskey and sat on the couch as the sad background of my life faded.

The last thing I remembered was the sweet sounds of Judah & The Lion. I smiled and I blacked out, ironically, to 'Why Did You Run?'.

PART VII
Alone Together

CHAPTER 55

Katie didn't handle the fight with a great deal of poise and grace either. Where I thought she coped with it quite well, that her outburst and argument was almost cathartic, I was wrong. This whole situation, this whole weekend which was designed to be a smooth, fun trip away did nothing but pick away at the emotional scab, finally exposing the festering wound that she needed saving from and I, in all the focus on my flaws and faults, I forgot to even ask her to go into detail. That being said, she was never overly keen to share when she was presented with the opportunity, so I'm going to take that as a "it's not totally my fault".

The incident with Sam, how I handled things, and then the whole Ryan thing, very much reflected a dark shard of her personality that I had inadvertently forced her to emotionally revisit. As it turns out, Katie was happily engaged a few years ago, and the prospect of her "happily ever after", her Hollywood life, was a reality in a rather unpleasant way.

Her husband-to-be was very much built in the mould of "a Sam" in that he couldn't keep his cock to himself. Throughout the majority of their rather lengthy engagement he had one-off flings with a multitude of women while away for work, or fishing trips, or when he was supposedly playing cricket with his mates "a few suburbs over".

The woman she eventually caught him with, a twenty something barista, had no idea he was engaged, and she's confident none of them did. I think the reason she'd been so aggressive with James when he came to collect the phone was because her fiancé's friends constantly backed him, covered for him and made excuses. They'd known what was happening and condoned it through silence.

Katie saw my reaction, one that she empathised with because it was similar to what she received when she caught her scumbag fiancé with this other girl. It was all good in his eyes, though, because he loved her with all his heart, but he just needed more … physically. It broke her and she found it hard to date after the wedding obviously went to shit.

Ryan was one casual thing that, despite her tough exterior, she was actually looking forward to. Why? Because it was casual, and because her best friend thought they would be good together, despite her feelings towards him. Knowing that I was the catalyst for the pain and that I'd forced her to revisit it through an uncanny series of events made me feel like the lowest form of life.

I should have been strong enough, through all the medication and support that she gave me, to give her the support and love that I had gotten from her. I hated myself even more.

I found out later that she made her way into town to the date with mixed feelings and reactions. Anger, frustration and fear all fought for supremacy and all revolving around me and how I had let her down. The saddest part was that she feared for me and for what would happen if everything broke down. The idea of me just bouncing from man to man all the while trying to find another friend to gravitate to, another cult of personality to follow and live through.

Luckily Ryan was late, no fucking surprise there, giving Katie a chance to adjust herself and ground herself emotionally. She had no intention of forcing this, of getting nothing out of this date more than lunch but the anger within her that still lingered whispered to her, suggesting she make this work, just enough to teach me a lesson. It wasn't spite, it wasn't to punish me but, instead, it felt like a "cruel to be kind", teachable moment … I was the child here and, at that point in Katie's mind, a harsh detention might have been just what I needed to come around.

Ryan showed up in a classy Ralph Lauren shirt and sports jacket, looking suave and cocky as ever. Unfortunately, Katie took a discreet photo. I was too afraid to ask the purpose of said photograph, but even I had to admit that he'd looked incredibly handsome, cute and ... who am I kidding, with all taste and class, old Hannah would just have referred to him as 'fuckable'.

Understandably, Katie indulged in a few cocktails over lunch and the conversation evolved from her humorous sarcasm to vulnerable semi-drunken venting to a guy she barely knew. As it turns out, Ryan was actually quite scared of me, which gave me a nice, inflated sense of satisfaction, and was too fearful of my reaction if he did ask me out. Apparently, he'd considered it at one point, but I call utter bullshit. Lunch evolved into afternoon drinks and stories of failed romance with Ryan's charm eventually convincing a rather drunk Katie to go back to his place for 'coffee'.

Now, we all know what that means ... even teenagers in remote, rural high schools know that "coffee" after any type of date has very little to do with actually enjoying a hot beverage. Men really need to change their language a little here, just to freshen things up.

'Would you like to come in for an apple juice?' or 'Come in for a chai latte?' or my personal favourite, 'Come and join me for a frangipani tea and a butter biscuit?' That shit right there ... that's a lot more appealing after a booze riddled date than a generic, instant coffee.

Katie took him up on his pathetic offer of coffee and ended up in his little terrace house about two blocks from the waterfront ... probably worth a few million, easy. Turned out he was given some substantial money by daddy when he and step mum moved to Portugal. So, he was now a *rich* arsehole. Apparently, he didn't even get halfway through his coffee before they were undressing and making their way to the bedroom.

This was only late afternoon ... not even dinner time and I'd messed this girl up so much she was about to sleep with a guy she'd known for a few hours and who was already throwing out red flags. The main one being continuing to ply her with multiple cocktails while he sat on one beer most of the afternoon.

As she told the story, they were the better part of naked, lying on his immaculately made bed and he removed his underwear, the universal code for 'I'm done with foreplay, let's get the main event started'. Even in her drunken state, she was taken aback by his complete lack of tact and, in a stunning turn of events, size. This in itself wasn't funny as, despite popular belief, the average girl isn't a size queen, it was more that his frequent not-so-subtle hints as to how gifted he was in that area made that crumb of knowledge even more pleasant. What happened next pretty much reinforced every preconception I had of this man ... Total. Utter. Arsehole.

'I don't wear condoms ... it just doesn't do it for me,' he said, proceeding to kiss her on the neck. Katie gently pushed him away and told him in no uncertain terms that, if that was the case, there would be a problem.

'Okay, that's nice, thanks for sharing, but if you don't want to go down that line we will end this here. Look, I've even got one in my handbag.' She reached for a bag and with all the arrogance of a former U.S. President he continued to refuse.

'I don't wear them, that's not who I am' – What a wank of a line that one is, thinking he is important enough to make that decision for both parties – 'and I've never had a problem before.' At this point, he apparently began to caress his own abs in a way of supposedly attracting his potential mate.

'Okay, that's great, but I guess we are done.'

She got up and proceeded to track down her clothes, but the level of self-obsession and narcissism of this man meant he just had to continue down the futile line of argument.

'Really, just like that? After all those drinks? Not even a blowjob?' I could actually picture with 5K clarity the look of sheer disgust on Katie's face this point.

'Arrogant fuck! Hannah underestimated the level of arsehole you actually are. Let me guess,' she said as she continued to get dressed, 'you're pretty much only nice to a girl to try and get something out of them? Sex, an undying allegiance and willingness to jump when you say so? I say this with all my heart ... you're nothing but a stuck up, arrogant cu—'

He cut her off, unfortunately before she could finish the sentence. 'Typical ... just fuck off then and know that you were pretty much going to be nothing more than an easy, afternoon distraction anyway.'

She stormed out, but before slamming the door, she had to have the final say. 'By the way, your cock is unusually small. You probably should seek medical attention.'

Before calling for a cab, Katie had checked she had everything and stood on the curb contemplating what she just went through. There was nothing like an encounter with an arsehole to sober you up and bring forth a feeling of intense anger, birthed from the very core of your being, to the surface.

She wished she'd listened to me, but also knew that giving in to my manic change of heart was not beneficial to our friendship in the long-term. At this point, in those moments after she left, I didn't even think there would be a friendship anymore because in Hannah's maelstrom of a mind, one fight meant things ended.

While waiting for the cab on that lonely, grey, urban street, Katie did something I could never do, she reached down and sought her empowerment. She knew she needed to leave one more thing as a big, royal "fuck you". So, in a brainwave worthy of social media "likes", she found her red lipstick and, with all the control and neatness of a kindergarten teacher she proceeded to write all over his beautiful white door. She took a photo as a reminder of this amazing piece of justifiable graffiti ... no, art.

In massive, ruby red letters scrawled for everyone to see, Katie exacted a penance from our boy Ryan: 'I am a womaniser with a small cock.'

Finishing just in time for the cab to arrive, she smiled through the remnants of her tears and jumped in the back seat, making sure to point out her masterpiece. As the car sped off, she grabbed her phone and sent me a simple message.

K: Hey, we need to talk.

There was no reply, nor would there be ... I was too far gone.

I don't remember much of anything in those brief moments of consciousness I experienced that afternoon. I do remember feeling completely numb and that sensation of not caring, of not thinking and of not worrying actually that provided me a sense of subdued happiness. I wouldn't say it was a Hollywood 'out of body experience' but I did have a sense of looking at myself from another perspective, look at what I had resorted to in an attempt to try and not hurt. There was, afterwards, a vague recollection that brings me to tears whenever I think about it ... it was a feeling of shame.

CHAPTER 56

After not hearing from me by the time Katie got home, after a rather hefty taxi fare I might add, she messaged me again ...

K: You there, Hannah? Get back to me.

... and again, under the impression that I was deliberately ignoring her.

K: Hannah, txt me back.
We need to talk

Each message was seemingly more desperate than the other. Reading through those messages after the fact, I could almost feel her growing desperation.

K: Please. Just talk to me or I'm coming over ...
Or worse, I'll call you.

She did know me and my distaste for using the phone for an actual conversation and was using it as a threat ... a threat ... to get me to respond. Because of my desperation and feelings of sheer hopelessness, she had no chance.

Then she called, and called again, and the phone kept ringing out and going to voice mail. By the time she'd gotten out of, what she now referred to as, her "silly sundress" and into something more sensible and less shameful in her eyes, she kicked into nurse mode. All because of one, very simple, minute little detail: the phone stopped ringing at all, it just went straight to messages. The phone was dead and for all my faults, my phone was never fully dead.

At that point, once again waiting for a Uber, Katie had felt so very helpless and totally alone. She had to do something because she was in the dark and had no idea whether this was just a bipolar tantrum or something more. All she could do at this point was call the police. She didn't know the neighbour's numbers, which would have been quicker, but she did know police took requests for urgent wellness checks pretty seriously. The history and Katie's status as a nurse added credibility to the phone call that she made, still waiting for her cab, and the operator she spoke to dispatched someone immediately.

Katie breathed.

Katie arrived at my house to flashing lights and a scene of organised chaos. Luckily for me, I hadn't locked the door after Katie had stormed out and the officers, making out my limp, unconscious body on the floor at the base of the couch, invited themselves in. They were met with a scene that was probably far too familiar to them. Music still playing in the background, there was a half empty bottle of whiskey on the coffee table and a container of opioids next it.

It didn't take Sherlock fucking Holmes to put two and two together, and they had the ambulance there pretty quickly to, in their mind, what was an obvious suicide attempt.

Idiots. If only they knew I just wanted some peace they mightn't have wasted public resources. I was being stabilised and put in the back of the ambulance when Katie arrived and she couldn't do anything but look on in fear.

Even the "I'm a nurse and her friend, let me help" didn't work, probably because of the puffed, teary eyes and an obvious scent of booze. They let her ride in the back and, if I was remotely aware of what was going on, her presence would have provided me with a sense of calm that I so very much needed. When I sat there, alone and made that decision to 'do what I did', I once again thought of Hannah and the easy road.

To be incredibly clichéd, I took the easy way out and I failed to acknowledge how others would react. At no point, and it hurts to look back on it, did I think of the few that actually cared about me ... it was just about me needing to be in a place where I didn't have to deal with "me".

CHAPTER 57

I woke up with no sense of time or place, in a bright room filled with a whole bunch of people I didn't know. It was subdued and, at first blurry and it hurt my eyes.

Fuck, I'm dead! This isn't so bad I guess.

Wow, what a great place for my brain to go after being "reactivated", for lack of a better word. I registered the "bleeps" and the "bloops" of a number of machines and the drip hooked up to my swollen arm. Fuck, I'm in hospital, that's worse than death ... depending on the suburb.

I regained a physical sense of touch as I felt someone's hand squeeze mine, ever so gently. I looked up and it was mum, with a tear in her eye and the biggest smile I have seen on her face since Manu won *Dancing with the Stars*.

Her first words to me weren't even judgemental or critical, they were a simple, 'I love you, Hannah.'

I had two nurses surrounding me, checking obs and all those fancy medical readouts in a matter of seconds but Katie wasn't one of them. Then I registered the discomfort, nope ... the pain. I hurt all over and despite being unconscious for some period of time I was exhausted.

'Hannah, why? That's all I want to know and I won't ask again ... I promise.' Mum sounded sincere and there was a sense of care and empathy in her voice I hadn't heard from her in a long time. 'I know I'm hard on you, Hannah, and I don't mean to be and I know I could—'

I had to interrupt her, I didn't think I could deal with her emotions at the moment. 'Mum, I love you too but I didn't try to kill myself, despite what the doctors are probably telling you. I don't want to talk about it right now. Can we just leave it there?'

She nodded, registering that she wasn't going to get anywhere with this line of questioning but, she didn't sulk, she just sat there, holding my hand in the most comforting way.

Doctor ... Williams ... I think ... but I was more than likely wrong, gave me the verdict on my condition less than an hour after I woke up. I'd asked mum to leave, because deep down I knew I'd fucked-up pretty badly and I didn't really want mum to know just how stupid and dangerous, i.e. potentially fatal, what I did was.

'When you mix excessive alcohol and opioids, it causes what we call respiratory depression, essentially your lungs stopped doing their job as efficiently and effectively as possible. That leads to damage to the brain, and organ failure leading to death, if not picked up soon enough.'

Wow, I'd known it was bad, but fuck! For someone not wanting to kill myself I did a pretty good job of failing at that enterprise.

'Okay, where to now? When can I go home?'

The door burst open and Katie, scrubs and all, came in completely unannounced ... to the apparent dismay of the doctor.

'Ummm ... I'm going to have this conversation with you later, but you'll basically be allowed to go once I'm happy and I strongly suggest some form of rehab. Nurse ... we'll discuss your "entrance" later. I'm consulting.' Katie gave me a massive hug, unfortunately knocking my canula in the process, and a smile that was trying to hide what I hope was tears of joy and not 'fuck, she survived'. 'Do you have someone at home,' the doctor asked, 'because that would be best.'

My face sunk and I was brought back to the reality of my sad, lonely existence ... maybe I'd just have to get a one-night stand for every night of the week ... that would be like living with someone. As humorous as that was intended to be, it didn't bring any relief from the inevitable.

'I'm going to stay with her until she gets back on her feet. I'll make sure she's all good.'

I hadn't seen that coming and Katie gave me a look of ,'I hope you don't mind and please agree'.

'Yeah, roomies … it's all sorted.' I was sure the look on my face was one that showed just how comfortable and at ease I was at having people stay over at my house (insert "facepalm" emoji here).

CHAPTER 58

Coming back home to the scene of my existential crisis, I was met with a relatively undisturbed scene. Someone had turned the music off but the bottle of whiskey, now empty unfortunately, had been placed neatly on the coffee table and my oxy, well, all that remained was an empty box and a vague memory of that numbness.

'Well, I guess I don't have a great chance of getting a new script for these then?' I threw the box over the breakfast bar, hoping to somehow score a "Kobe" moment and land it in the kitchen bin. Unfortunately for me, the bin had a lid and, basically, I was a shit shot.

'So, how are we going to work this? I know you're not a big fan of "sleepovers".' Katie put it out there straight away, stating the bleeding obvious as she closed and locked the door. 'I promise, there won't be any truth or dare or pillow fights in our underwear,' she said with a wink, dumping both suitcases near the door. 'Sit down, think about it. I'm going to put the kettle on.'

There seemed to be a sense of forgiveness, of understanding, since she'd picked me up and we shared a far from pleasant Uber ride from the hospital. I actually felt like any more time in that back seat and I would have caught an STI.

'I guarantee there will be no milk or, even worse, the milk will be now a solid.'

Katie opened the fridge and pulled out a fresh carton of milk and I caught a brief glimpse of actual food on the shelves. 'I went shopping, I figured we probably shouldn't live off Uber Eats and two-minute noodles for very long. I'm actually a good cook ... somewhat.'

The couch was heaven, and it quickly readjusted its shape to coalesce with the structure of my arse. I hadn't really said much, I was still a little taken aback to be honest. I hadn't even made a sarcastic joke or cynical comment ... that's how out of sorts I was. 'I figured I'd just sleep on the couch, it looks comfy enough. Unless you've hidden another bed somewhere.'

She said with a glimmer of hope in her voice as she poured the boiling water into my amazing, non-matching coffee cups. 'No, that's not happening.' *Deep breaths, Hannah.* 'Just share the big bed with me ... it's pretty big and I'll try and remember to put on clothes.' She just looked at me with a "did a little piece of your brain die in the hospital?" kind of look. 'Seriously, but you have to promise not to laugh at me when I build a pillow wall between our different sides.' There it was, a crazy statement just to remind her that the old Hannah was still in the building.

After all the talk of cooking, we ended up just ordering pizza which, to be honest suited me just fine. Katie wouldn't let me have a glass of wine with dinner which was probably a good thing, to be fair.

As we sat there, with another cup of tea and a rather average vego pizza, she told me in a very subdued fashion, about her experience with Ryan and, more importantly her engagement and how fucked-up it was.

I felt uncomfortable during this rather lengthy story because everything about it, in some way or another, was caused by me. They'd only met because of me messaging him a photo while drunk, they only went on a date because I said it was okay when it clearly wasn't and ... possibly my worst involvement, it was because of me that she went to the date an emotional wreck. Outside of "story time" we didn't talk about that afternoon, I was too embarrassed and for some reason, I think Katie felt responsible;

or at least that was the vibe I got. There were apologies of course and the verbal back and forth that was 'it was my fault', 'no it was totally my fault' etc., but we largely just left it as what it truly was: a catalyst for change.

Despite viciously, yet quietly, cursing the girl for making me wait for a shower, that first night was a lot more acceptable than I expected.

What I dreaded was that I knew I struggled to sleep in any type of "pyjama" or any item of clothing for that matter, so when I slid into my side of the bed flanked by the mighty, unbreachable wall of pillows I had expertly erected down the centre of the bed, I shimmied out of my shorts and baggy shirt, took my bra off and pulled the covers up as far as possible. I figured I'd deal with the panties but there was no way I was sleeping in a bra. I lay there, staring blankly at the roof as Katie sat on the edge of the bed, pulling her hair back in a sensible ponytail, looking stunning as always in floral night shorts and a plain singlet.

That taught me one thing, it appeared she also slept with no bra and that it was a little colder in here than I expected.

'So, what time do you start tomorrow?' I was obviously still on holidays which was great, meaning I didn't have to deal with Ryan again at this point.

'I don't work tomorrow. I thought we might go down to that café near the bus stop for breakfast.' I'm guessing she means that hipster joint where Lizbeth works. 'Jam and Bread, I think it's called.' Fuck ... hipsters and, to top it off, a girl who was hitting on me and to whom I'd never made the effort to even speak to again and say 'hey, I'm straight, but thanks anyway'.

'Okay, sounds good, but you do know how overpriced and pretentious that place is, right?' She nodded. 'So, when is your next shift? Just so I know what day and time to meet up with my black market opioid dealer,' I said it with a smile and a slight sarcastic tone so I was hoping she picked up that I wasn't being serious.

She got up, put the brush down on the bed side table and slid between the covers.

'I'm not going back to work, I quit yesterday.' With that she turned the lights off, rolled over and left me laying they there with a great big 'what the actual fuck?' look on my face.

PART VIII

Thelma & Louise

CHAPTER 59

The "Jam and Bread: Roastery and Talkhouse", of which whose full name I had thankfully forgotten, was unusually quiet. I guess that might have been because I'd deliberately delayed our arrival to avoid the pre-commute Latte crowd. That being said, there was still a fair few pretentious hipster with their obscure European Indie band shirts and deliberately hobo-esque facial hair. Lizbeth was there and she gave me a welcoming smile as we walked in and sat down. It was slightly more subdued than what I received on my last visit, so I was going out on a limb here in thinking that she thought Katie and I were "together".

We both ordered the vegetarian breakfasts loaded with sourdough, avo, mushrooms, tomatoes and perfectly grilled haloumi and a coffee. Mine was as large as one could legally order as, expectedly, I didn't sleep particularly well ... especially after Katie's bombshell work situation. We kind of danced around the topic of work and the "how the fuck do I deal with Ryan" situation when I return to work, which hit me last night when I couldn't sleep. Poison in his coffee was a real option ... or maybe medical grade laxatives.

We mostly watched the world go by and commented on which hipster would be remotely attractive if they dressed properly and tidied themselves up. Yes, I knew I was being a judgemental bitch but I really struggle with that particular group.

'So ... quitting work hey? Ummmm' – Now, there was a massive uncomfortable pause because I had no fucking idea how to be tactful – ' ... why?'

She'd been expecting this question, I could tell, and I was a little proud of myself for not adding addendums to the question surrounding money, rent, bills etc. 'Okay, so you nearly died. Like, I don't actually think you realise just how close your body was to saying "fuck you, I'm done" and shutting down. That, coupled with the fucked-up date with that arsehole, really got me thinking that since the engagement debacle – and no, I'm not even mentioning that scum's name – I've done nothing. All my dreams and hopes of what I wanted in life died and I had accepted it and put my life into nursing.' I took another sip of the coffee, which really was a good brew, and tried to tell myself that I really didn't need that last piece of haloumi. 'I know you, Hannah. You're a beautiful mess and I know that deep down there is something inside you that you gave up on. Something that being "grown-up" got in the way of.'

I went cold and the expression on my face visibly shifted from listening intently to "fuck, she's got me". She pointed at me and with an amazing Katie smile, she saw through my really bad attempt to hide.

'I knew it! There it is. Tell me, what is it? What part of you did "life" kill? You show me yours, and I'll show you mine.' I knew this girl knew me better than most but, I didn't see this coming.

I'd buried that dream, that aspiration years ago on the day I walked away from Will. Damn, that was someone I hadn't thought about in a while. I'd have to look him up and see who was unlucky enough to be partnered with him these days. Back on topic, Hannah ... focus.

'Share it with me ... help me out by showing it's not just me.' Katie gave this expression that was almost one of pleading ... she was asking for help and, in a small, miniscule way, for someone to start to save her.

'Writing.' I couldn't have been more stoic. 'I just wanted to write books and tell stories.' I'd substituted my usual wine for coffee and I finished what was left in an attempt to compose myself. 'Shit happened ... *I* happened. Shitty relationships, shitty choices and then, after making excuse after excuse, I gave up. I settled for a shitty government job, a lonely, cold house and the occasional one-night stand.'

There was silence, even a lull in the background noise of the customer base. Not a single mention of renewables, edibles or vapes. I could hear myself breathing. I could feel my heart beat faster and I did my best to keep it all together. 'It doesn't matter ... I'm too messed up to write, I don't have the focus and I learned that—'

Looking down at her coffee, Katie interrupted me. 'I want to travel. I always wanted to leave everything behind, just fly away and explore what is out there beyond the confines of these fucking city streets.' There was a pause and I was really hoped this wasn't going the way I thought it was. 'That's what I'm going to do, that's why I quit ... I'm going to finally follow through.' *Deep breaths, Hannah.* 'Don't melt down, Hannah, give me a bit.' *Deep breaths, Hannah.* I was pretty sure Lizbeth could hear my deep breaths from the other side of the café.

Katie continued, 'I want you to come with me. I know, big step, but I want to do this with you. The added part of this dream was travelling with my best friend, and the one I had in mind years ago is now pretty into the meth thing and living up north with about six kids and a twenty-year-old "partner". You're my best friend now and have been since pretty much that first coffee.' That one statement settled me and it brought me back to reality. After everything that happened, I still had a best friend.

'Okay ... travel. That's big ... ' She expected a straight up 'no' from me, I could tell by the look in the eyes. There was genuine heartbreak there. ' ... I obviously can't give you an answer straight up but, to be honest with you' – That look of inevitable heartbreak deepened – 'I'm not totally against the idea. The whole "nearly dying" thing makes you rethink your prospects.' The biggest issue here really was not even if I wanted to do, it but could I do it. An unsuspecting hint of hope appeared on Katie's face.

'No pressure, obviously. My place is getting packed up next week and pretty much everything is being taken to a rather sketchy looking storage facility. It's cheap though.'

The whole idea of completely putting every aspect of your life on hold to travel was kind of life changing ... understatement of the century, I know. I sure as hell wouldn't get leave so I'd have to quit. I'd have to store my shit and get out of my lease.

Well, I guess compared to some people that wasn't that daunting and, besides, it would have the added bonus of me finally telling Ryan to "fuck off".

'Just think about it. Also, can I keep crashing at yours until I, or we, leave? I'll obviously pay my way ... possibly by cleaning, washing and making sure I don't make you wait for the shower.'

In all honesty, I'd actually appreciated the company last night ... even taking into consideration the awkward sleeping arrangements. If she stayed long enough I was just going to have to sleep naked and we'd both have to deal with it because I sure as hell couldn't continue this way. It was just so unusual ... I just didn't know how people managed.

'Hannah, just know that if you choose to stay, this isn't going to be the end of us.' I could tell she genuinely meant that.

We finished up, paid and leisurely walked up the street, taking in the morning sun and ignoring that ever present, rotten city odour which you can never quite place. All the while I was going over things in my head; I had a valid passport from that aborted New Zealand holiday from a few years ago, I had a fair amount of money locked away that I wouldn't classify as "life savings", one of the advantages of not having dependent children I guess, and there was nothing here really holding me back ... except for the ever present anxiety and all seeing eye of my mother. Could I actually do this?

CHAPTER 60

The pain from my knee hit new levels of shittiness that night, probably from the complete lack of oxy in my system these days. I ended up getting out of bed at about 2am and having another shower, completely oblivious to the fact that I, in the words of a young kid, had a friend sleeping over. There I was, partially in a trance, walking through the house in nothing but a pair of underwear for a glass of water, stopping by the shower of course to get that steam and heat happening. I really wished the land lord would sort their shit out and get a system sorted so it didn't take five minutes or more for the hot water to come through at an acceptable temperature.

'Bill Murray, play me some music.'

I grabbed a clean towel and pushed my war through the wall of steam as the sweet, emotive voice of BLÜ EYES followed me, adding to the surreal experience. The voice, the lyrics, they just all resonated with me, bringing me to tears on occasion. I couldn't help but hammer out my pathetic version of the bridge, to scream the lyrics and give me that sense of 'fuck, I'm good' from nailing every single line.

Everyone said
You look fine from the outside
But in my mind I was upside down and
screaming
What the hell is wrong with me?
Tryna make it make sense, making my head spin
Now I pray to forget 'cause I'm still here

screaming
What the hell is wrong with me?

I must have been a little too loud on that last line because, not long after, while still enjoying the subtle embrace of the shower, Katie came barging in with a concerned, faraway look in her face.

'FUCK!'

I'd obviously had forgotten she was sleeping a room or two over, because she scared the bejesus out of me.

'What, are you okay? What's up?' I stood, as naked and wet as the day I was born, hopefully with my bits obscured by steam. I had no idea what to say. 'You forgot I was even here, didn't you?' Katie seemed somewhat relieved as she turned and walked away, she'd obviously thought I'd had another crisis and was having a breakdown in the shower.

In all honesty, the depressing nature of the song probably hadn't helped that impression. I got out, dried and turned off the music to try and turn the house back to 'go to sleep' mode. I walked into the room, towel wrapped tightly around me to see Katie lying in bed, back turned to me.

'I won't look, I promise.'

I dried off quite thoroughly and, once again, slipped into bed. 'I'm sorry. I woke up in a daze and I guess that I'm so used to being here alone that I didn't even register you next to me … dick move, I know.' I slid into bed and turned the light off ready to once again try and actually get some rest. Despite all good intentions, I could feel through that wall of pillows and darkness that we were both laying there, eyes wide opening staring blankly into nothing.

'So, even if you don't come with me … are you going to write again?' Katie asked.

That was a good question, one I'd never considered. The whole immature pipe dream had hurt me a little more than I expected, reminded me that I lack the motivation and drive to even do what I want to do. Katie sat up straight and looked over it me, my eyes wide open staring at discoloured patch on the ceiling. 'So? Give me something.'

I didn't know what to say or do for that matter but I did have to give her something. She was like a rabid wolverine, insatiable, unrelenting. I paused, as long as I could ... I delayed and considered everything for what seemed like hours. It was like time slowed, just for me, giving me an opportunity to consider ... would I ever try and write again?

Deep breaths, Hannah.

I opened my mouth and the first thing that came out surprised even me. 'I'll come with you.'

What followed was a very awkward hug with too much of my skin touching too much of hers, but she was happy and, surprisingly, so was I. Somehow, her asking me about writing again had made it a hell of a lot easier to become a part of Katie's plans.

Was this me helping her? Was this going to be my contribution to saving her? Either way, I didn't have to think about writing anymore.

CHAPTER 61

The next twenty-four hours were wild. The first thing I did was something I had wanted to do for so long but never had the opportunity or courage to do so. I quit and in what I hoped was a massive "fuck you" to Ryan I didn't even tell him. I filled out all the online paperwork, clicked "yes" to payout my long service leave and in the box that's asks why you quit, I wrote, and I quote, 'I had an arsehole of a boss'.

He did eventually try and call and expressed his disappointment to my voice mail but, ultimately, he had no option but to accept my resignation. I emailed on my work email, one last time, in which I told him he can, with all respect, toss or burn everything on my desk because I wanted no memory of that hellhole. I did, however, also email Marg and thank her for being that cynical, sarcastic mentor that I'd needed.

As far as shutting down the rest of my life, it was scarily easy. The landlord was happy to let me go early from the lease as he was toying with selling the place anyway.

Mum and dad, who took the news surprisingly well, agreed to store all my stuff and deal with my mail and within the space of a day on the phone and in front of the computer I had basically cancelled my life. That, in itself, was sad.

I was now jobless, homeless and locked in to travel with a girl I had known for not very long at all, in the grand scheme of things. Every part of that scared the shit out of me but, as Katie said, sometimes you need to feel the fear, you need to 'be cruel to yourself to be kind'. One thing I did know for sure was that after everything we'd been through, I trusted Katie implicitly.

I started to clean up the place that very day, pack up my life, and get things together as I was worried that I might change my mind at any moment. The landlord was great but I wanted to be out within two weeks. Katie was right in that the more I thought about this, the more problems I'd find and the more anxious and insecure I'd become. Rip the bandaid off, let's get all of this happening and try put our lives here behind us, even if just temporarily. That in itself raised a good point, I had no fucking idea how long we would be gone for. There was stepping out of one's comfort zone and then there was this ... this was me jumping head first out of my comfort zone into a giant pit of "I have no idea what's going to happen".

Currently, my version of tidying up was piling my clothes into three rather large areas, what I called "zones of despair". I was categorising them as "keep", "pack" and "what the fuck was I thinking ... please throw it out!". The latter pile became increasingly large which, in many ways, made things easier because with it all being in good condition the local op shops could really benefit from it. They actually did picks ups as well so I had organised for them to swing by in the next few days for the clothes and some furniture that I didn't think was worth storing.

Mainly, my dining table and chairs, and I used this term very loosely, because I couldn't remember the last time I'd actually eaten at the table. I was pretty sure my last interaction with the table was actually quite adult in nature and involved a very, very passionate "skirt up" adventure. Great date, that, I think he'd been in my house for a grand total of less than an hour.

Thankfully I had no knick-knacks and very little clutter, and what I had Katie was either throwing out or putting in storage boxes for me. The really sad thing was that it didn't take long to organise and pack all my possessions except white goods, a bed, some basic cutlery and clothes into roughly one-third of my living area. Katie and I were sensible enough to leave out the laptop and a fully functional Bill Murray.

Over a glass of wine or two (Katie actually let me drink!) we sat down in front of the computer with some shitty Chinese takeout, and tried to plan things out. First thing was to set the date, to lock it in and get organised enough to book flights ... my time to shine! After surprisingly little deliberation we decided on flying out on a Friday, a little over a week from now.

'Pull the bandaid off, Hannah. That leaves plenty of time to cancel insurances and electricity. Plus, what really are we doing at this point other than sitting around all day, going back and forth from the coffee shop and working our way through the entire *Police Academy* movies.' I didn't have the heart to tell her I actually quite liked those films ... always made me laugh. 'Don't forget, the countless long showers and 'private time' that you need in you room quite frequently.' She laughed and I blushed like never before ... surely I was stealthy and discreet. 'I saw what's discreetly hidden under that pile of clothes on the floor and I really don't care. Just announce it to the world, I won't bother you ... promise.'

'Okay, I need to end this conversation and move on immediately.' If it came across desperate, it was because it was. 'Destination? I need to know because I need to book these flights ... I REALLY need to know.'

Deep breaths, Hannah. I could feel the anxiety of the unknown suddenly build.

'Calm, Hannah. Maybe you need some 'quiet time' alone—'

I interrupted her with all the vigour and force of ... well, an anxious woman. 'Nope, no jokes .. not the right time. We need to do this now, or I'm going to go full "Hannah" in no time at all.' There was silence broken only by the sounds of my attempts at controlled breathing and the hypotonic vocals of Brandon Flowers ... thank you Bill Murray!

'Okay, I'll do you a deal ... I was planning on going to Europe and I'm not going to tell you which city I was going to fly into. You, Hannah, pick a city, book the flights and let's go ... your choice. I'm going to have a shower and some "alone time"' – she paused, fishing for a reaction –' ... jokes Hannah, I'm going for a shower and to boil the kettle.

In honesty, It didn't take me long for me to settle and before Katie come back, not adequately dry enough for my liking, with a cup of tea, I was ready to go.

All I had to do was click that magic 'buy now' button. Katie looked over my shoulder, one hand on my arm comforting me as she could see me trying to regulate my breathing.

'Why there?' She took a sip of my tea, giving it to me to see if I'd register ... I didn't. I was just staring at that screen ready to make the biggest step of my life with the single click of a button.

'I was supposed to go there, years ago, and I couldn't do it. I pulled the pin and gave in.' I could feel a little tear forming as Kate put her hand on mine and, together we moved the cursor over the button and clicked.

'London, baby.'

CHAPTER 62

A week later and I was sitting at 40,000ft and alternating between surprisingly calm and fucking terrified. All I had was a bag of clothes, my passport a phone and a bank account ... oh, and travel insurance. For some reason, I also had my laptop which Katie insisted we bring along. I wasn't sure if she suspected or not. It wasn't until that moment, sitting here three hours into the second leg of a long-haul flight to London, that I came to the realisation that things were now very different. I had just pretty much discarded what remained of everything that, until that point, had made up who I was and, on a whim, made what was essentially a life-altering choice.

I was on a plane to Europe, something I couldn't bring myself to do for Bianca's wedding but, here I was. I'd taken a leap of faith, a metaphorical step, and I had, at for the moment, locked all that toxic anxiety away, somewhere. Even if I folded, if I surrendered, if I gave in and came home and rebuilt my castle to the point that it was before, it wouldn't matter; everything would still be different. I would be different. I'd be starting again, needing to find a new job and a new place to live at forty. I would need to salvage my possessions from dad's back shed, smile and admit defeat.

I could see the smug look on mum's face right now but I know, that underneath it, there would be feelings of pity but, more importantly unconditional love. Thoughts kept circling in my head, my internal monologue reminding me, in a surprisingly calm voice, that things were changing and that it might be for the better.

Change was probably an understatement; a violent state of flux was probably more accurate, to the point that I had no idea where I would be in two weeks' time, let alone two years.

This was so not who I was, this was the actions of someone existing as a complete antithesis; an anti-Hannah, for lack of a better phrase. I was scared, petrified, positively pissing myself, but I didn't think I could, or would, go back in time and change my mind if given the chance ... there would be no *Back to the Future* moment written into this story.

I think that, deep down, I needed the fear. I needed it to feel alive and bring me out of a state of existence that was, in many ways, contributing to how broken I was.

Was it something as simple as that I had been living my life for others, building an existence and identity around what I saw and felt in other people, and in everything going on around me? Had I always gravitated to one person, one friend and created my own dependence on a "cult of personality" to supress any drive and motivation behind a feeling of self-inflicted inferiority? Honestly, I had no fucking idea and, at this point, I was too scared to think too much about it, too scared to reflect on past choices and what brought me to where I am. *Look at me, psychoanalysing myself ... this is brilliant, I may have missed my calling.*

I looked over at Katie in the seat next to me, 38B. She was fast asleep, drooling in a way that somewhat distracted from the porcelain perfection of her features. I sat here next to a girl who I'd met completely through happenstance and bad decisions, and I was, now openly willing to acknowledge and celebrate that she was my best friend and that she'd changed me for the better. What made me smile a little was that, deep down, I thought maybe I'd changed her as well ... maybe we really had saved each other.

The cabin lights were dimmed. I considering the purpose of the laptop and how it would allow me to do something that, for a long time, I never thought I could. I was jetting off into the unknown with not even our first night's accommodation planned. Here I was, about to start another journey, parallel to this flight, one that, despite past aspirations, I never thought I was ever capable of taking.

This one, I kept quiet, because I needed to start this on my own. This one had to be on me.

I'd had that tiny push and 'you'll be fine'. Now it was my turn to jump.

My life had all led to this in some way or another, I had been thinking about this for as long as I can remember but I never had the self-belief or drive. Now? Now, I had someone to support me in this crazy, and possibly futile undertaking.

Deep breaths, Hannah.

I opened my laptop, temporarily blinded by the brightness of the screen, but a few clicks here and there quickly remedied this. I opened a new document and adjusted the alignment, font etc. to my rigid standards. I paused, considered what I was about do and I laughed, loud enough for Katie to turn her head and subtlety poke me in the ribs before drifting back to sleep.

I took one last pensive look at the blank screen, the last time I would see this document devoid of words and feelings. I was going to write and for once, every part of me knew this; that even at my age, I could finally do this.

Deep breaths, Hannah.

My fingers rolled over the keys with ease, with practiced precision and grace and I'd taken that massive first step. I'd broken the ice. For once I was about to change my own internal monologue, to alter my own path and hopefully become the person I have always wanted to. It felt so good, so cathartic ... better than a shower!

It wasn't much. Just a few words that, at this point, meant nothing to anyone except me. All that was there was a title, which some said was the hardest part of writing, but I knew exactly what it would be and, deep down, I always had.

I considered the words, how they were merely pixels illuminated in a way that formed letters and meaning. The cursor, blinked, almost daring me to continue. Is that all you've got?

He had no fucking chance and I was finally up for a scrap because on this rare occasion, for one of the few moments in my life, I knew exactly where that title was leading and how the story would end.

Films have given me trust issues. By Hannah Gardiner.

THE END

New Found Books Australia Pty Ltd
www.newfoundbooks.au